Priced to Move

Priced to Move

A NOVEL

Ginny Aiken

Revell
Grand Rapids, Michigan

© 2007 by Ginny Aiken

Published by Revell
a division of Baker Publishing Group
P.O. Box 6287, Grand Rapids, MI 49516-6287
www.revellbooks.com

Printed in the United States of America

Library of Congress Cataloging-in-Publication Data
Aiken, Ginny.
      Priced to move : a novel / Ginny Aiken.
         p.   cm. — (Shop-'til-you-drop collection ; bk. 1)
      ISBN 10: 0-8007-3227-8 (pbk.)
      ISBN 978-0-8007-3227-1 (pbk.)
      1. Gemologists—Fiction. 2. Shopping—Television—Fiction. I. Title.
PS3551.I339P75 2007
813'.54—dc22   2007023070

Published in association with the literary agency of Alive Communications, Inc., 7680 Goddard St., Suite 200, Colorado Springs, CO 80920.

For wisdom is better than rubies, and all the things one may desire cannot be compared with her.

Proverbs 8:11

$1\underline{\underline{00}}$

NEW YORK, NEW YORK

It's so not fair. Why doesn't anyone tell you ahead of time your dream job's going to morph into a nightmare if you stay in it long enough?

Like I have.

"C'mon, Roger," I reason. "You can't ask me to take off for New Delhi tomorrow. Give me a break. I just got in from Hong Kong last night."

My boss, the oh-so-distinguished Roger Hammond, frowns. The gears in his steel-gray-haired head practically spew smoke from his warp-speed thinking. Then he smiles.

Uh-oh.

"But that's why it's so perfect, my girl." Have I ever noticed the ultrabright whiteness of his teeth? "Now you don't need to unpack. And you know you're the very best. No one, but no one, can compare. You're simply the only one I can trust with this deal."

Yeah, right. Butter up the fall girl again. You know I don't say it. You also know I cave. Especially after Roger describes, in flamboyant Technicolor, the loot I'm supposed to bring back.

What can I say? I'm a sucker for the beauty God plants under layers of plain old mud.

"Here." Roger plunks his index finger on a fax on his desk. "Take a look at this. Sudhir Singh says the new find's the finest vein of top-grade garnet found in Orissa to date. That's saying a lot. We've bought how many of his parcels in the last few years?"

My vivid imagination paints a series of picture memories. "Have you seen samples of the new material?"

"No, and that's why I need you in Orissa." Roger slips his right hand into the pocket of his custom-tailored Italian suit trousers, strolls to the meager excuse for a window in his office, and pauses. He doesn't bother to check out the view; the high rectangle features a grimy back alley.

He goes on. "Sudhir's not about to leave this new find to bring us the goods, Andrea. Poachers, of course. And I would go, but for this . . . this . . ." His voice trails off while he waves his free hand in helplessness.

I really, *really* have to fight a laugh. "Do the words *dinner party* escape you?"

When he turns, a red haze creeps up onto his chiseled cheekbones. "Well, you do know Tiffany. She makes such a production of everything."

Oh yeah. Do I ever know the infamous Tiffany, the trophy wife. Roger treated himself to Tiffany after his first wife left him for their starving-artist pool boy four years ago. At first, he was understandably livid. Then he turned morose. By the time he'd dabbled in all the colors of emotion, the ink on their amicable (*not!*) divorce had dried. Three months later, the beauteous, extravagant, and too young Tiffany became the second Mrs. Hammond. The rest, including lavish parties and astronomical Saks, Macy's, and Cartier bills, is now history.

I don't remark on Tiffany.

"Well, Rog," I say instead, my hip propped against the corner of his desk, "it's not nice to invite the mayor and senator to din-din, then stand them up while you take a trot around the world, now, is it?"

His sigh of relief is funny—almost. "I knew you'd understand. That's why I pay you the big bucks."

I wish. "Does he have anything else you're interested in right now?"

"Sudhir said something about a parcel of emeralds. But you know how I feel about Indian emeralds. They just don't compare with the Colombian material or even that from Zambia. I'll leave it up to you."

Swell. "What price range do you have in mind?"

He takes a couple of steps, then gives my shoulder an awkward pat. "I'll trust your judgment—within reason. You know your gems. Better than I do, actually."

Well, yeah. Roger owns a store in New York's diamond district; I own a BS in geology and a Gemological Institute of America certificate that declares me a master gemologist. But why quibble?

"Ohh-kay, then." I grab the fax and head for the door. "I guess I'm off to India bright and early in the morning."

The smile blazes again. "That's wonderful, my girl. I always know I can count on you. You're the most valuable employee a man could ever have . . ."

I am thankful for all Roger has taught me over the years, but I still block out the effusive flattery. You see, besides that BS in rocks and piece of paper from the GIA, I also have a torn-up gut, the result of seven years' work in the stress-filled gemstone industry. My mangled middle lies in wait until something like this stirs it up, and then that holey gut of mine starts in with a zesty hula. Like it does right after I agree to New Delhi.

So once I chow down a fistful of extra-strength Tums, I grab my Coach handbag and head home. What passes for home, that is.

Do you have any idea what rent runs you in New York City these days? No? Well, let me tell you. It's downright bad for your health. Big Apple rents'll take a juicy bite out of you each and every month. Sometimes I feel like I work just to keep my landlord in Jaguars and homes in the Hamptons and Bahamas.

As always, the subway jostles me the whole ride long. That motion joins the gyrations of my twitchy digestive system, and together they—*bam!*—kick it all up a notch. Gotta love that Emeril, you know.

When I reach my stop, a sea of humanity shoves me out onto the platform. Every morning and every evening I spend a good chunk of time in prayer over that platform. Well, not the platform itself, but rather the track. There's nothing there to keep a girl from getting crammed off the narrow platform and flung down onto the rails just as the next steel behemoth belches in.

Not a pretty picture.

Then there's what passes for my apartment. You can't do a whole lot with five hundred square feet of space. I'm sure that my petite pad has a posh past as a dressing room in the vast apartment home of a well-to-do Roaring Twenties flapper. Now? Let's just say that Murphy and his famous hide-in-the-wall bed save me from the hassle of inflating an air mattress on the floor every night.

Brrriiinnng!

I run inside that expensive cubbyhole of mine and yank the receiver off its cradle before my caller can hang up—I'm call-deprived, you know.

"Hello?"

"Where you been these last ten days, sugarplum?" My Aunt Weeby's homey southern-flavored voice flows over me like a balm.

I drop my Coach bag on the floor, then I wince. That bag didn't cost me chump change. But my daddy's sister trumps Coach any day. "Hang on. I just walked in."

I throw the deadbolt, slip the doodad into the chain lock's slot, then turn the tab in the regular doorknob before I feel safe enough to relax. That's when I flop back on my diminutive armless slipper chair—all I could fit in my "living room" after I placed a love seat against the one wall—and finally smile.

"Aunt Weeby!" How come when a two-year-old dubs a relative something too cute, it sticks forever? "It's so good to hear you. How've you been?"

"No, no, no. That's not how we play this game. I asked first. You tell me, and then I'll tell you. So where you been?"

"Hong Kong, remember? It's almost the end of June. The gemstone show ended only day before yesterday."

"That's right. My, my, my. Time plumb flies by too fast when you move into the Metamucil and Centrum Silver lane." She clucks her dismay. "So, tell me now, did you get yourself any

11

a' them chopstick thingies? You gonna teach me to use 'em? How 'bout any pretties? You get yourself anything special?" Aunt Weeby is a world-class shopper.

"Nope. Prices were outrageous this time around. I didn't even buy a whole lot for Roger. He wasn't any too happy with me, but there was nothing I could do with the budget he gave me."

"So what's the hottest stone a' the moment?"

I shrug and toe off my classic black pumps. Aaahhh . . . "It depends on who you ask. The big four are always . . . well, big." My mind ticks off the list: diamonds, rubies, sapphires, and emeralds.

"*Phhhht!* I know that, sugarplum. I don't wanna hear about the usual. I'm after hearing about new and fabulous finds."

I tell her about my trip, which, to anyone but me, sounds exotic and exciting. Me? I just relive the exhaustion. But Aunt Weeby's Aunt Weeby. So while I describe the goods I saw in exquisite detail, I leave out all mention of my adventures with the cab driver who hit another cab on the way to the hotel from the airport, the subsequent argument—midstreet, mind you—my lost suitcase, the emergency room visit for my torn-up gut, and my overall sense of burnout.

Aunt Weeby tends to worry about me. I strive to prevent that worry.

"So why don'cha tell me what kinda fun things you gonna do tonight in that Big Apple a' yours?" she says when she's had her fill of gemological tidbits.

Fun things? Me? "Uh . . . I'm about to wash my underwear so I have enough clean, since Roger's sending me to New Delhi. I leave tomorrow."

Dead silence.

Then, "You sure that's wise, Andie?"

"I happen to like my undies clean."

"That's not what I mean! It's that deli thing. Is it wise?"

"Hah!" I say before I can stop myself. "Wise doesn't enter into my job. Wisdom's not why Roger pays me, as he says, the big bucks."

More silence.

Uh-oh. I know my father's much older half sister and my dearest friend in the whole world too well. My little outburst has plunked me square in the middle of trouble.

"Aunt Weeby? You still there?"

"'Course I'm here, Andrea. I'm not the one Roger's sending to some new deli. Can't that boy get hisself his own lunch? And you really should have enough clean undies to get ya through a week. I'm sure that mama a' yours taught you much better'n that. Besides, where else would I be but in good ol' Louisville?"

"It's New Delhi, *India*, Aunt Weeby." What am I doing, trying to explain? Somewhere in that brain of hers she knows what I mean, but she plays the ditz when it works in her favor. What I have to do is change the course of our typically loony, hopscotching conversation. "And you could always be off somewhere junking with Miss Mona."

"Now, Andie, you know better'n that. We don't go junking at all. What Mona and I have done is refine the art of flea market shopping. You have no idea what kinda treasures some stump-dumb folks are so blind they can't even recognize. Why, the last time Mona and I took off, we found a . . ."

And now she's on a roll. Aunt Weeby's descriptions have even more detail and far more color than I'll ever manage to put in any of mine. And that's just fine.

But then, "So now we've talked out all that other hoo-hah, how're ya doing, sugarplum?"

Tears well in my eyes. "You really want to know?"

"I wouldn'ta asked if I didn't, now would I?"

"I'm pooped, bummed, and corroded."

"Come again? What's that corroded bit supposed to mean?"

Time to fess up. "*You* know. After all this time working in the diamond district, I've figured out that I'm not really a Type A after all. I'm more a leisurely southern-speed kind of girl. All I have to show for those years is three—count 'em, three—ulcers."

"Ulcers! Andrea Autumn Adams. How could a bitty little thing like you get herself three ulcers? Why have you not bothered to tell me about even one a' them? And you're most certainly one a' them Type-A types. Why, just look at your initials, sugarplum. AAA."

One must navigate a minefield of choices when responding to Aunt Weeby. "What's there to tell?"

"You do sound a mite peckish, now you mention it." She clucks. "That's what happens when a body moves to that scandalous Apple a' yours. Why, I hear say they don't even eat their greens there."

I smile. "No. Not as a rule, they don't."

"What you need is a good mess a' turnip greens and some a' Great-Grandma Willetta's favorite cod liver oil. That stuff's so good they still make it even after all this time. It's not smart to mess with success, I always say."

The shudder rips through me, hard and heartfelt. Over the years, while staying with Aunt Weeby, I've been a frequent victim of Great-Great-Grandma Willetta's health doctrines.

Not that she's done the dosing herself, since Willetta Wither-spoon went to her Lord many decades before I came along. It's just that Aunt Weeby doesn't hesitate to lubricate at the slightest sneeze, limp, blush, blanch, or general peckishness, as she calls it.

"That's okay. I did see the doctor recently." Never mind that I didn't understand a Chinese word the lovely lady said. "I'm doing just fine. And my trip to New Delhi should be . . . good. Yes, good. And productive too."

I ask the Lord's forgiveness for that one. I prefer not to fib, but when it comes to Aunt Weeby—even over a phone line—skating on the outer edges of the truth is sometimes for the greater good.

"What you also need—"

"For goodness sake, Olivia Adams Miller!"

The rich alto voice in the background sets off my suspicion-o-meter. Before I can comment, however, a tussle for the telephone ensues.

"Give me that thing already," my auntie's flea-market buddy, Miss Mona Latimer, demands. "You've been chewing the girl's ear off for an eternity and still haven't told her—"

"Don't pay no never mind to Mona, sugarplum. She doesn't know what she's talking about—"

"Of course I do. Andie knows that, don't you, dear? But I've not been able *to* talk. Livvy here's the one who's hogged up the phone this whole time."

"Have not."

"Have so."

If my ears don't deceive me, the wrestling match for the receiver resumes.

"She is my niece, you know."

"And that's why she has to know—"

A loud *KLUNK* in my ear reveals the fate of the phone.

I've heard enough. "Aunt Weeby!" I try to count to ten but give up at three. "What is going on? I'd begun to wonder about the superlong call, but now Miss Mona's made it clear something's not right."

Instead of Aunt Weeby, Miss Mona responds. "It's that medicine they got her on for the pain, dear. It gives her the runs . . . of the talking-too-much kind. I wish we were calling you for a better reason, Andie, but this old fool here won't get to the point even if you lead her right up and stick her on it."

"So what *is* the point? Is Aunt Weeby okay? Are you?" Then I draw a sharp breath. "Oh no. Is it Mom? Dad? Did something happen at the mission?"

"Oh, honey, I'm so sorry we scared you. Your mama and daddy are fine as frogs. You know the good Lord watches over them and their naked natives all the time. And I've never had me more fun than I'm having these days. It's your auntie here that's got herself in a fine kerfuffle."

Their antics tell me the circumstances can't be life threatening. Even after Miss Mona won the phone fight, my aunt seems her usual wacky, lovable self. Which might, of course, be the problem in the first place. I don't want to ask.

But I have no choice. "What's wrong with Aunt Weeby?"

"She broke her left leg."

"Say *wha-ut*?" Under stress, my southern roots show up and multiply the syllables in my words.

"You heard me, Andie. Livvy broke her leg."

The possibilities are endless. Still, I have to know. "How?"

"Well . . . you see—it's like this . . ."

Miss Mona isn't given to hesitance, so I know what's coming has to be good—or bad, depending on how you see things.

"Go on," I urge.

"Yes, well, it's like this—"

"You gimme that phone right now, Mona Latimer."

After a chorus of grunts and groans, Aunt Weeby wins this latest scuffle. "It wasn't no big deal, sugarplum. I just took one of them Day-at-a-Horse-Farm tours. You know, you go and do what-all them horse farmers do every day."

Visions of mayhem dance in my head. "And how did the tour lead to your broken leg?"

"Let's just say that it did." She sniffs. "It's not the kinda thing a lady likes to talk about."

Now she has my curiosity in a headlock. "Come on, Aunt Weeby. Tell me what happened."

"Fine! I wrassled me a stable hand for his pitchfork, and lost on account of that big, nasty horse standing up for his human pal."

"Huh?"

"That's what I said. I had me a close encounter with the business end of a horse's snout. He didn't like that I wanted to . . . what do they call it? Oh, that's right—muck out his stall. Silly thing."

I still don't get it, a common occurrence around Aunt Weeby. "Did the horse spook? Did he trample you?"

"Pshaw! 'Course not, Andie. He just lowered his big fat head and . . . ah . . ."

"He shoved this busybody's butt out of the stable hand's way!" hollers Miss Mona.

My mind conjures up myriad images—all ridiculous, none

flattering. "Okay. Let's get back to what really matters. How are you? Really, now. No goofy stories. I want the truth."

"Oh, all right. I didn't want to worry you, but this big galoot here wouldn't let me be until I called."

My aunt's sudden seriousness tells me the situation isn't quite as good as she would have me believe. "Go on, Aunt Weeby." I make my voice super gentle and extra reassuring—no trouble at all. I love her. "Tell me what's going on."

"Well, sugarplum, the doctor's operated already and he stuck one a' them metal plates in my ankle. It looks like something outta that Frankenstein's monster kinda movie. There's all these metal gizmos what stick outta the plate right through my skin. But the cast he put up the rest of the leg's a real pretty purple color."

My torn-up gut chooses a belly dance for this occasion. Surgery, plates, pins, *plus* a cast—multiple fractures, you understand—are bad, very bad. And Aunt Weeby lives alone in the Adams three-storied family mausoleum . . . *er* . . . home.

"Is Luke in this hemisphere?" I ask.

"Not right now." Aunt Weeby's voice shakes just a touch. "My boy's somewhere out in the Middle East, sugarplum."

Cousin Luke is a career military officer—Special Forces, no less. His deployments are never to peaceful hamlets populated by happy folks.

"How about Mom and Dad? When's their next furlough?"

"Andie! Did you forget already? They were home over the summer. They won't be back for another two years."

Sure, it slipped my mind. Keeping up with Aunt Weeby doesn't leave much leftover mental nimbleness. But before I can come up with a comment, Miss Mona regains the phone.

"What your aunt's trying real hard not to say is that she's all alone right now, and she needs help. She's mule stubborn too. I told her to move in with me while her leg heals, that it'd be fun, like a running pajama party, but noooo. She has to stay right in her own home, no matter what."

I know where this is going. And I waver . . . oh, for all of about a nanosecond. You see, when your perforated digestive system starts in on a samba with a touch of rumba, you know you have to seize the moment.

"Roger can go to New Delhi himself. I'll see you both bright and early tomorrow morning."

Between Aunt Weeby's objections and Miss Mona's thanks-filled effusions, during the exhausting call to my now former boss, and through all my haphazard packing, I find myself reaching for assurance—I no longer have any visible means of support, you see.

Lord? Have I done the right thing?

Since he doesn't answer right away, much less out loud, I squash a twinge of unease and accept reality: I'll have to find out as I muddle along.

With Aunt Weeby in a cast and pins.

Oh, and armed with my BS in rocks and that paper from the GIA. Not to mention in *Louisville*, of all places. No Mecca for the gemstone trade, our lovely Louisville.

Sure, sure. Is this my wisest career move or what?

$2\underline{oo}$

Nine whirlwind days later—I couldn't get it all done over-night, like I'd told Aunt Weeby—find me staring at a hospital room door. I pause, take a deep breath, knock, and enter after Aunt Weeby's "Come in."

Medieval torture equipment attached to the bed from one end to the other makes me hit the brakes. "Whoa! Those are some fancy toys you have there."

"Sugarplum!" The shiny metal quivers and rattles. "You've just brought the smile to my day."

A rectangular, inverted chrome U rises from the headboard across to the footboard of the bed. I maneuver around the triangular trapeze thingy that hangs from it over her middle, and lean down for a hug. In spite of where she is, Aunt Weeby, as always, has her lipstick and eyebrows on, and the classy floral scent of *Joy* gives me the feeling of everything right with my world.

I chuckle. "You are too much. A broken leg, surgery, all those . . . those . . ." I wave at the shocking hospital bling. "And you look ready for a gala night."

Aunt Weeby pats the perfect champagne knot on her crown. "I've told you since you were little, Andrea, my girl. A lady's always gotta look good. You never know who's going to see you, and that first impression . . . it's awful hard to change, sugarplum."

I plop her another kiss, this one on her forehead, and then drag the slime-green vinyl chair over to the side of the bed to collapse into its not-so-welcoming embrace. "What's all that stuff for?"

"You just try to sit yourself up when your leg's been crunched into bitty pieces—and honey? They get you up on your feet right after they've patched you back up around here. No mercy at all." Aunt Weeby reaches up and waggles the trapeze triangle at me. "This is what I need to help myself sit."

"Okay. So that explains the fixed metal bar over the bed. What's the other one all about?"

"That one's kinda fun, you know? They used it with the nicest woolly slings to hold my leg up, and now . . . well, I see it like it's some kinda award. On account of my surviving all the other, you see."

I see no medal of valor; I see a free-arm chrome rod with a chain that ends in a bar that separates a wicked pair of open-ended, bent metal rectangles. Each thick wire end curls up onto itself, and I can see where something can be hung from the hooks they form. I shudder.

"It's been rough, hasn't it?"

Although Aunt Weeby tries to hide it from me, the slight wince tells me more than her words. "Oh, it wasn't so bad. It broke and had to be fixed. But let me tell you. Once I get my hands on that farmer boy . . . *whoo-ee!* I'm fixing to give him a good piece a' my mind."

Poor guy. "Maybe stables, pitchforks, and farm hands aren't your kind of gig. I'd stay away."

"*Pffft!*" She crosses her arms. "Enough of that. Now that you're here, mind telling me about that corroded gut a' yours?"

I take a second to check in on its current condition. The dumb thing surprises me. "It's an ulcer. It's there. But not so bad today."

"Humph!" The blue eyes never leave my face. "If you say so."

I rattle my purse. "Never fear. Have pharmacy, will travel. I'll be fine."

A dark-haired guy in maybe his mid-twenties, dressed in khakis and a cream polo shirt with the hospital's logo embroidered on the pocket, walks in right then. "Knock, knock!"

Aunt Weeby preens. "Timmy. Aren't *you* just in time? Here's someone I want you to meet." She points at me. "Andie, sweetheart, this is Timmy Holtz, my physical therapist—or rather, my torturer and taskmaster."

I smile and shrug.

My irrepressible aunt continues. "And Timmy, this is my darling *unmarried* niece, Andrea Adams. She's a New York gemologist. Poor thing." Aunt Weeby tsk-tsks better than anyone. "Andie plays with fabulous diamonds all day, but, wouldn't you know? She's still looking for the man who'll put one on her ring finger. I think she needs help"—she winks—"therapy, in a sense."

Swallow me, earth. "Looks like the pain meds KO'd her loose tongue's internal editor. Forgive her."

The therapist laughs. "It doesn't run in the family, does it?"

"*We* are nothing alike."

Aunt Weeby's torturer laughs way too much for my comfort.

"That's not what I hear," he finally says, winks, and then goes to the broken-leg side of the bed. "Okay, Miss Olivia—"

"What's that?" I shake my head, pat my ear, gape.

He looks at me as though I've grown another head. "I just said Miss Olivia. Isn't that her name?"

I stare at the too-innocent senior in the bed. "Sure, but no one's called her Olivia since I began to talk. I mean, I didn't do it on purpose, but she hasn't heard that name in—" Ooops! This guy doesn't need to know about the upcoming three-oh, does he? And I'm no fool—I'm not about to tell him. "I didn't think she even remembered her real name by now."

Aunt Weeby blushes, thrashes around, and grabs her trapeze. "Now, don't you pay her no never mind. She just has this pet name for me, and thinks everyone should use it—"

"'Morning, Weeby!" A nurse in a black top with Pink Panthers and pink hearts all over crosses to the wide windows. "How's the pain? What number are we if zero's none and ten's the worst torture you've ever endured?"

I grin. "Busted!"

Aunt Weeby groans. "Erin, honey, you sure do choose your moments, don't you? First you wake me up to give me a sleeping pill this morning, and now you go and blow my cover."

Erin narrows her clear green eyes. "What cover? What are you talking about, Weeby?"

I howl. "Serves you right!"

The therapist, a very confused-guy look on his face, ping-pongs his gaze from one to the other of us. Finally, he zooms in on me. "Did you really say . . . Weeby?"

"Oh, you know how it is." I shoot Aunt Weeby a grin. "Toddlers are notorious at making up names. She's been Weeby instead of Livvy ever since I turned two. Nobody calls her anything else."

"Okay," he says in an uncertain voice, then turns to the nurse. "So what's up, Erin? Does Miss Olivia—er . . . Miss Weeby?"—he gives me a did-I-get-it-right? look—"have something else going right now? I came to start her PT exercises, but if you need her, I can come back later."

Talk about strategic retreat!

"Well . . ." Erin fills Aunt Weeby's water pitcher at the sink. "I had planned to give her a sponge bath—"

"Why, Erin honey, that's just perfect." Aunt Weeby's eyes twinkle—uh-oh! Incoming trouble. "Andie? Why don't you go along and keep Timmy company while Erin here gives me one a' those nice sponge baths she's so good at? I'm sure he'd love to hear all about you when you were small. You were such a sweet little peanut."

"Aunt Weeby!"

She ignores my objection, reaches for and catches her therapist's hand, then gives it a pat. "You shoulda seen our Andie here growing up. All that red hair and those beautiful gray eyes. Uh-huh. And smart? Whoo-ee! This girl's always been sharp as a tack."

Instead of the ubiquitous deer, we have a medical professional in the headlights. "Ah . . . well, you see—" He squares his shoulders. "I'll go take care of Mr. Warren while you have your sponge bath, Miss Weeby. I'll be back after we're all done with what we're doing . . ."

His voice trails off as he flees the nuthouse. Aunt Weeby

can empty a room just by opening her mouth. Which she does with alarming regularity.

"So there you go." I stand. "Tell you what. I'm going to do you a favor. I'll pretend you didn't do what you just did and go to the family waiting room while you two do the sponge thing. Last time I stuck my head in there, the coffee pot was still dripping. A fresh cup would hit the spot."

"With an ulcer?" Horror doesn't exactly work with Aunt Weeby's lovely elderly lady looks. "Why, Andrea Adams. No wonder you've got yourself that corroded gut. Like Great-Grandma Willetta use'ta say, you're just pouring oil on that fire. You oughta go get yourself a nice glass a' milk instead."

"Actually, Weeby," Erin says, a thick white towel, fresh linens, and another pillow in her arms, "the milk thing has been discounted. Milk protein does have an initial neutralizing effect on gastric acid, but because of its high calcium content, it's also a potent accelerator, and stimulates excess acid production."

My eyes glaze over. I've heard it all before. "You guys don't need me here," I say. "I'll be in the family waiting room."

Once there, I pour my cup of coffee, then plunk my butt down on one of the hard upholstered armchairs. True, coffee isn't the best beverage for an ulcer patient, but if I only drink a cup or two a day, my torn-up gut doesn't abuse me too badly.

Four welcome sips later, my cell phone rings.

A gruff male says, "Miss Adams?"

"Speaking."

"This is Al, here, ma'am. With Two Men and a Truck, you know? I . . . umm . . . thought I better call about your stuff."

Visions of an overturned truck kick my pulse up a notch. "Oh no! What went wrong?"

"Nah, lady. Easy, okay? Nothing's wrong, just that we can't find the address you gave us. Can you, like, give us some directions?"

I talk them off the freeway, around Louisville proper, and out to Aunt Weeby's three-story white colonial. I tell Al—again—that yes, they are to unload everything into the detached garage behind the house; that I left it open so they can do just that; that no, there is no room in that huge house—Aunt Weeby's a devoted collector—and that I'll be there shortly.

When I snap shut my clamshell cell phone, it sinks in. As does my stomach, so to speak. "What *am* I going to do with all that stuff?"

The rumpled woman who is crashed on the sofa across from me opens one eye and mumbles, "Whassup?"

"Nothing, nothing. Just muttering."

Sure, sure. Why shouldn't she look at me like I need help, of the straitjacket kind? I've been reduced to mumbling sweet nothings to myself.

Is this that big payoff my career was supposed to bring? What am I going to do with myself? I have no job, no income, and no raging desire to twiddle my thumbs.

My phone rings again. "Yes, Al. What else do you need?"

"Al?" Roger asks. "Who's Al?"

"My mover, Rog. You know, the guy who's brought all my things from my closet-sized apartment here for me. I'm fine, thanks for asking. And how are you? How's Tiffany?"

"Ah . . . well, yes. How did your trip go?"

"How nice of you to ask!" What can I say? I'm far from perfect, and I fail to stop my smart mouth from smarting off. Lucky for me, this time no one sticks me in a corner to ponder the error of my ways—like all those times back in my schoolgirl days. I shake my head, shoot a prayer for self-control heavenward, then go on. "But I do know one thing. You didn't call to see what kind of mileage I got on the drive, or to see how much wreckage Al and his pal wrought on my stuff. So what's up?"

"What do you mean, what's up? I called to see if you'd worked this tantrum out of your system yet."

"I'm sorry, Roger. I am a smart-mouth, and that's not so cool." Okay. I've faced up to my part. But I hate it when he pulls his daddy-thing on me. "Tantrum? I'm not throwing a tantrum. I just couldn't go on. I worked, worked, worked, and didn't have a life. It all just got to me."

"Oh, all right." His long-suffering sigh rings alarm bells. Roger is known for his determination. "How about a 25 percent raise? Will that do it?"

Wow! Twenty-five percent . . .

Temptation lasts about two seconds. "I wish it were as simple as money. It's the stress, the ulcers that don't heal, the crazy rents that had me living in an apartment smaller than my aunt's downstairs powder room."

The woman on the couch glares. I shrink into my chair and lower my voice. "Where was I? Oh yeah. New York, I've come to believe, is a great place to visit, but not one for me to inhabit. Sorry."

"B–but . . . what about . . . ." His words trail off. He sighs. He gulps. He stays quiet for a moment, two . . .

Roger is really upset. I've always known he respects my work but never thought he cared much about me as a person, an acquaintance, a friend. Or is it my gemological knowledge he loves so much? After all, a time or two, when he was gung ho on making a questionable purchase, I stepped in and managed to save his bacon. Big time.

"Andie, I really need you here." The sincerity in his voice

catches me by surprise. "I don't know anyone else with your talent, expertise, and honesty. You can spot a flaw a mile away, never mind a fraud. Where am I going to find someone else who can do that? Besides, we've always worked very well together."

I take a gulp of coffee . . . two. "Thanks for the compliment. It means a lot. Really. It does. But you know the GIA graduates top-notch gemologists all the time. That's where I learned what I know. Call them. I'm sure they'll hook you up with the right person."

"They'll know their stuff, but will they care?"

"Sure. Gemologists love rocks."

"But will they *care*? About business. About negotiating."

"I can't make any promises."

"See? I need you back."

"No, you don't, Roger. And I can't go back. You might never understand." I pinch the bridge of my nose. "Even though you think I went temporarily insane when I jumped at the chance to come home again, I had been praying for a change. Aunt Weeby's accident just gave me the push I needed."

"But what about your career? All those years of studying?"

Aargh! The guy does know my weak spots. As I think of an appropriate response, I glance at the woman on the couch. She shuts her eyes fast in a lousy effort to pretend sleep. I feel bad for disturbing her, but I can't handle cell phone and coffee and walk all at one time. So I tell Roger, "Thanks for the free trip down the guilt aisle, Rog. It just won't work. I quit."

"I really need you, Andie. Take a couple of days to think it over. I can postpone the trip to New Delhi while you reconsider. I won't hold it against you once you come to your senses."

28

Big of him, huh? And here I thought I'd come to my senses the minute I decided to come to Louisville. "Don't, Roger. Don't hold out hope. I'm staying here."

"Not for long, you won't. You'll get bored in days, and besides, what are you going to do for a living? Can't imagine there's a huge need for gem experts down there."

"I don't know one way or the other." I tamp down the panicky butterflies in my stomach, and give the by-now irate woman on the couch an apologetic smile. "But I do know I'm staying here. Now, hang up and call the GIA. I'm sure the perfect gemologist is out there, waiting for you to find him . . . or her."

"Andie, really. I—"

"Good-bye, Roger. Give Tiffany my love."

This time, the snap of the closing phone sounds more like the thud of the floor falling out from under me. What *am* I going to do with myself? Does anyone need a gemologist in Louisville? If so, where? Who? And if not, then what else does my skill with expensive sparkly stones qualify me for?

My nerves detonate another stomach salvo, one unlike the earlier butterflies. This one threatens to wake up my dormant ulcer.

I burst up out of the uncomfortable chair. "Well, enough of that."

Your choice, your choice, your choice. My footsteps seem to mock me as I march down to Aunt Weeby's hospital room. She has to be done with that sponge bath by now. There isn't a whole lot of her, so how long can a lick-and-a-promise swab-down take?

I slam the door on every thought that even considers popping into my head as I put foot in front of foot.

$3\underline{00}$

At the door, I hear a familiar, throaty laugh.

I grin. "Hey, there, Miss Mona! I didn't know you were coming."

"But here I am, and I need me a hug."

As always, Miss Mona Latimer looks like a million bucks, somewhat less than she's reported to be worth. Her sage green suit brings out the green in her hazel eyes, and her hair is in its usual sleek silver bob. By comparison, I feel ready for the next episode of *What Not to Wear* in my boring blue-on-white pinstriped button-down shirt and gray pencil skirt.

After I extricate myself from the solid, comforting hug, I catch a glimpse of Aunt Weeby. Uh-oh. The tricky twosome is up to something, and this time, I don't think it has anything to do with matchmaking. That's Aunt Weeby's thing. Miss Mona would rather eat ground glass than mess with someone else's love life. And she's said so. About a million times.

"Okay, you two." I frown and waggle a finger. "Spit it out. I can tell when you're making trouble."

"What?" Aunt Weeby can't pull off the blasé thing worth

beans. "Can't a woman be happy to see her best friend and her favorite niece both at one time?"

"*Favorite* niece? What's up with that? I'm your only niece, you fraud, you. And you and Miss Mona fight more like sworn enemies than best friends. So tell me what's up."

Aunt Weeby turns to Miss Mona. "It's your idea, so go ahead and tell her."

"Of course it's my idea, but she's your niece, and you think it's a pretty good idea too, so *you* tell her."

I roll my eyes, something I do around these two way more than anywhere else. "Why don't you both do what you always do and talk over each other? I'll figure it out."

"Why, Andrea Adams, that's rude. We don't talk over—"

"My, my, Andie! Your auntie and I would never engage in such—"

Both zip up at the same time, their eyes huge, their cheeks rosy.

"You don't, do you?" I shake my head. "So what's the big deal? Why don't you just tell me what you're up to?"

Miss Mona stands and gestures for me to sit in the pleather chair she's just vacated. "Oh, all right. I'll tell you. But I just want you to know that I know you're the perfect woman for the job."

I sit, but the stiff, hard chair almost spits me back out. "Job?"

"Yes, dear. Job." Miss Mona squares her shoulders. "Do you remember when I bought a really bad television station a few years ago?"

There go my alarm bells. "Television station? I know nothing about broadcasting."

"You don't have to," she says. "Let me tell you what I've

gone and done. You do know that television's all about cable nowadays, don't you?"

I nod.

"Well, honey, I knew that local news would only keep the station sagging along as it was. So I decided to go into the big time."

"What do you want me to do with your TV station?"

"Nothing, dear. Just pipe down and hear me out. You're almost as bad as Livvy here. I invested a good chunk of change—I tell you, it was so much, it had even me scared for a bit."

"Mm-hmm," Aunt Weeby says. "The whole thing had me shaking up a storm. And it wasn't even *my* retirement that was about to run off with all them infomercial doodads she bought to sell."

My pulse kicks it up one more notch. At this rate, I'm going to need all kinds of blood pressure meds to stay alive around these two. But I don't say a word; the ladies are doing a pretty nice job of doing all the talking.

Miss Mona crosses her arms. "I reckon you can tell by now I didn't lose my shirt, and now I own a cable TV shopping network."

I sproing out of my chair. "You what?"

"You heard me. I own the Shop-Til-U-Drop Network."

My eyes goggle. "No way. You mean *you* are the brains and bucks behind the 'All women, for women, by women' channel?"

"So you've seen us."

Fists on hips, I tap my right toe. "They do have TV in New York, you know. Of course, I've seen you. I've been known to channel surf every once in a while."

"But you haven't stopped to shop."

"Oh, I've stopped. But I haven't shopped. I hardly ever cook, so I don't need pots and pans. And clothes? Well, as tall as I am, I really need to try things on. If I'm not careful, five foot ten means lots of floodwater pants."

"You do know we have a 100 percent money-back rule, no questions asked, don't you?"

"I remember hearing something like that."

"And you still didn't buy anything. Can you tell me why?"

"I just told you. I don't need a whole lot, and although I did like the clothes I saw, it's the sizing thing that nails me every time. I can't shop catalogs either, if that makes you feel better."

"We offer lots more than pots and pans and clothes."

Aunt Weeby gives a most unladylike snort. "Mona! Let the girl be. Isn't there something more important you wanted to talk to her about?"

"Oh. Well, yes. I'm just so passionate about my business. You do understand, don't you, Andie? That's how you feel about your gemstones, right?"

"Totally."

"I knew you'd understand. And that's why you're my girl."

This is getting scary. "I wouldn't be so sure, Miss Mona. What is it you want?"

"Well, honey . . . This, to me, looks like the Lord's just put before me the perfect opportunity to expand my network's gem and jewelry catalog. I want you to be my new jewelry and gemstone show host."

I can't possibly have heard her right. She hasn't just put bling-bling, me, and a TV show together in the same sentence. Has she?

Her expectant look says otherwise.

When I finally speak, I rival a bullfrog. "You want me to be your what?"

"You heard me," Miss Mona says, her gaze clear and direct.

So I didn't hallucinate it. Miss Mona is as nutty as I've always thought. As nutty as the nutcase on the bed not two steps away from her, a matching goofy grin on her face.

"But I know nothing about TV shows or anything like that."

"True, and that's where I come in," Miss Mona says. "What you do know all about, and what I do need, is a hot-shot gemologist. And there's none better than you."

"Just think, Andie." Aunt Weeby clasps her hands at chest height. "You're gonna get to teach your viewers all about your bing-bing—"

"Bling-bling." My voice nearly wimps out on me this time.

Aunt Weeby chuckles. "That's it! Anyway, you'll be teaching all you know about gemstones, and where they come from, and all that. Isn't that just plumb wonderful?"

As wacky as it is, she does have a point. The whole scheme has a certain appeal to it. But the on-TV part? That sure doesn't give me the feel-good cozies. Nuh-uh. That part makes my teeth itch.

"I can't go on TV. I don't know what to do, what to say."

"Whoo-ee!" Aunt Weeby gives Miss Mona a thumbs-up. "See? She's not run halfway back to New York like you said she would. I know my girl. She's gonna be great—the best. You'll see."

Miss Mona holds out her right hand. "I won't take no for

34

an answer, you know. So let's shake on it, and get to getting. There's a whole world of things you have to learn."

Lord? I know I prayed for a change of pace. But this? What is this?

F-16s dive-bomb in my gut. I stare at Miss Mona's perfectly manicured hand. Tympani *bong-bong-ba-bong-bong* in my temples. I did want out of the New York rat race. I still need a job. And Miss Mona says she needs a gemologist just when this one has fled her wormy corner of the Big Apple.

Do I shake? Do I run?

Do I dare?

I swallow hard against my inner wimp and take Miss Mona's hand. "I can't promise I'll be any good at it."

"Oh, thank you, thank you! See how the Lord answers prayers?" she cries. "I'll take my chances, dear. And it sure seems the Father's gone and given me a natural instinct for this kind of thing. He hasn't let me fail yet."

Swell. Talk about pressure. "I sure hope I'm not your first one then. Failure, that is."

"Pshaw! You couldn't be a failure if you tried."

I am so not going there. Besides, I'd been glooming and dooming about my shaky earning prospects not even a half hour ago. It looks like God has a sense of humor, after all. Did you ever imagine he'd answer like this?

I didn't.

"Well, I still hope I don't let you down."

That's when it all hits me. Like a ton of bricks, it hits me. I *am* home. Really and truly. In Louisville—well, the outskirts, but a whole world closer than New York City, that's for sure.

New York . . . Louisville. New York . . . Louisville. Oh,

geez! Al and his pal and the truck with my stuff. Knock, knock! Reality calling.

"Ladies, ladies! I gotta go. The movers are at the house, Aunt Weeby. They called while I was in the waiting room. Something about some papers they want me to sign."

"Everything's ready for you at the house," Miss Mona says. "I was so excited, and just couldn't wait till you came home, and since Livvy couldn't do a thing, I had me the best time shopping and doing for you. I hope you like what I prepared."

What can I say? They're wacky ones, but they're *my* wacky ones. I love them to death.

After hugs and kisses—the real kind, not those oh-so-chic air deals—I make my way to the parking garage, drive home, watch Al and his pal do their thing, sign papers, go inside, drink a tall glass of Miss Mona's killer sweet iced tea, and then collapse on the parlor sofa.

If you ask me how I did any of it, I can't tell you, it all happened so fast, like a blur.

And blurring out's scary. Almost as scary as . . . the *other* thing.

The TV thing.

Did I really agree to work for Miss Mona? Did I really agree to hawk jewelry and gemstones on TV?

Do I need a frontal lobotomy?

I've never had a problem with Wednesday mornings. I do now.

Let me draw you a mental picture: Aunt Weeby . . . her metal contraptions . . . the trip home . . . helped by Miss

Mona. How's that for scary? That's what I'm facing today. I'll take a blue Monday any day.

Oh yeah. I'm ready to pull my hair out over these two. But before I get to my new do, I have to help Erin talk Aunt Weeby into the required wheelchair ride to the parking garage, where Miss Mona is waiting in the Shop-Til-U-Drop Network's limo. Aunt Weeby's comfort on the ride home is assured.

Just not her cooperation.

She frowns from head to toe. "What good's this cute little cast they gave me if I have to ride down to the car in that dumb ol' thing?"

Erin pushes the chair closer. "Weeby, it's hospital policy. Remember? We have lots of those around here, and I can't break the rules. I like my job. What if someone's spilled water, and you slip on it? How about grease in the garage? The cast won't keep you from breaking something else if you fall. You want to keep this super-luxurious suite awhile longer?"

Aunt Weeby crosses her arms. "I'm done with being sick. And I can walk outta here just fine too, thank you very much."

There's my cue. "Aunt Weeby? D'you want to go home?"

"Why, sugarplum, you know I do."

"Well, then. Piece of cake. Sit in the chair."

"But—"

"It's the chair, or it's the chair."

Her sigh deserves an Oscar. "Now, you two girls have just ganged up on a poor, defenseless old lady. I ask you, is that right?"

Before I roll my eyes, I catch myself—I did tell you I do that way too much around Aunt Weeby, right?—and only shrug. "Them's the rules, ma'am."

She clamps her lips together, the edges rim white. "I just

plain hate this. I can do for myself. I'm not really that old, sugarplum."

The lightbulb goes on in my head. So *that's* what this is really about. I drop to my knee next to the green pleather chair where Aunt Weeby's been ensconced during our argument. "It's losing your independence that worries you, isn't it?"

When her eyes meet mine, fear burns loud and clear in the blue. "I've never had to depend on anyone"—her voice cracks—"not even on your dear Uncle Harris. And I don't intend to start something like that at this point in my life."

Her hand is cold against my fingers. "You and Uncle Harris were partners, the real deal, I know. But this is different. Look at it this way. If I was in your place—the broken leg deal—I'd have to accept the same kind of help and limitations you do right now." I wink. "It's really *not* all about you!"

She covers my hand with her other one. "I guess my head knows that, sugarplum. But it's my gut what hates this being so weak, so needy. I see so many friends who're in warehouses now—you know. Them nursing homes."

"Oh, ick! What a nasty thing to say."

"Listen to me, Andie. I know I'm kinda creaky, but I've got me some eyes and ears too. And I know how folks feel when their friends and families muscle 'em into them nursing homes. They feel they've been shelved in a warehouse—that's Paulina Madson, Doc Madson's older sister, what came up with the name when they stuck her in that Happy Days Acres place. Happy Days Acres! What kinda dopey name is that? I can't stand it, and I'm gonna fight it to the end."

No way will she wind up like that. At least, not so long as I'm around. I'll take care of her. But no matter how strong my reaction, Aunt Weeby's words scare me more than I let on. I

38

can't stand to think she's aged so much. I can't stand to think of the day when she'll go home to be with her Lord, even though I know it's coming. *Not too soon, Lord, please.*

"Weeby," Erin says, "what kind of logic is that? You're going home, woman, not to a nursing facility. You'll have all the independence you want there. Well, all that your cast gives you, but the cast's not so bad, right? Staying here, fighting hospital rules, that isn't independence."

It's just stubbornness, Aunt Weeby's specialty. Something I'm just a wee bit familiar with myself. "C'mon. Miss Mona and the driver are waiting for us. You should be happy, not so down. Let's get you home."

"Oh, my, my, my!" She shakes her head. "I shouldn't've put my troubles on you girls. I'm so, so sorry. That's not right. I do get to go home, and I should be celebrating. Besides. Just look at my darling new cast, Andie. It's pink!"

My aunt, the pink obsessed. "I can see that. Whose palm'd you grease to get that kiddy cast?"

With a ton of effort, she stands, then tips up her chin and looks down her nose at me—kinda hard to do, since I'm about six inches taller. "I did no such thing. Dr. Takashi told me to choose, and I chose."

So as not to further irritate her sensibilities, I fight my urge to hold her elbow to help her walk as she crosses to the wheelchair. Instead, I walk next to her, matching her every step, close enough to catch her, if needed.

Finally, she sits, hugs the vase of pink roses I'd sent her, and we head on out. When the elevator finally lands at the appropriate parking garage floor, I take a deep breath.

Almost. I'm almost home.

4<u>00</u>

Miss Mona spots us. "Why, Livvy! And here I thought you said you wouldn't ride the wheelchair, no matter what." She winks. "You going soft on me already?"

Aarrgh! See what I'm up against?

Aunt Weeby glares. "You bite that flappy tongue a' yours, Mona Latimer. You don't know beans. This"—she smacks the armrest—"is all about them hospital rules. Can't have sweet Erin here losing her job over a silly little ol' wheelchair, now can we?"

"Of course not, dear, of course." She grins. "Now let's get you in this car. Davina's ready to help us get you home."

The tall, uniformed driver gives me a brief nod. Whoa! This girl's got at least two inches and a good forty pounds on me. It takes a lot to make me feel petite. Davina does it without breaking a sweat. Bet you shopping's no treat for her.

Davina turns to Aunt Weeby. "You ready, ma'am?"

"Can't wait to get home."

To my surprise and Aunt Weeby's horror, Davina the driver scoops her up and heads to the limo. Aunt Weeby sputters like a steamed-up teapot but gets nowhere with Miss Mona's benign giant.

"Why . . . you! Davina! You put me down right this minute." To Miss Mona, "Call off your goon-girl. And here I always thought her such a sweet thing." She shakes her head. "I'm perfectly capable a' making my way to that fancy car a' yours, Mona. Tell her to put me down right this very minute. Immediately, Mona Latimer!"

Davina's shoulders shake with silent chuckles. I glance at Miss Mona, who's got the laugh she's fighting plastered all over her face, and finally at Erin. Then I get it.

They'd planned this. I'm going to have to give Miss Mona more credit. Aunt Weeby's no enigma. What you see is what you get—goofy, feisty, lovable, and recovering from a badly broken leg. So it wouldn't have taken much to figure how she'd react when faced with the wheelchair. But I'm still glad they planned it; Aunt Weeby's not ready to walk, no matter how much mileage she wants to put on her cast.

Davina, deadpan, bends to slip Aunt Weeby into the car, her movements gentle, as tender as those of a mother for her child. When she stands back upright, I come close and touch her arm. "Thanks."

"No problem, Miss Andie. Miz Weeby's a favorite of mine."

"You can drop the Miss with me. I'm just Andie. And my aunt's something, all right. Just don't ask me what."

The disco-style, color-changing lights in the limo keep Aunt Weeby fascinated, as does the small fridge filled with juices and sodas. Once home, she doesn't fight Davina, and we get her settled on the parlor sofa.

After everyone leaves and it's just the two of us, though,

a tug-of-wills war eats up the rest of our day. Aunt Weeby being Aunt Weeby, wants to do everything she's always done the way she's always done it, never mind the broken leg in its Pepto-pink cast.

By the time I settle her into bed—you don't want to know about that hike up those stairs, since she refused to sleep on the queen-size, double-decker AeroBed I inflated in the study—I'm exhausted. Drag-down, knock-out beat. My every muscle screams when I go back to the kitchen to make myself a cup of cocoa. But in spite of my exhaustion, something about this house makes me crave the comforts of childhood. Aunt Weeby's always been a firm believer in the power of prayer and chocolate therapy, not necessarily together or in equal measure.

When the phone rings, I groan and ignore it for two shrill shrieks, but then my call deprivation gets the better of me. I answer with little enthusiasm.

"Andie?"

The woman's voice is familiar, but not so much that I recognize it. "Yes?"

"It's Peggy. Peggy Sanders. Remember?"

Oh. My. Goodness. "Of course, I remember. We spent too many summers planning and plotting how to ditch our chores and go swimming not to. How are you?"

Her relief comes across loud and clear. "I'm fine, but I'm not Peggy Sanders anymore. At least, not technically. I married Josh Ross, from youth group. Do you remember him?"

"Wow. I do remember him. That's great. What are you two up to these days?"

She laughs. "I'm not so sure you really want to know, but

42

since you asked, I'm up to my eyeballs in dirty diapers, dirty dishes, and dirty kitty litter."

"Girlfriend, are you sure the ammonia fumes from the diapers and kitty litter haven't pickled your brain?"

"Oh, I'm sure they have. But enough about me and my pickled brain. How are you? Last I heard, you were jetting all over the world buying up the crown jewels of third world countries."

"Not exactly. I did score a ton of frequent-flyer miles buying exotic gemstones for my boss, but I never got close enough to sneeze at any crown jewels. I usually hung around boring business offices and the occasional muddy mine entrance."

"That's way more interesting than dealing with multi-species poop."

As we both laugh, I realize how much I lost when I gave my all to the pursuit of my supposedly awesome career. Memories of lonely nights in New York return with a vengeance. Ouch!

How could I have left such a fun friendship in the dust I kicked up in my mad scramble up the success ladder? And even now, after I return home, it's Peggy who calls, not me. Color me mortified.

"Hey, Peg," I say, suddenly serious. "I owe you a huge apology."

"What do you mean? I haven't seen you in ages. How could you owe me anything?"

"That's just it. I lost track of what really matters. I never stayed in touch with you or anyone besides Aunt Weeby and my parents. And let me tell you, the Big Apple may be great for retail therapy and Broadway, but there are just so many Coach bags and show tickets a girl can consume.

Besides, when you're alone, your best bet is a cat. And then mine died."

"And you think *my* brain's pickled? That's awful, Andie. Didn't you find a church home? And how about your neighbors? What was wrong with them?"

"Church was Sunday. The rest of the week was work, work, work. And you don't know New York. It's like a beehive—well, the apartment buildings are. You know, every worker bee buzzes home to the correct cubbyhole, slams the door, and hunkers down. It's so not *Mr. Rogers' Neighborhood*."

"Better you than me," Peggy says. "I couldn't have done it. But you must have liked it some. Otherwise you'd have come home sooner. Right?"

Would I? Not then, I wouldn't have. "It took me a good long while to figure out I'm not like that either, but I'm here now. I did love the gemological side of my New York life, though. That's about all I did love. And it wasn't enough."

From there the conversation leaps all over the place. Finally, we agree to have lunch on Saturday, when Josh has his guy time with their two little boys. We hang up, and I smile.

What an awesome feeling to know I still have a friend, a good one. *Thank you, Lord, for looking out for me when I didn't have the sense to do so.* I even have a home—the real deal, not my glorified closet in a très chic building in Tribeca.

Halfway up the stairs, I turn to check out the parlor and foyer one more time. They haven't changed; they haven't had to. The classic furniture radiates that aura of quality—good simple lines and rich, warm taupe upholstery. The Asian rug, with its traditional gold, black, and cream pattern, couldn't

44

be more ideal. The cherry side and dining room tables were Great-Great-Grandma Willetta's grandmother's once upon a time, so they're probably worth a bundle, and the drapes are ivory silk, luxury again. The soft scent of fresh flowers on the foyer console reminds me of all the other times I've walked into this house. Aunt Weeby will go without coffee, biscuits, or country ham before she'll forego her flowers. And they're fresh. Only fresh works for her.

I'm so not a New Yorker. Except for the shopping: Macy's, Saks, Bloomies, the designers' boutiques . . .

As I go upstairs, I glide my finger over the silky-smooth banister. Memories of family vacations, holidays, lazy summer afternoons, and above all else, love, blossom in me like a field of daisies under the summer sun. At the landing, I hug myself, and turn a slow, happy circle.

Then I grin. Forget about that approaching three-oh hill. No one's around. No one's gonna bust me. So I hike up a leg, and . . .

"Yeah, baby!" The banister's as slick as ever, the exhilaration the same. *Thank you, Jesus, for Aunt Weeby, Miss Mona, and the faboo banister too.*

That was then, three days ago. This is now. I've crash-landed into *The Twilight Zone*.

Time? It means nothing. Days zip past me in a hazy blur. I now have a good—bad, actually—idea of what sleepwalking feels like. And I never wanted to know in the first place. Now I'm in this new dimension—well, my body is—and I hear and say all the right things, but my mush-for-brain can't quite get around it all. Day after day of meetings with gemstone vendors and jewelry suppliers go well. I know most of them from my years in New York, and I do know my gemstones.

But then there's the other. You see, I'm suddenly the victim on a manic version of *What Not to Wear*. It's not one of my fave shows anymore, not after what I'm going through. What's worse, my survival isn't assured in this *Groundhog Day* cycle of planning meetings, rehearsals, and millions of fittings for the clothes Miss Mona and Aunt Weeby want me to wear on-screen.

But surprise, surprise! By the time two weeks of this madness have gone by, they have disagreed over every shirt, skirt, dress, and pants each has suggested.

And I wouldn't be caught dead in anything they choose. Starting with the inverted lampshade Aunt Weeby calls "darling." When she pulls it out of the dress bag, I go into shock. My reaction hovers between laughing, crying, and running back to New York and a fresh new ulcer. It's the exact shade of her cast and that diarrhea medicine.

What was she thinking?

"If you like it so much," I tell her, "buy yourself a lamp base and stick it on top. It's not going on me."

"But it's the perfect dress for your launch show, sugarplum. See how the lights make it glow? And retro's back in style."

I look again at the shiny pink satin, extreme Audrey Hepburn shirtwaist with the bouffant skirt. There's enough reflective fabric here to turn me into the world's tallest, crinkliest, pinkest lamp. Let me backtrack. Ms. Hepburn wouldn't have been caught dead in this thing. "Not this kind of retro."

"But pink's wonderful for a woman's complexion."

This shade of pink doesn't work for anyone—except maybe Miss Piggy. And I'm not that short.

By three o'clock, I dig in my heels. Enough is enough. "I'm *not* wearing pink! Would *you* buy diamonds from a Charlie-Brown's-little-girl-with-red-hair lampshade? News flash! I'm not in third grade anymore. And pink's toxic for redheads. No way."

Aunt Weeby's no pushover. "But it's such a happy color, sugarplum."

Miss Mona clears her throat. "I told you she should stick to cool colors like the greens, blues, and purples rather than your pink."

Aunt Weeby crosses her arms. "*Everyone* wears blue, green, and purple. We want her to stand out."

"Oh, she'll stand out in pink all right. I'm just not sure I want a Pepto bottle look-alike to try and sell my gems."

After a couple more go-rounds of this, I'm ready to offer them—and their pink monstrosity—to the first pasty troll I find. With two index fingers in the corners of my mouth, I whistle. Life comes to a standstill in our little corner of suburban Louisville.

A girl could get used to this kind of power.

"Here's a novel idea, ladies. *I* choose what I'm going to wear. And how about I stick to neutrals so viewers can focus on the gems and jewels?"

Amazing how brilliant my two geriatric fashionistas suddenly find me—about the neutrals, that is. They still don't trust me with my on-screen wardrobe, and nix my solo shopping spree.

Know what I find out? Louisville's got some primo shopping going on.

The next day, I do like a homing pigeon and hit Ann Taylor for a fab black floral jacquard jacket and pencil skirt, a caramel knit wrap sweater, and black wool pants. One day later, at Macy's I pick up a yummy BCBG dark green wool jersey dress with a cummerbund of the same fabric, a V-neck, and buttons all the way down the front.

Finally, after a twenty-four-hour hiatus from our extreme shopping safari, we hit the mother lode. Miss Mona drags me into a small, exclusive boutique—think Marc Jacobs, Donna Karan, Monique L'Huilhier, and a bunch of English and Italian design stars too. Suzi, the owner, finds me a Diane Von Furstenberg silk wrap dress, then leads me straight to the racks of killer shoes.

But by the time I get there, exhaustion zaps me. Try to do all I've done the past few weeks, then add helping Aunt Weeby clump around with that massive cast. It feels as though it weighs as much as she does. And she's not above playing on my sympathies to get her way when I dare suggest an extended break.

"Oh no, sugarplum," she says. "We're not done. Everything has to be near perfect. It's all because I love you."

I can almost hear the violin strings in the background, but what can I say? It is Aunt Weeby we're talking about here. You know I'd do just about anything for her, even cut off my nose . . . you finish the cliché.

Let's face it, anyone can tell I'm not myself when I balk at shoe shopping. I'm so all about shoes. But get real. Who's going to see my shoes behind the host's desk? I could do my shows in—*shudder*—Birkenstocks, and no one would know the difference.

And while I'm at the point where I'd rather wrap myself in my five-hundred-thread-count linens than shop, and the geriatric fashionistas give me no vote on the colors or styles,

I do fall in love with the shoes they choose for me. I score a pair of dark green velvet Stella McCartneys, some Manolo Blahnik beige patent leather Mary Janes, and a pair of Stuart Weitzman Kiss black kid leather pumps.

The best part of the shopping frenzy? Miss Mona insists on charging it to the network's American Express card. I usually hit either Marshall's or Filene's Basement for my designer fix, so the number of zeros on the bills leave me gasping.

Then, bright and early the next morning, they drag me back to the studio. Just shoot me.

Miss Mona's camera people subject me to multiple screen tests, makeup makeovers, and manicures. If the extreme shopping hadn't worn me out, I might've enjoyed the beautifying spree—I do have my well-developed girly-girl side.

On the other hand, I do get to plan my shows, to choose gemstones, jewelry pieces, and diamond semi-mounts for shoppers to mix-and-match according to their individual taste. I even get to choose my backdrops, which is too cool.

It's all about the gems, right?

Hah! Not by Aunt Weeby's reckoning.

"There's millions a' single men out there, sugarplum," she says on the way home after the remake Andie dog-and-pony show. "You have to look good. You never know when you'll catch one's eye."

I did tell you she's nuts. "On a *women's* shopping channel?"

"Their mothers shop, don't they?"

Oh goody. "If these men are still at home watching Mommy's shows, then, trust me, I don't want 'em."

"So, there you have it, sugarplum! You're plumb too picky for your own good."

49

"Discriminating. I'm sure if God wants me to marry, he has a great guy out there for me." I hope.

"Ah . . . so you're waiting for the perfect hottie."

"Yuck! I hate that word. It's tacky. And I'm so not looking, or waiting, for a guy, any guy."

No matter what I tell her, she can't believe I'm not the rosy-glowed romantic she is. Maybe I am, but would rather wait for my Prince Charming than stalk him down. But don't you dare tell her.

Then again, I'm not the driven executive Miss Mona has become, either. Who'd a thunk? Once upon a time these two were just small-town matrons with a weird thing for flea markets. Now one's the female Ted Turner of cable commerce, and the other one? I'm not sure what Aunt Weeby's really up to these days.

At least I get to work with nice people. There's Allison, my makeup artist. She knows her business, and can erase under-eye circles and create cheekbones where the Lord forgot to put any. But when it comes to me, the dangerous duo fights to hijack her color choice every time—toward the pink spectrum, you understand.

Then there's Julie Tuttle, Miss Mona's retired military rent-a-cop for the vault. She's the proud mama of twin girls. Every time I go check out the product, she talks endlessly about those sweeties and their daddy, her eyes full of stars.

I'm jealous. And the owner of a ticking biological clock. *Forgive me, Father.*

The other hosts—Tanya, Marcie, Wendy, Karen, Danni, and Rosemarie—are okay, but usually too busy to pay much attention to me. Well, all of them except Danni Sutherland. The dainty blonde has an Alaska-sized chip on her petite shoulder. The moment Miss Mona heard I was coming home, she yanked Danni from the weekly jewelry and gemstone show and stuck her with a couple more underwear—er . . . *lingerie* shows.

Eeuww! Can't say I blame her. Tell me, would *you* like to look into a camera and tell the whole, wide world how much you loooove your underwear and why?

Nuh-uh. Not me.

Which makes me wonder. What kind of woman buys bras and panties off a TV screen while the whole world watches? Beats me, but there must be gaggles of them out there, since the Shop-Til-U-Drop Network sells truckloads of the frilly, stretchy, cottony, slimming, or colorful things.

Something tells me I'm soon going to know those TV shoppers pretty darn well. My on-screen debut isn't too far off.

Heaven help me.

5<u>00</u>

It's D-day. Debut day.

So here I finish hair and makeup, my palms sweat, and I can't force down more than two sips of java, no matter how delish the fumes. It's not Starbucks, but when a woman's desperate, she copes.

But today there's just no coping going on, *capisce*?

As I walk from the green room—Hey! I know what that is now. It's the room where stars and lesser beings like me wait for our cue.

Where was I? Oh yeah. As I walk from the green room to the set, the list of product I'm scheduled to offer in hand, I try to tame the buzzards crash-landing in my gut. But they're so into their own thing that they pay me no attention. And a woman who talks to imaginary, carrion-eating raptors is certifiable, which I must be, since I agreed to this TV host gig in the first place.

What was I thinking?

"There you are!" Miss Mona says in a loud whisper.

I hurry toward her, but shoot a glance at the set. Danni is

still on, a pair of puce silk panties in her hand. "Is something wrong? Did I miss something? And why are you here? I thought you were interviewing someone for a camerawoman position."

"She called to tell me her flight from New York was delayed, so I came instead of sending Carla after you. I didn't want you to be late for your launch show."

The deep breath I take is none too steady, but I'm not about to 'fess up to my nerves. Somehow, this whole TV gemologist thing has grown on me in the last few weeks, and I'm as excited as I am nervous. I figure I'm either as loony as Miss Mona and Aunt Weeby, or else their brand of madness spreads like athlete's foot in high school locker rooms.

"No way was I going to be late. Does Sally have everything ready for the show?"

Miss Mona points to a stainless steel cart stacked high with tray upon tray of gorgeous gemstones. "She's as excited as you are about the launch. You should've seen her. She looked like a little girl at the candy counter."

"I don't know a woman who can honestly say she really, really doesn't like jewelry. And gemstones are what jewelry's all about."

The network's theme song starts to play, and my excitement ditches my bad case of nerves. Oh, I'm psyched, all right. All the gemstones I could ever want, and a TV audience full of potential gem collectors. What more could a true-blue gem geek want?

A rustle of activity breaks out behind me, and Miss Mona's face lights up like Times Square on New Year's Eve. "Oh, Andie! Do I have a surprise for you."

Uh-oh. Something about her excitement scares the pants

off me—figuratively speaking, you know. "Can it wait until after my show? I don't want to let anything distract me."

"Your surprise *is* the show, or part of it, anyway."

I clutch my lists to my green-silk-covered chest. My rose-polished nails dig into the pages for dear life. I take a breath and pray for strength. "Go for it. What's my surprise?"

Miss Mona unfurls her hand in the most dramatic, most Aunt Weeby–like gesture. My gaze follows that hand, and my jaw drops.

During the last three weeks, it's become more than obvious that the Shop-Til-U-Drop Network's feminine atmosphere is part of Miss Mona's genius. So imagine my reaction when what to my wandering eyes doth appear but a blond West Coast surfer and two comfy armchairs.

He smiles.

I shiver.

Wow!

The tall, Barbie-doll counterpart, towhead blond, silver silk-suited, tanned, blue-eyed surfer boy in Carla's clutches heads toward me, hand held out. I gape like a goldfish. Then I start to hyperventilate.

Carla grabs the armchairs and brings them to the edge of the set, clearly ready to wheel them into place once Danni and her panties are done. I'm so not ready for this.

Finally, when he's inches away, I get a grip. "Who're you?"

"Andie, honey," Miss Mona says.

I glance at her and catch sight of her canary-feathered grin. Why, why, why, why, why did I ever agree to do this?

Oblivious to my condition, she says, "I'd like you to meet Max Matthews, your brand-new cohost."

"My who?" Okay, so I'm not proud of the squeaky voice. But what's a girl to do when she gets a bombshell dropped on her head?

"You heard me. Max will be at your side for all your shows."

"B-but this is all about us. We're cable TV's estrogen pack!"

"Sure, honey, that's what we've been so far, and I know we've been very successful. But have you taken a good look at the network's name? There's something not quite right about the way we've been doing things around here. And then I had me a brainstorm. I figured out how to fix things. Max is my fix."

Brainstorm? Try monsoon. And just as dangerous. In that scary, red-blooded American woman's dream-man way. "How so?"

"Sugarplum—" Aunt Weeby's voice comes from behind me—"how can the S.T.U.D. Network be the S.T.U.D. Network when we've got us no stud?"

Gulp. No way was I going to try to answer that sneaky little rat's question. She was supposed to be home, watching me on her brand-new, flat-panel, hi-def TV. And I had no answer. Other than another question.

"The Stud Network?"

Miss Mona grins. "Isn't that so cute? That's what our customers call us. You know, S for Shop, T for Til, U for . . . well, for you, of course, and D for Drop. S-T-U-D. The S.T.U.D. Network."

I smack the palm of my hand on my forehead right between my brows. I've been had. Hornswoggled. Bushwhacked. I knew this job was a bad idea. From the very start.

What do I know about TV? For that matter, what do I know about studs? And I'm so not talking horse. Trust me, I know nothing of horses, networks, brass tacks, or human studs. Especially not the dream-man kind of stud. My track record with the other half of the human race isn't exactly stellar, as Aunt Weeby will be happy to tell you in mortifying detail.

That's why I haven't gone on a date in years.

When I agreed to this, no one said I'd have to take turns talking about jewels with a guy who's prettier than me *and* the gems. How am I going to squeak out a sound, much less pretend coherence?

"The best thing," Miss Mona says, "is that Max will take care of all your worries about on-camera experience—your inexperience. He's been doing TV weather for years."

"Really?" I croak.

"Really," the S.T.U.D. Network's token stud says in a really nice baritone. "I've worked for WZZP in Willandell, Missouri, for the last five years. It's good to finally meet you, Andie. I'm sure we're going to be great."

Carla drools.

Aunt Weeby swoons.

Miss Mona rapturizes.

Missouri . . . Who-Knows-Where, Missouri. Groan. And he says we're going to be great. He's sure of that how?

I hold out my hand. His long, tanned, sinewy fingers nearly swallow it up. And that's when I get the shock of my life—literally. A current sizzles up my fingers, arm, stomach, and rushes straight to my head.

Do I have to tell you I'm in trouble? Or did you figure it out?

"Uh . . . yeah. Great."

Eloquent, I am not. And great we are. *Not.* On camera.

You see, Max the Magnificent, stud or otherwise, knows nothing, *nothing* about gemstones. Which ignorance he proceeds to demonstrate to our customers. And which ignorance lights up my redhead's temper in fifty seconds or less.

How bad is he?

Let me count the ways.

Lights, camera, action! Here we go.

"Good afternoon, ladies. My name is Andrea Adams. I'm so thrilled to join the Shop-Til-U-Drop Network"—no way am I calling it that *other* name—"as your new jewelry and gemstone host. And here to my right is . . ."

"I'm Max Matthews, new to the lovely state of Kentucky . . ."

How does he do it? I can't take my eyes off him. He looks great and sounds even better, with that chocolate-rich baritone voice. Something warm swirls in my middle, and my tongue thickens to the consistency of a cotton ball. How am I supposed to do a show with him sitting so close?

I feel for the women of America, dropping like flies.

Then I realize he's staring at me, Aunt Weeby and Miss Mona are waving like windmills, and Hannah, the camerawoman, is smacking her four fingers against her thumb like a beak in the universal gesture for "Talk."

So I do. And for a while, we take turns giving the viewers our bios. Mine is short and sweet. Hometown girl goes Big Apple, but returns home wiser and happier to sell gemstones on TV. Then Max takes his turn. I tune out. He goes on and on and on.

When I notice Hannah doing her duck imitation again, I realize the show's dying, and I'd better do something. Like sell the gems I'm supposed to sell.

Fortunately for all of us, Sally, the show's merchandiser, had clamped a set of adjustable jeweler's tweezers around a magnificent solitaire stone and left it ready for me to launch the show. I pick up the tweezers to bring the stone in front of the white velvet drape we chose as a backdrop for the product. It trembles a little—just like I do.

"To start us off for real," I say, that nervous southern thick in my voice, "and so that y'all will get to know me quickly, I want you to know I'm a GIA certified master gemologist, and I'm about to introduce you to my favorite gemstone. Anybody know what this is?"

My cohost—*aaack!*—leans closer to get a look at the stone. The scent of his spicy masculine cologne surrounds me, ties my tongue in knots, and makes me hanker for those simpler days of rat-race stress and gnawing ulcer pain in New York.

Oh my.

The camera zooms in on the brilliant orange gem and off me. I'm so in trouble. But so is the ditzy duo when I get done here.

Does the word "setup" ring a bell?

Thanks to the zillion rehearsals, I stutter out my spiel. "This . . . uh . . . this is one of . . . ah . . . the earth's rarest stones." *Get a grip, woman.* "It was first discovered in the Spessart Forest in Germany in the 1800s, and since that time, pockets have been found in Nigeria, Namibia, and even California and Brazil. The finest stones, though, have come from Namibia. The color can range from a bright yellow, through a citrusy orange, to a burning-embers shade of red. The most valuable—and desirable—hue is the exact mandarin orange I'm offering you today."

My heart rate decides to settle down when Max leans back into his chair. Phew! I can get to my job again.

"Since there's never been enough supply for this stone to go fully commercial"—my voice is still embarrassingly breathy—"I'm sure most of you are wondering what it is."

Miss Mona makes like a traffic cop. I humor her and stop to create dramatic effect. Something clatters to my right, but I refuse to let Max distract me any more than he already has. "You may be surprised to learn that this intense, yummy color belongs to a . . . garnet!"

For some inexplicable reason all his own, Max finds my statement hilarious. I shoot him what I hope is a stern glare. But before I can gather my wits and go on with my presentation, he oh-so-generously shares the reason for his humor.

"Everyone knows garnets are red," he says. "Come on, tell us. What is it? For real."

A gemstone host who doesn't know garnets? I'm so in trouble.

"You're such a kidder," I say through gritted teeth.

"I'm not kidding. *You* are. Garnets are red."

"Not *just* red."

"Red."

"And green and orange and yellow and purple—even color-change, like alexandrite. They come in every color but blue."

"No, they don't."

"Yes, they do."

"Red."

What am I doing? My job's to sell gems, not to argue with a dud. A hunk of a dud, but a dud to the—oh yeah—max.

Get with the program, Andie. "Max's response shows the common misconception about garnets. I can guarantee that this gorgeous jewel *is* a garnet, a spessartite garnet. The difference between this one and an almondine—that's the red kind—is the absence of iron and presence of manganese in the chemical composition. Iron turns the material red, or worse, brown."

"Huh?"

Did I say we're doomed? No? Well, I'll say it now: We're doomed.

I turn my face so the viewers don't think I'm totally rude, but I stare at the way-less-distracting stone. "That small difference, Max, makes the manganese-colored stones rare—and pricey." Back to the camera. "But our wonderful vendors have negotiated for us an incredible price. And when we get a good deal, we give you a great deal. This internally clean, two-carat stone is priced at only four hundred and seventy-five—"

"*That* little thing?" Max roars. "Four hundred bucks?"

If I had a weapon, and if I was the violent kind, and if I wasn't a Christian . . . well, you get the idea. I consider ducking under the desk. But I'm not that big a coward.

Yet.

"I think we can safely assume that Max has no experience with gems. A fine spessartite garnet like this"—I turn the tweezers to better show off the stone—"internally clean and beautifully cut, can go for up to twelve hundred dollars per carat. And this one is two full carats. Quite a bargain—for a mandarin orange garnet."

"That's insane!"

"That's an investment."

He snorts. "An investment's stock in that . . . that Jimmy Buffet—no, not Jimmy, *Warren*—that Warren Buffet guy's investment company."

I ignore his blather. "Ladies and gentlemen, I can report that statistics show gemstone collecting as the fastest growing hobby in our country, and as an up-and-coming favorite investment too. So at only four hundred seventy-five dollars? How can you pass up such a great deal?"

Max wriggles in his chair. Out the corner of my eye, I see a flash of silver. Good. He's picked up the tweezers that hold the gemstone I'm scheduled to feature after the garnets on this nightmare of a launch show. Maybe he'll learn to use them and do something constructive.

"Here." I angle my hand in front of the white velvet drape, then hold the tweezers so the garnet lines up with my ring finger. "See how fabulous the mandarin orange garnet looks on the hand? It's so gorgeous that many women are choosing colored stones like this one for engagement and wedding rings. Now what girl wouldn't want to wear a beautiful bit of captured, fiery sunshine on her finger?"

"Diamonds are a girl's best friend . . ." Max's baritone does a decent job on Marilyn's trademark song. Not that I need it.

Time for damage control.

"Max has a point. But let me tell you, diamonds have gone up 30 percent in recent years. Know what a so-so two-carat diamond sells for? Way more than four hundred and seventy-five dollars. You can take that to the bank."

"You think you can talk women into going cold turkey on diamonds?"

He's so incredulous, it sounds as though he's mocking me. Not cool. Maybe I can talk Aunt Weeby and Miss Mona into going cold turkey on *him*. "I find colored stones just as exciting as diamonds."

His muttered response isn't—thankfully—clear. I try to ignore him and get on with my job. "So how many of you lovely ladies out there are going to be so lucky as to own one of these gorgeous stones? I see on my monitor that a bunch of you have already taken advantage of this great offer. You're smart shoppers. And we still have some quantity left for the next few callers—but not a lot. I don't even have enough for two per state, so hurry, grab yours before they're all gone."

Five feet behind the camera, Carla, Miss Mona's assistant, mimics a phone with her hand. Relief is good.

"Let's go to the phones." I squint against the studio lights to read the monitor screen on the desk. "Hello? Is this Sissy from Alaska?"

Giggles titter over the air. "Yes! I can't believe I got through!"

Even a giddy viewer is better than Max. "I'm happy you called. What do you think of the spessartite?"

"Oh, dearie, it's just precious! I saw it, and just had to elbow Charlie. I told him I had to have it. So he bought it for me. Told him it'd keep me thinking of him while he's on the road all those days at a time."

"Are you a collector, Sissy?"

"Oh, dearie, I collect *everything*. I haven't met the teapot I haven't loved. And porcelain dolls? Why, they're my babies. Well, aside from Fritzi and Mitzi, my Pomeranians. And then there's the plates and the quilts and . . ."

Her list boggles this mind. "So tell me, will you be setting the stone? Do you need a diamond semi-mount? Because if you do"—I lower my voice to girls-sharing-secrets level—"I have a faboo tray of them to show you. Six, six beautiful diamond semi-mounts."

"And we're off to the races! Giddyap!" Max says. "What's a semi-mount?"

I spin my chair and face him, distracting or not. "You don't know a spessartite from spit, and now you ask me what a semi-mount is? You don't know a thing about the gem trade, do you?"

Tweezers in hand, he shrugs. "Never said I did."

"But—how . . . you're supposed to be a gem expert!"

"Why?"

"Because we're selling gems."

"No. *We're* not selling gems. *You* are selling gems."

"Fine. But then what good are you?"

Just beyond the camera, Miss Mona is making like a football ref calling for a time-out. Everything about her blares STOP. Okay. I'll stop. For now. But just wait until this fiasco is over . . .

"We have three more stones available. Who's going to pick them up? Who's going to own a stone that's close to extinction from the earth's crust? Who wants—"

"Ooops!"

Max's tweezers clatter onto the desk. Something sparkly skitters across the surface, falls off the edge, and I see it bounce toward the camera tripod. My jaw drops.

Did he really just do that? And Miss Mona thought he was a good idea because . . . ?

When I collect myself, I point at Max. "You! How could

you? What kind of idiot drops a princess-cut diamond? What were you thinking?"

"Before you get a chance," he says in that ridiculously wonderful voice, "I'll say my kind of idiot. What's the big deal? I dropped it. It's not as if I tossed it through the goalpost uprights, then did a victory dance on top of it. I'll just go pick it up."

"NO!" I leap out of my chair. "Don't you even think about it. Don't move."

As I kneel to pick up the gem, the channel's theme song starts up again. Relief turns my knees to overcooked linguine, and I plop down onto my butt.

Thank you, Lord. The launch show is over. The nightmare has ended. I can get back to the rest of my life. Far, far away from the S.T.U.D. studios.

You know it.

6 <u>00</u>

Decision made, I scramble up, shaking. I'm so mad. Diamond in hand, I stalk off the set and, like a bride on Filene's Basement gown sale day, make for Miss Mona. "I quit! There is no way I'm working with that joker ever again. He knows nothing, *nothing* about gems."

"Oh, Andie!" She chortles. "You have no idea. This is *the* most successful show we've ever had. You and Max are wonderful."

"Huh?" I stick a finger in my right ear and jiggle. "What'd you say?"

"The phones haven't stopped ringing since the two of you went on. We sold out of the spessartites, all the semi-mounts went too—sight unseen—and the viewers want to know when you and Max are on next. They don't want to miss it!"

Now I'm really living in a nightmare. "But he doesn't know a thing! He said some really dumb stuff on the air. And he dropped a diamond. A diamond, Miss Mona. The one we were supposed to feature next—but couldn't. He messed up the show from the start."

Aunt Weeby clumps up, a radiant grin on her face. "Sugar-plum! You and Max are a hit! I was in the call room with the customer service girls, and I heard all them phone calls. You're a hit! The viewers love you and Max. They think you're a perfect couple—you know: Hepburn and Tracy, *Moonlighting*'s Maddy and David, Miss Piggy and Kermit."

Oh great. Her plan really is for me to join the ranks of pink-obsessed pig puppets. "But—"

"It's everything I wanted and more," Miss Mona adds. "Sparks! Fireworks! Chemistry! I knew it would work."

Chemistry? Did these two ever think to check my past? I'm the one who got kicked out of chem lab once for setting the place on fire. I hardly think their plan included spontaneous combustion of the redhead-with-a-temper kind.

"You two are nuts. Keep Mr. Chemistry. I'm outta here. You can teach Max the Magnificent a thing or two about the gem trade. Oh, oh! And how 'bout this? I'm sure Miss Piggy would love to stage a comeback and be his sidekick. I hear she's between projects these days."

With no dignity left, I don't care that every employee stares at me as I stomp out of the studio. I can't believe I set myself up for this. And to think I gave up that fab career of mine in New York for a pair of lunatic seniors, the chance to humiliate myself before millions, and a know-nothing pretty boy. I thought that was a good idea because . . . ?

"But you were great . . ." Miss Mona's wail follows me all the way to the door.

We were great, all right. A great, big, fat flop.

I should've known better than to let Aunt Weeby and Miss Mona take over my life.

Now what, Lord?

In the parking lot, I realize something's cutting into my palm. I glance down and groan.

You got it. I walked out with the diamond Max dropped. And while I can return it in the morning, once I'm not so mad, I don't feel right taking a three-carat treasure home with me.

But would you want to go back to the scene of that crime? I don't either.

And that's when my conscience kicks in, right on schedule. I'm convinced that mental tyrant of mine is hitched at the hip to heaven. So I try to reason. Why? I don't know. I've yet to win a single argument. But I give it a go anyway.

"Okay, Lord. I know I have to take it back. But it was such a perfect exit!"

I take three steps toward Aunt Weeby's old, clunky VW Jetta—she loaned it to me until I find myself a decent set of wheels to buy. Mine bit the dust when I pulled into town.

Where was I? Oh yeah, praying. *God?*

Since he doesn't answer me, my discomfort grows.

"Aw, c'mon. You know I'm honest. I'm not going to run away with Miss Mona's property. I'll bring it back. Besides, I'm too embarrassed."

Then it hits me. No matter how much I want to flee, there's nothing I can do about it. There's a very good reason the Bible calls anger a no-no. I let mine get the better of me, and I stormed out without my purse. Uh-huh. You know it.

No purse, no keys. No keys, no Jetta getaway.

Bummer.

"Oh, okay. I get the message. I gotta go back in there and

eat humble pie. And when I see anyone, today or tomorrow, I'll have to confess and ask forgiveness. As always, you're right. Just don't leave me now, Lord. Help me through it all."

Not feeling a whole lot better, I retrace my steps, push open one of the massive glass doors, and reenter the building. In the lobby, a tall brunette in a gorgeous black suit stops me.

"Are you Mona Latimer?"

I laugh at the stranger's question. "You've got to be kidding. She's my great-aunt's best friend. I'm Andie Adams, one of the hosts here. Who're you?"

She waves. "No one, really. I mean, I'm supposed to meet Miss Mona for an interview. I'm a couple of hours late because of my flight."

"Aha! So you're the one. She'll be happy to see you." Especially since it'll take her mind off the debacle Max and I just staged. "Why don't you go down that hall on the left, and keep going to the end. Her assistant should be there. She'll get you to Miss Mona."

I turn to get back to my business, but then say over my shoulder, "Good luck!"

She doesn't smile back but only nods.

Back to righting my latest wrong—I told you trouble follows me, right? Oh, well. First I have to deal with the purse and then return the diamond to the vault. While I don't have the car keys, I do have the vault combination memorized. At least I don't have to go back to the scene of the debacle just yet. I can take care of the diamond first, and then face the music.

I find my dressing room door about an inch ajar. Strange. I'm pretty sure I closed it all the way before I headed for makeup and hair. But that's no big deal, I guess. I don't have anything anyone would want.

I walk in and my ears are assaulted.

"*Squawk! Shriek, shriek!*"

My ears ring and my heart does a hundred-yard dash. "What…?"

Then I see it. And what a sight it is. I now know for sure, without a shadow of a doubt, that I've walked into one of those parallel universes Trekkies talk about.

Who's ever heard of a birdcage in a corporate building? Especially a birdcage that comes complete with what looks like a beautiful miniature parrot swinging on a perch.

"*Squawk! Shriek, shriek!*"

How can something so beautiful make such a nasty noise? And the little loudmouth *is* gorgeous. Bright orange-red head feathers blend into yellow ones on its neck. Those shade toward red again down the body, but then melt into the yellow on the wings. The most extreme wing feathers are blue-green and match the long tail feathers—I'm talking long as in as long as the body itself. The bird's chest is that same orange-red as its neck. Beautiful.

The critter tilts its head and with its round black eyes peers at me, as if wondering who I might be and why I'm suddenly here. If it weren't for the diamond, I'd be wondering the same thing myself. I do notice the pointy beak and sharp claws, also black—in sharp contrast with all the brilliant color. They don't exactly reassure me.

"*Squawk! Shriek, shriek!*"

"All righty then. I get the message. I'll keep my distance."

But I do have to move the cage to get to my Coach bag, which I left on my small armchair. Whoever brought the feathered invader in here stuck the cage on top of the purse. The little pile of feathers objects to my efforts to retrieve my handbag—at ear-splitting decibel level.

"Okay, okay. I'm sorry." I drop the cage out of my way right next to the chair. "Don't get your feathers all ruffled now. You're fine."

Sadly, my Stella McCartneys aren't. The cage, small though it is, has a tiny water bowl, which sloshes its contents all over. Some drops—enough—hit the lovely dark green velvet. All that extreme shopping down the drain.

My earlier frustration returns. What a rotten day. "I can't wait until it's over," I tell the showy bird. "And don't complain again. I'm no happier than you are. And by the time I come back tomorrow, you better be gone."

Purse in hand, I hurry to the ladies' room—yepper, that's right, the bathroom. In their never-ending, way-out-there wisdom, Aunt Weeby and Miss Mona figure no sane robber would think to check out the restroom for a vault. So right between the last of six sinks and the hot-air hand dryer, behind the walnut wall panel, one finds the Shop-Til-U-Drop Network's vault.

That's right. I'm with ya. Crazy.

When I walk into the bathroom and don't see Julie at her post, I get that hinky feeling of something not quite right. But ready to go hide out in my room at the house, I press the exact spot that activates the spring-loaded panel. It swings out and the massive steel door gleams at me. The lock, with its coded numbers, is the last hurdle before I can ditch the diamond and go home.

Once I plug in the right sequence, the tumblers click into place, and I give the huge wheel-shaped lock a spin. Good. I'm just that much closer to home.

But when the door swings toward me, I stumble. My eyes pop. My mouth opens, but nothing comes out.

My hands shake.

My stomach heaves.

I grow cold, then hot as I lean over to get a better look at the man sprawled facedown on the floor of the vault, a puddle of blood under his head. Horror gets the best of me, and I let out a wrenching, heartfelt scream.

"HELP!" Then quieter, "Oh, Lord Jesus . . . please, *please* help."

I don't know if I blacked out or if my brain just blocked out the awfulness, because I remember nothing more until the door bursts open and Julie runs in. Behind her are Miss Mona, Aunt Weeby, Carla, Sally, and Max.

"Andie! Are you okay—" Julie cuts off her own question with a gasp. She goes for her pistol, holds out her free hand to keep the others from crowding after her, and then steps into the vault. "Call 9-1-1."

The irregular *thump-thump* of Aunt Weeby's walking cast comes up behind me. She wraps her arm around my waist. "What happened, sugarplum?"

That's when I realize my teeth are chattering so hard I can't even form an answer. The trembling spreads down through my body. I feel chilled, colder than I have ever felt before. My head spins. My knees go watery and my stomach turns into a vast pit.

A rumble of furniture pierces the fog in my brain. Then, "Here," Max says.

Next thing I know, I'm in the armchair that usually sits in

the left corner, just inside the ladies' room door. Miss Mona is kneeling in front of me, her hands rubbing mine. Aunt Weeby stands behind me, her hands on my shoulders.

"Is he . . . dead?" Sally whispers.

I try to draw in enough breath to answer, but my body still refuses to cooperate, not that I know what to say. The best I come up with is a weak shrug.

"Hush!" Miss Mona admonishes. "Andie's in no kind of shape to chitchat right now. Besides, Julie's checking out the . . . the person. Did anyone call the police?"

"I'm on it, Miss Mona," Max says. Despite my earlier anger toward him, all I feel right now is a swell of gratitude.

The room, eerily still and silent, then resonates with Max's beautiful voice. What he says isn't so beautiful.

". . . We have a person in the vault. Security is with him, so I can't tell you much about his condition. What I did see is blood under his head, and he's not moving. Please send us help—and fast."

Somewhere in the gray desert that my mind has become, I register his calm demeanor. How can he pull that off? I've been aware of . . . *it*, the man on the floor, longer than he has, I'm sitting, and I still feel as though I'm going to shatter into a million pieces.

I don't want to hear about gender differences, okay?

A very green-around-the-gills Julie steps out of the vault and pushes the steel door back a bit. I'm glad to not have to see that broken body on the floor anymore.

"He's dead," she says, her voice strained. "But I don't know who he is. Of course, he doesn't work here, and shouldn't have been in the building at all. But I do know something about how he got in here."

72

I draw on all my determination and push myself to the edge of the chair. Everyone stares at me.

"Does it . . ." My voice fails me, and while they all make comforting noises, I'm not willing to play the wilting lily any longer. I suck in a rough breath and square my shoulders. "Is that why you weren't here when I walked in?"

Julie nods. "Davina called to tell me she saw a stranger walking around the building. She asked me to check it out, since I'm better equipped"—she pats the pistol she's sheathed again—"to handle an intruder than she is. Now we know he came inside and slipped in here while I was looking out there."

Miss Mona stands. "Too bad you didn't find him."

The bathroom door bangs open. "What is going on here?" Danni asks, her voice shrill.

My feathered friend makes his . . . her . . . its arrival known. *"Squawk! Shriek, shriek!"*

Everyone jumps. I gulp and a nervous giggle pops out. "Uh-oh."

Miss Mona, white as a sheet, draws herself up to her full, statuesque height. *"What* is that?"

I point to the cage in Danni's hand. "That's what I found when I went to my dressing room for my purse. I grabbed my bag and came here to return the diamond Max dropped during the show. I never gave the bird another thought. Anybody ever seen it before? Danni?"

She shakes her head. "I just went to my dressing room—minding *my* business—the noise was just awful, so I went to see what you were up to. I've never seen the bird before. And you know I'd never forget something like"—she lifts the cage for all to see—*"this."*

This time, I'm not the only one with a nervous laugh;

everyone seems to welcome the chance to diffuse some of the tension in the room.

I recover first. "Anybody else think our flashy little visitor has something to do with the guy in the vault?"

From somewhere far away, the sound of a siren approaches. "Thank you, Lord," I whisper. I lace my hands together and hold on tight. Even though I'm glad the police are nearly here, something tells me I'm in for a wild and wooly ride.

Julie heads for the door. "I'll go get the officer . . . officers. I'm sure they'll have sent more than one patrol car."

Again, everyone falls silent. The only sound in the room comes from the bird's claws skittering across a bar in the cage. When the bathroom door opens again and Julie leads in a middle-aged uniformed man, the bird lets out its now-familiar *"Squawk! Shriek, shriek!"*

The startled cop shakes his head and narrows his eyes, but doesn't get a chance to say a word.

"Oh, Donald, dear!" Aunt Weeby hurries to his side as fast as her klutzy cast will let her. "I'm so glad you're the one who's come. Something so very, very nasty has happened here. I . . . I've never seen anything like this before."

The officer—Donald—takes Aunt Weeby's hand, tucks it into his elbow, and with his other hand, gives it a pat. "It's going to be okay, Miz Weeby. We'll just get to the bottom of this . . . whatever it is, right quick here."

He gestures to the two officers in the doorway, and the man and woman enter the bathroom. It's getting mighty crowded in here all of a sudden. And to think that before today no male had breached the doors of the Shop-Til-U-Drop Network's headquarters. Now we have three of 'em in

74

the building—four, if you count the dead one—and they're all in the ladies' room, no less!

I have to admit, I don't mind. The more the . . . well, not merrier, considering the circumstances, but it's much better to have company at a time like this.

Officer Donald—since I don't know his full name—goes into the vault, followed by the other two cops and Julie. The rest of us wait, the silence again thick and heavy. Until the bird does its thing again.

I shoot it a glare, and realize he—she?—is growing more restless, or maybe frantic's more like it, by the moment. It crabs along the rough white perch attached to the right side of the cage, then bites one of the slim steel wire bars and, fireman-like, slides down to the floor. There it waddles from wire bar to wire bar until it reaches the back of the enclosure, where with beak and claws it climbs back up high enough to reach the almost empty water bowl. It dips its beak into the water, throws back its colorful head, and swallows. Then it looks to either side, flaps its wings furiously, and lets out another series of screams.

As the little critter does all this, I notice what looks like a piece of paper stuck to the back of the cage. How I didn't spot it when I first found it in my dressing room, I don't know.

Well, I do know. I was too busy worrying about how embarrassed *I* felt, and how little *I* wanted to accept responsibility for *my* hot temper. But enough about that for the moment. I'll deal with that—me—later.

The piece of paper turns out to be a small envelope with a card inside. My midlength nail comes in handy to open it, and from my right side Miss Mona says, "What do you have there?"

"It's a card—oh! It's addressed to me. But how could that be?"

"If you read it," Max says, a hint of humor in his voice, "we might all find out."

What I read breaks my heart. "I can't believe this." A tear rolls down my cheek. "I know who the man in the vault is—was. And he's nice, the nicest vendor I worked with in New York. I'm so, so sorry . . ."

"A vendor?" Aunt Weeby looks confused.

Can't say I blame her. I'm pretty confused too. "Mr. Pak deals in the most fabulous rubies, Burmese material, the finest in the world. Roger and I met with him at least four times a year to buy stock."

Miss Mona steps closer. "Did he come here to see you? Did you know he was coming?"

"I had no idea he'd be here, even though he says in his card that he came to wish me luck in my new job."

"Squawk! Shriek, shriek!"

"What about the bird?" Sally asks, her eyes big dark pools of questions.

"That's what's so crazy." I shove a bunch of hair that's come loose from my chic on-screen updo off my forehead. "The bird's supposed to be a gift for me. What would make Mr. Pak think I'd want a noisy bird?"

"Tsk, tsk, tsk!"

Did I tell you Aunt Weeby tsk-tsks better than anyone else? Do I need this? Now?

"Andrea Autumn Adams! You know better than that, young lady. Why, it's not one bit polite to question a present. I don't know what's come over you since you left for that Sodom and Gomorrah city a' yours."

76

Stunned by my aunt's outburst, I notice the crease between her brows, the white line around her lips, and the tight grip of one hand on the other. A swell of sympathy rises in me. And then I realize she's still talking to me.

"... I'm so thankful the Lord saw fit to let you get yourself all rusted up while you were out there. I reckon you wouldn't've come home otherwise. And you do need yourself a good dose a' Great-Grandma Willetta's wisdom—and maybe some a' her fish oil too."

Heaven help me—and my stressed-out aunt. "I'm not questioning a present, and I'm not being ungrateful, Aunt Weeby. But I never said anything to Mr. Pak to make him think I'd want a parrot—"

"A parrot?" she asks. "That bitty thing there's a parrot? I thought they were big ol' things with can-opener beaks."

I hand the card to Aunt Weeby. "See for yourself. According to Mr. Pak, this is a Sun Conure, a small breed of parrot."

"Hmm . . . ," Aunt Weeby murmurs.

Sally leans over my aunt's shoulder. "Oh! Look here. He says the bird's name is Rio, Rio de Janeiro, like the city in Brazil. How cute!"

Carla, who's been silent up to now, chuckles. "Would you look at that? He just pooped."

Max laughs.

Miss Mona leans over to look at Rio. "He is beautiful, Andie. And I'll bet you very, very expensive. It's mighty . . . unusual to have a parrot for a pet. I never met a parrot owner before, you know. I'm sure it's going to be real interesting too."

The vise that took hold around my forehead when I first saw the bird—Rio—squeezes harder. I'd thought I'd be leaving my troubles behind in the Big Apple. Instead, I seem to be attracting new ones here faster than my little black dress does lint.

I mean, think about it. First, I agree to work for Miss Mona, trouble if anything. Then, Aunt Weeby and Miss Mona decide I'm a paper doll in need of a makeover. Next, Max the Magnificent and his gemstone ignorance blindsides me. And that's when things really get . . . what did Miss Mona call it? Oh yeah. Interesting.

Right.

Can we agree that finding a dead ruby vendor in the vault is trouble? *Big* trouble.

Someone somewhere must be laughing. But it sure isn't me. My heart aches for Mr. Pak. Plus there's a Mrs. Pak in Thailand, one who'll mourn the loss of a truly nice man.

And what am I supposed to do with a screaming, molting, pooping machine?

I'm in trouble all right.

Which fact permeates every corner of my being when Officer Donald comes out of the vault, locks his gaze with mine, and heads right for me, a piece of paper—yeah, another troublesome piece of paper in less than five minutes—in hand.

"Any idea, Miss Andie, why this dead fellow would have your name and the address of the network in his hand?"

Dorothy's tornado seems to have lost its way. Instead of Kansas, it's decided to strike Kentucky this time. And instead of a cute little mutt named Toto, it's decided to pick me up, spin-cycle me to bits, and then spit me out in the middle of yet another episode of *The Twilight Zone*.

And right into trouble with the law.

I gotta get a life. For real.

Oh, wait. That's what I thought I was doing when I came back home. Where did I go wrong?

7:00

The next morning, when the alarm clock goes off, I force one eye open a crack, reach a hand out from under the comfy down comforter, and smack the beeping bully silent. But for some strange reason, the alarm screams again a second later.

My head pounds in response. "Why . . . ? Why today?"

After the day I had yesterday, I don't want to wake up, much less deal with a dysfunctional alarm clock. Miss Mona had said I didn't have to do today's show, but after everything that went wrong during that disaster of a launch, I don't think it's in my best interest—or the network's—for me to pull a no-show. I do need sleep, though, before I can face that camera—and the whole wide world—again.

What Max the Magnificent does is his business.

The relentless alarm continues to rattle my brain. "*Aaarrgh!*"

There's no two ways about it. I have to do something about that noise. Inch by inch, I drag my exhausted body upright, and rub my eyes to clear them of their early morning sleep fog. And then I notice that the clock isn't beeping at all. But the screams haven't let up one bit.

"What on earth—" I tap my forehead between my brows. "Ugh. Rio!" I wish he was a nightmare. If he were, now that I'm awake, he'd just—*poof!*—disappear.

No such luck.

"Pipe down! It's too early for this. Go back to sleep."

A wild batting of his wings against the cage bars accompanies another barrage of shrieks. I slump down onto the bed again, my back against the padded headboard. Sure, he's a beautiful animal, but I can't stand his racket, and I don't know a thing about birds. What does one do with a parrot for a pet?

At the very least, I know he needs water, so it's good I refilled his bowl before I went to sleep last night.

I shudder. What a night . . . day! Donald Clark—*Chief* Donald Clark—raked me over the interrogatory coals until late into the night. If nothing else, he's thorough and determined.

In that whole time he never let his eyes drift away from my face. "And you say you didn't come up with some kinda plan to have him meet you here at the network?" he asked me for what must've been the thousandth time.

"Oh, for goodness sake, Donald!" Aunt Weeby finally burst out. "The girl's told you and told you she doesn't know a thing about this here Pak man's trip to Louisville. If she doesn't know, she doesn't know, and it doesn't make no never mind how many times you ask or how many different ways you ask it. Why, I'm about ready to swing my purse at your fat head and give you what-for. Ten thirty came and waved us good-bye, and you're still asking her the same ol' thing. I'm tired, she's tired, and we want to go home."

He slapped his hands against his thighs, then stood. "Well, Miz Weeby. It might not hurt if you looked at it from where I stand. Your niece comes to town, and next I know, I have me a dead Thai in Miss Mona's vault."

Aunt Weeby waved. "Coincidence, Donald, dear. The one doesn't have a thing to do with the other."

"Beggin' pardon, ma'am," he said, dogged and unfazed by her scolding. "The victim brought Andrea Adams a mighty pricey present, and he even had her name and address on a note in his hand. That to me doesn't spell no coincidence."

By then, I'd had it. Aunt Weeby was right. I was tired. And the chief's questions felt a gnat's hair away from police harassment. Plus Aunt Weeby needed to rest. With what little oomph I had left, I pushed myself to my feet. "Chief Clark?"

Once I had everyone's attention, I went on. "Can I make a couple of points clear here?" He nods, and I go on. "When Julie got to Mr. Pak, and even when you and your officers checked him out, he was still warm and the blood wet." Oh yeah. I grossed myself out when I thought of that, but the thought of jail time grossed me—freaked me—more. "So if we use even as little logic as a pigeon in Central Park boasts of, we all know I couldn't have hurt Mr. Pak."

He brought heavy silver brows close over the bridge of his nose. "And how would your city pigeon and I know that?"

"I have what might be the world's best, tight-as-a-two-sizes-small-shoe alibi. I was in front of a camera—live, you know?—in plain view of millions of America's shopping-crazed women."

He pushed his square jaw out. "Who's to say you didn't kill him before you went on to start up with your show?"

"I didn't have time." I tugged on a bunch of hair slicked

into the updo. "This took about forty-five minutes to cook up, and then I went straight to makeup. You can check with the hairdresser, Cecelia, and Allison, the makeup girl. I was on time for my show too. All that doesn't leave much time for me to kill Mr. Pak and stick him in the vault."

He narrowed his eyes. "How about after the show? When you stomped off the set all by yourself?"

"I wasn't out of sight of the rest of the staff for more than five minutes. I don't know a thing about killing, but I'm sure it must take more than five minutes to kill someone and stash him away in a vault."

Julie, whom the chief had held hostage too, stood. She looked as pooped as I felt. With a shaky hand, she wiped her eyes, and started for the bathroom door.

"Where d'you think you're heading, Julie?" the chief roared. "I'm not done here."

"You're done with me," Julie answered. "And you're done with Andie. She's right. She had no time to kill that man, and what's worse, you know it. Just because you don't have a quick answer doesn't mean you can force one out of where there isn't one."

"You're vouching for her?"

"We all are, Chief." She opened the door. "And my girls had to go to bed without me. It's the first time ever I haven't been there to hear their prayers. Had it been for a good reason, I wouldn't be so steamed. Go home and get some sleep. You might do better figuring things out in the morning after you've snagged some shut-eye."

Julie's no-nonsense statement gave everyone else the push we needed. In spite of the chief's sputters, we all said good night and went our individual ways.

82

At home, it took all my wiles to duck a dousing of Great-Great-Grandma Willetta's fish oil.

Now I have this charming wake-up call to deal with.

Why me? Why does trouble stick to me like lint to black velvet? Oh, did I ever mention it does? Well, now you know.

It occurs to me the poor parrot might actually be hungry. But what does a parrot eat? Aside from the clichéd "Polly wanna cracker" bit, I don't know what to feed it. And that might be why he keeps complaining. I figure I'd squawk too if I hadn't had a bite to eat since the night before.

Come to think of it, I haven't had a bite to eat.

When I drag myself to the bedroom door, I catch the *thump-thump* of Aunt Weeby's cast moving around down in the kitchen. "Hey, there! Do we have any crackers?"

"What d'you want crackers for?" she asks. "I'm making us eggs, bacon, grits, and fruit. Isn't that better'n any ol' crackers?"

For my taste buds? Oh yeah. My arteries? Oh my.

"Breakfast sounds great. The crackers aren't for me, but the bird might want some. He's been letting the universe know he's not happy, and I don't know what one feeds a parrot. I didn't give him anything last night. He's probably starved."

"Maybe it wasn't such a great idea to haul him up to your room. Whyn't you bring him to the kitchen? It's sunny, and I seem to recollect parrots are from hot, steamy, sunny places."

"They're tropical, Aunt Weeby. I'm not sure Kentucky's ever going to fake him out, not even if you use the electric oven like a space heater." But since anything's better than rooming with the feathered earsplitter, I grab the cage and head down.

"Maybe we won't pull no wool over his eyes," Aunt Weeby

says, "but at least he'll be outta your room. When he kicks up a fuss again, he won't wake you up."

I snort. "Hey, this is no stealth bird we have here. I'll hear him coming miles before I see him. How could anyone not hear that awful noise?"

As if on cue, Rio lets out an ear-shattering "*Shriek!*"

"Oh, sugarplum. He sure is loud. Gotta say that much for him." She shakes her head. "Wonder why that foreign man came all that way here, and to give you a parrot, for goodness' sake. Isn't that the most peculiar thing ever?"

Aunt Weeby's talking about peculiar? I love it when pots call kettles black.

"I've wondered myself. And aside from wishing me good luck with the new job, and telling me a little about Rio, the card still leaves things clear as the tax code."

She arranges four strips of sizzling bacon, a field of sunflower-colored eggs, and a perfectly pillowy biscuit on a plate, and then, next to all that, builds Mt. Kilimanjaro out of fluffy grits. My mouth waters and my stomach growls on cue.

"Well, I sure do hope Donald gets to the bottom a' this whole hoo-hah. Who'd've thought we'd find us a dead man in the vault?"

I dig into the fat-fest she puts in front of me, and wonder if it wouldn't be more efficient to just trowel the stuff onto my hips and thighs. This living with Aunt Weeby deal could prove risky for my wardrobe. And thinking of wardrobe, what am I going to wear today? To counteract that fiasco yesterday, I have to look way more professional than usual. Maybe the Ann Taylor pieces will seal the deal.

But the thought of the show gives me the worst case of cold feet I've ever had. Who'd want to face the world after *that*? I could never have imagined my first day on the job would go off with such a series of disasters.

And the death of Mr. Pak is a real tragedy. It puts things into perspective. Even Max's ignorance doesn't seem so outrageous by comparison.

I push my hair behind my ear and shove away from the table. I take the dishes to the sink, run water, and then wash up. "Maybe if I talk to Mrs. Pak, I can figure out why Mr. Pak wanted me to have that bird."

"Do you know her?"

"No, but he always talked about her. He really loved her."

"Well, there you go, sugarplum. You just toddle over to the S.T.U.D. and give the lady a call. I don't have long distance here at the house. Not since you gave me this cute little toy thing."

Toddle? Yikes!

She points to the cell phone in front of her plate—I gave it to her last Christmas when I got worried about her being all alone in this great big house. "It's not a toy, and you know it. Besides, isn't it more convenient to have a phone you can carry with you all the time?"

"Why, sure it is." She patted the device. "It was right handy when I found myself at the mercy a' that horse and the horse's behind of a stable hand what's supposed to have been showing me how to muck the stall."

My stomach plummets when I think what could have happened to her. Aunt Weeby's only a hair over five foot three, and while she's sassy and spry, there are limitations to sassy and spry—like a ton of farm horse dancing on her head.

"I'm just thankful you got help fast. From what I've figured out so far, that leg of yours is a real mess."

85

She leans down and raps her knuckles against the pink cast. "It's a battle wound. Life's nothing more than a brand-new battle after the last battle you fought ends. If a body doesn't collect herself a war wound or two along the way, why, then she isn't really living, now is she?"

What a way to look at things! "Gotta tell you, Aunt Weeby. I'm allergic to pain."

"We all are, sugarplum, but if things don't come up against us enough to rub our noses a bit the wrong way, then we aren't doing our part. And that goes twice for Christians. God didn't put us all down here with cotton balls around us. He told us to go out and salt up the earth for him, and if that means we rub someone or something the wrong way, well then, the Lord's just gonna have to deal with us and them."

How our conversation about a parrot's shriek issues made its way around to Aunt Weeby's theology, I'll never know. But I do know she loves her Lord without any holding back, and lives her life fully for him.

And, scary thought, she kinda makes sense.

So before I catch any more of the Aunt Weeby brand of nuttiness, I snag a cracker, break off a piece, and learn that Rio does love crackers. I also learn that little parrots aren't just way too loud.

"Good grief, Aunt Weeby! What a messy eater. Are you sure you want him in your nice, clean kitchen? Look at all the cracker crud he's flicked out of the cage."

My aunt, practically mesmerized by the bird, nods. "Sure. It's not any big never mind. The floor's good ol' pine, and it cleans up right nice. Don't you worry yourself about Rio and my kitchen. I know we're going to get on real fine."

That doesn't exactly reassure me. Then again, nothing much about Aunt Weeby does.

But I'm not a woman of leisure. I can't stick around and babysit . . . er . . . keep an eye on things. I have a show to prepare for. Thank goodness Sally and I determined ahead of time what I'd sell in the first six shows. Last night's events are renting too much room in my brain for me to go in and choose a whole show's worth of material right now.

As I head back upstairs, My cell phone rings. I hurry, and am thrilled to hear Peggy's voice. "How are you?" I ask.

"Great. I loved your first show. Who's the guy?"

"Don't go there! Miss Mona sprang him on me as a surprise five minutes before I went on. And he's no great bargain."

"He looks great."

"That's about it for him."

"Aw . . . I'm sure you'll find a good side to him."

When she falls silent, I get a bad feeling I know what's coming. And she doesn't disappoint.

"Listen, Andie. Are you okay? I read the paper this morning, and I figure you must be the person named as the 'new employee who found the corpse.' What happened?"

I tell her what I can, since I don't know much. She commiserates, we talk about her kids, and then I notice the time.

"Hey, listen. I gotta go. I'm due at the studio soon."

We agree to lunch next Saturday, and hang up. I hit the shower feeling way better than I have since before Miss Mona presented me with the S.T.U.D.'s stud.

I dress in the gorgeous black Ann Taylor jacquard jacket and skirt, and hit the road. By the time I reach the S.T.U.D.— can you believe that's what they call the studio and warehouse complex?—I've almost talked myself into believing I can, really and truly, do today's show.

But as I hurry down the hall to hair and makeup, I see my nemesis in the hall. Before I can duck out, he sees me too, and heads my way.

"How'd you sleep?" he asks.

What kind of greeting is that? "How'd I sleep?" I roll my eyes. "Like a log. I was drained. Why're you here?"

His cheeks turn a bronzy rust—did I mention he's got a to-die-for surfer-boy tan to go with the blond hair and baby blues?—and he blinks. "Sorry. But I don't get it. What do you mean, why am I here? I have a job, a contract. I have a show to host."

I snort. "And how do you plan to do that when you don't know gems from Jell-O?"

He takes a step back. "That's not exactly right. I know my diamonds, rubies, sapphires, and emeralds. Oh, and garnets too. The *real* ones, that is. Come on. Tell me. What was that orange thing you were selling yesterday? And don't give me that mandarin garnet spiel. We both know that's not really what it is—"

"You can't help yourself, can you? You have to go and show how little you do know about gemstones. What you saw on the set yesterday *is* a garnet. One of the rarest stones on earth."

"Look. I'm not some lonely disabled grandma with only the TV and a clicker to keep me company. I can see how they'll buy—in more ways than one—anything they hear from slick shopping network hosts."

"Ick! That's a nasty way to look at our customers."

He shrugs. "I bet it's a realistic one."

"And you would know how?"

He stands taller. "I've been on TV for a number of years. Something you can't match."

"True. I haven't been on TV before, but I've spent my entire adult life studying gems. Something *you* can't match. I *do* know what a spessartite garnet is."

He crosses his arms and studies me. I don't like the warm sensations that run through me when those baby blues land on me. He looks too good for my comfort zone.

Uh-oh. How shallow is that? Not good. Gotta pray about it.

And build a big, fat wall to protect myself from that scary effect Max the Magnificent has on me.

"Look," he finally says. "I didn't just barge onto that set yesterday. Miss Mona did hire me."

I don't like it, but he's right. "She did."

"And she hired you too. Didn't she?"

He better not think he's gonna chase me away. I tip up my chin. "She and my Aunt Weeby conspired and connived to get me to take the job. They want me for my gemological knowledge."

"But they don't want your on-screen ignorance, do they?"

Ouch! "Just as they don't want your gemological ignorance."

"But that's the beauty. I'm multifaceted."

He really does have a killer smile. *Why me?*

Then I realize what he said—the guy does distract, know what I mean? "Multifaceted? I didn't know we were going into weather changes now."

"We're not, but I am an expert on golf, basketball, football, skiing, and even NASCAR. See?"

Hope springs eternal. "Oh! You mean you're going to handle a part of the network's sports catalog."

"I should hope they don't waste my knowledge."

Relief is sweet and welcome. I smile. "I've never known Aunt Weeby or Miss Mona to let anything go to waste. I would imagine your days as a gemstone host are numbered."

"Fine by me."

And then I hear it. That familiar *thump-thump* that warns the innocent of incoming trouble.

"Awww . . ." Aunt Weeby sighs. "Isn't that sweet, Mona? They do look just like some of them dolls on a big ol' wedding cake. They make the nicest couple."

"I told you they would, right from the minute I saw him," her sidekick answers. "The good Lord's given me great instincts."

To his credit, Max gulps, turns a sickly shade of green, then backs away from me as fast as his shuffling feet can go.

Now wait a minute! I don't like Aunt Weeby's and Miss Mona's meddling, but I'm not a bubonic plague carrier either. I glare, and turn on the troublemaker.

"What are you doing here?" I ask my aunt. "Last I knew, you were settled in with your third cup of coffee, your second biscuit, and your HDTV blaring Tony Danza on his talk show."

"Mona stopped by on her way to work. I reckon being here's more fun than watching women what got their stomachs stapled and their boobs blowed up. That's what that boy's got on his show this morning. Besides, you showed me how to TiVo the thing so's I can watch my programs later."

Foiled by advanced technology. I'd bought her the TV thinking it would keep her entertained while she recovered. Great idea, right? See how well it worked? I call it the Aunt Weeby effect.

In the hope of regaining some control over the conversation, if not my current situation, I tip my head toward the set. "Who's on right now?"

"Wendy's hosting our Fat Busters segment," Miss Mona answers. "It's very successful."

"I'll bet," Max mutters. "Never heard of it."

Neither have I. "What exactly *is* Fat Busters? Is it diet products? Exercise equipment?"

"Why, honey," Miss Mona says, her eyes opened wide, "I can't believe you haven't heard of them. Fat Busters is the best thing in helping folks maintain their figures. It's from China."

Aunt Weeby nods.

Max gives me a don't-ask-me look.

"Oh-kaaay. It's popular and Chinese. Just exactly what is it?"

After a glance at her watch, Miss Mona points toward the set. "Since you and Max have plenty of time before your show, why don't you go watch Wendy for a moment. I'm sure she explains better than I can."

Wendy's soft southern accent reaches us as we approach the set. ". . . viscosity polymers allow an amazing stretch. So, girls . . . ? Listen to me"—she raps her scarlet claws . . . er . . . fingernails on the show-host desk—"y'all want to make sure you get your set of Fat Busters before they run out. The sooner you get them, the sooner you'll bust that fat around the gut and glutes."

In her hand, Wendy holds . . .

"It's a girdle!" Max exclaims just as tactfully as he denied the existence of spessartite garnets yesterday.

Everyone turns on him. "Shhhh!"

Miss Mona's frown is nothing to mess with. "That's not a girdle, Max. I'll have you know it's the finest and latest technology. Just listen to Wendy."

". . . for any of you just joining me now at the top of the hour, welcome! I'm so happy you can spend some time with me. Let's have some fun and help each other out here. Oh yes. Before we go any further, let me introduce myself. My name is Wendy, and I'll be with you for the next hour . . ."

Former cheerleader Wendy has the market cornered on perky.

". . . isn't it great? I'll tell you, there's not much advanced technology can't do. Fat Busters are self-contained, fat-breaking bands that do their thing while you do yours—and they do it *all day long*! Isn't that fabulous, girls? While you're sweeping, dusting, or even scooping the cat litter, your Fat Busters are working for you . . ."

Okay. I'm as willing to give technology a chance as the next girl, but . . . "It's a girdle."

Max grins. "Told ya."

"Can't argue with fact."

"And there's no such thing as an orange garnet."

"There is too."

"No, there's not."

"Just because you can tell a girdle's a girdle doesn't mean you know diaspores from diamonds."

"And I don't really have to."

"That day won't come soon enough."

"Amen."

Oh yeah. I'm with him on that—if not on anything else.

8.00

"Fine," I say, to avoid further confrontation. "I don't know about you, but I have a show to prepare for, and I really need Allison's fine touch with war paint after last night."

Forty-five minutes after I submit to hair and makeup's mercies, I'm—outwardly—ready for the show. That Max will again be at my side doesn't help.

How am I going to approach Miss Mona about this? I have to get rid of him, and soon. We want the jewelry and gemstone program to succeed. And a know-nothing blond version of Barbie's ex who used to read a weather teleprompter at some teeny local affiliate station in Who-Knows-Where, Missouri, isn't going to help.

But I can't go talk to her right now. I have to focus and do my best to overcome the six-foot-plus pain to my right.

With a prayer, I take my seat at the host's desk. Max joins me. At least today we're dealing in diamonds, not true exotics like the spessartite garnets. He says he knows what a diamond looks like.

We can only hope.

The show starts out fine. But so did yesterday's. We fly through the entire stock of white diamond solitaires in minutes. We go to the phones, and the viewers tell us all about their jewelry collections, especially the pieces they've bought during Danni's shows. There's a whole lot of bling-bling finding homes!

"Ladies," I say, "I'm thrilled you're so happy with your purchases from us. And I'm honored to show you top-quality goods. The Shop-Til-U-Drop Network's fabulous buyers negotiate to the penny, and that means we are able to buy the fine, VS clean, G-color white diamonds you've all snapped right up. I want to congratulate you on your excellent taste. Now let me show you another kind of diamond goodie."

In my left hand, I hold tweezers with a gorgeous full-carat white diamond clamped in place. With the other, I take a second pair of tweezers, and pick up an equally excellent, full-carat champagne diamond.

"See the difference between these two stones?"

Max, who up to now had kept his comments to safe "Oh yeses" and "Wows!" leans forward. "Yes, ladies and gentlemen," he says, "this is a perfect way to show you the difference between a superior diamond, like the one Andie has in her left hand, and this other, inferior, poor-color stone."

Huh? My chin nearly clips the desk when I gape. "What are you talking about?" I shake the tweezers with the champagne stone at him. "Do you have any idea what this is?"

"Even I know a dirty diamond when I see one."

"You've never heard of fancy-colored diamonds?"

"Everyone knows about J-Lo's pink one."

"But that's not the only fancy color. Diamonds come—"

"Don't tell me," he cuts in with a devastating smile. Women

of America drop like swooning flies. "Let me guess. I'll bet you're going to say diamonds come in all colors except blue, and that the rarest are the elusive mandarin orange spessartite diamonds."

His smile never falters.

My temper comes to life. "No, Max. There's no such thing as a mandarin orange spessartite diamond, and"—through gritted teeth—"you know it. Besides, as I'm sure all our savvy customers know, diamonds *do* come in blue. In fact, one of the world's most famous diamonds, the Hope diamond, is blue."

"Oh. Yeah. I guess I have heard of the Hope diamond. Isn't it in the Smithsonian or something? But are you sure it's blue?"

"It's at the Smithsonian, and I'm sure it's blue. Oh, and just FYI, the blue color comes from boron in its chemical composition."

"I got it. Boron, which rhymes with moron, does the blue." He rolls his eyes while I just stare, and then he points at my tweezers. "That, Andie, is no blue diamond."

Let it go, let it go, let it go.

"And you, Max, traffic in the way too obvious. This gorgeous stone comes from the Argyle mines in Australia, and it's what is known as a champagne diamond. See the golden glow, the orange, pink, and even red sparks when the light hits it? It's wonderful."

Max leans close. That clean, masculine scent of his cologne surrounds me. Too bad he's such a lunkhead.

"Now that you mention it," the lunkhead says, "it does kind of look like candlelight."

This unexpected insight stuns me—almost as much as

what I feel zip through me when he takes my hand to get a better look.

"Th—" *Whoo-ee!* He's dangerous, all right. I catch myself before I fan my face. "That's what this exact shade is actually called. Candlelight. How'd you know?"

"I didn't." He smiles into the camera. More women drop. "But just looking at it made me think of a romantic dinner, lit by tall, white, glowing candles."

Oooohh, he's good. From behind the camera, Sally gestures that the phone lines have gone ballistic thanks to Max. I've got to put the brakes on before this show turns into *Romancing the Max.*

"And that, ladies," I say, "is exactly what you'll be wearing on your finger . . . or near your heart. A memory of romance, of elegance, and that certain excitement that comes with life's special moments. Now what girl wouldn't love that?"

The show unravels from there on out. The good news is that we put a number of gushing customers through on the phones. The bad news is that they proclaim Max and me their favorite show hosts. I can't believe there are people out there who can stand this seesaw between knowledge and . . . well, *you* decide. But they do buy diamonds. A lot of diamonds.

So we score a debacle again. A debacle about which everyone raves. You can't account for taste.

By the time the network's theme music brings the show to a close, I'm shot. It takes a lot out of you to keep up a conversation with America while you also do damage control for a lunk's bloopers.

And, as if that's not bad enough, when I reach the green

room, where I left my briefcase before the show, my day takes a turn to the even worse. How, you ask?

Chief Clark is waiting for me.

Miss Mona and Aunt Weeby are with him, as well as what must be a plainclothes detective. I don't really worry about the loony two—well, I do worry about them, just not the same way. They know I had nothing to do with Mr. Pak's trip or with his death or even his turning up in our vault.

"Miss Andie," the lawman says, "the coroner finished the autopsy, and Mr. Pak died of blunt-force trauma to the head, just like I figured he had."

I fight the sadness, sigh, and then say, "Okay. I'm sorry he's dead, and I will miss him. He was great to deal with, and he handled the finest rubies on earth. What I don't get is why you felt the need to come all the way over here to share this."

"Maybe"—he draws an envelope from his pocket—"this will help you 'get' why I came on over today. The coroner found it."

I take the envelope, an official-looking, heavy vellum deal, with my name written in exquisite calligraphy. "How weird is this?"

The geriatric pals hustle over. Miss Mona peers over my shoulder and Aunt Weeby takes hold of my hand to bring the envelope close.

"Ooooh . . . ," Miss Mona coos.

"Aaaah . . . ," Aunt Weeby sighs.

"Whoa!" Max comes to a standstill just inside the door. "Did someone *else* die?"

Does this guy ever think before he blurts?

I jiggle the envelope in my hand—and Aunt Weeby's. "No,

Max. No more corpses around here. The chief brought me this. He says the coroner found it on Mr. Pak while doing the . . . the autopsy."

I just can't get my head around the thought of someone cutting up a dead person to figure out what killed him. How can people do that day in and day out? I couldn't, that's for sure.

I mean, really. Think about it. Mr. Pak is dead. By the time a coroner gets a corpse, it's cold, stiff. Certainly not the person anyone has known in life. A shudder runs through me. Dead bodies . . .

Then I realize everyone's staring at me. "What? Did I do something wrong? Say something?"

"No, sugarplum." Aunt Weeby pats my cheek. "But you just seemed to . . . oh, I don't know. You seemed all spacey-like. Are you feeling peckish?"

Peckish . . . Great-Great-Grandma Willetta's fish oil! Ugh.

I give her a hug and drop a kiss on her cheek. "I'm sorry. I was just thinking about Mr. Pak."

"Well?" Max says. "Are you going to open it? Everyone's waiting on you."

"I doubt the chief is waiting with bated breath. He—or someone in his office—already opened it."

I suspect they also checked it for fingerprints, even though I don't see any of the black dust you see used on those CSI shows. The cover of the card has an ornate seal engraved in gold. My heart does a tap dance against my rib cage as I run my finger over the seal.

But that measly little tap dance is nothing compared to the stampede that breaks out when I read the message inside. "Oh! Oh, oh, oh! I—Oh. My. Goodness. I can't believe this!"

"Andrea Autumn Adams! Get ahold a' yourself, sugarplum. You're spitting and spurting and making no sense at all. What is that card there all about?"

I'm near hyperventilating, and I really don't want to pass out. Not in front of Max the Magnificent, that's for sure. But this is incredible—for a gemologist, that is.

"Oh, Miss Mona, look. You're not going to believe this. It's an invitation. I just don't understand why he would have this with him, and why they'd invite me—us—in the first place."

Miss Mona plunks her fists on her hips and gives me a stern look. "Who invited you? Who's 'us'? And what'd we get invited to? And where?"

I keep blinking, but the words still read the same. I hold out the card. "Here. You read it. I'm afraid I'm dreaming or hallucinating or . . . or something."

My boss takes the card and seconds later she's spitting and spurting, as Aunt Weeby said, just like I did.

"Andie, honey! Is this real? The government of Myanmar is really inviting us to visit their mines? You do know what kind of politicking trouble's been going on out there, don't you?"

"Of course I know. Mr. Pak, Roger, and I talked about Myanmar more'n a million times. It's awful the oppression going on there—you know, the government squashes political parties, there's forced labor of adults and kids, human trafficking. It's bad."

"And now this . . ." She waves the card.

"It looks real, don't you think?"

She studies the card again. "I wouldn't know real from not, but it sure does look like it's official, at least someone important must have put it together. But I reckon we can check to see if it's real. We can call the embassy—oh, that's right. No diplomatic relations. They don't have an embassy in the U.S., do they?"

A scrap of info tickles the back of my memory. "You know . . . the last time Mr. Pak came to New York, he mentioned that Myanmar had begun to offer thirty-day visas for tourist travel inside the country. They might have an embassy now." I wave the invitation. "Do you think this might be part of that effort to open things up?"

"Who knows? Who cares? All I know is that this invitation is a golden opportunity for us, for the S.T.U.D. Network."

"Okay," I say, still unconvinced. "Tourism or not, that military dictatorship's not crazy about Americans and Brits—one of those sanction deals. And our government isn't crazy about them—that communism and organized violence against their people—the whole human rights issues thing."

A shrill whistle pierces my eardrums, my brain, total consciousness. It makes both Aunt Weeby and Miss Mona stumble.

Max, of course. His whistle's almost as good as mine.

"What's that for?" I ask.

"Because from what you and Miss Mona have said so far, we can figure out you've been invited to something-or-other in Myanmar—something to do with mines, but you two haven't let the rest of us in on the whole thing. "

I give Aunt Weeby an apologetic smile. "I'm sorry. But this is so exciting, I can't get my brain to unscramble. It says it's from the Myanmar government—Myanmar's what most people know as Burma—and they're inviting me, and the S.T.U.D. Network, to feature the Mogok Valley on the show. That's where the world's most fantastic rubies come from. But the deal is, they aren't good buddies with our government."

"You're still telling me you didn't know the victim was coming here, Miss Andie? Or bringing this invite to you?"

Only now do I remember Chief Clark. And his silent shadow. "Of course I had no idea. I've told you over and over I didn't know he was coming."

The chief's not about to let it go. "When was the last time you spoke to that there Mr. Pak?"

I think back. "About six months ago. He brought my boss in New York a small lot of Burma-ruby solitaires, a few good Ceylon sapphires, and some nice Cambodian blue zircons. We only bought the rubies, since the price has gone up so high. Besides, not many customers are willing to pay for the Burma material when they can get stones from Madagascar with almost the same quality, and for a fraction of the cost. We passed on the sapphires and the zircons."

"I still smell me a skunk," the chief says. "You come to town, and this dead guy follows."

"Why, Donald! That poor man there didn't follow Andie *dead*. Someone killed him once he got here. And that's who you'd do better asking all these questions, don't you think? Not Andie."

"I mean to find me that someone, no matter who it turns out to be."

I give him a leery look. "Do you *still* think I had something to do with it? After all I've told you?"

He shrugs. "I can't arrest you since I have millions of witnesses."

Talk about a non-answer.

Max laughs. "So that's the perfect alibi—a TV show."

I give him a crooked grin. "I guess I scored, huh?"

"With the show and that invite. Are you going?"

I shrug. "It's up to Miss Mona. But I'll tell you what. Because Mr. Pak is dead, and he did bring me that invitation, and fewer than few gemologists ever get to visit those amazing mines, I'm ready to jump at the chance."

I don't mention that I really want to look around, check out what's up in Myanmar. For real. Mr. Pak's problems must have started back there. And I want to wipe that suspicious look from the chief's face. It doesn't bode well for my future around here.

What can I say? I suppose if I'm really pushed, I can't say I blame the chief for trying to make a connection. Not only did I find the dead man, but I'm also the only one who knew him.

The chief doesn't look half as thrilled with my prospects as I am. "I gotta say, I don't cotton to this trip of yours. If I had my druthers, I'd lock you up. But you're Miz Weeby's niece, you work for Miss Mona, and I'd have a hard time arresting you."

His stubbornness and that silent pal of his are really getting to me. "You also have those million viewers to deal with. Max is right"—did I just give him credit?—"I have an ironclad alibi." I gotta grin at my TV cop line.

"Donald, dear," Aunt Weeby says, "go on home or the station or the donut shop, you take your pick. Andie's innocent. And you know it. I know you're hankering to have yourself a big ol' case to break, but you're not going to break it right on Andie's back. Go do your job. Find yourself some real clues.

Catch us a real killer. We're going to My . . . Mia . . ." She waves in defeat. "We're going to that ruby place."

"We?" I ask. "I don't see where there's a 'you' in the 'we' here."

"Oh, indeed," Miss Mona says. "*We're* going to Burma. But I'm afraid you're going to have to miss this trip, Livvy. You can't be going with that cast—"

"You're not leaving me behind, Mona Latimer!" Aunt Weeby's frown scares even me.

Miss Mona counters with a bulldog look of her own. "You aren't up to travel of this sort. You'll go on our next trip. Besides. Who else am I going to trust to keep things going here at the network while I'm gone?"

Aunt Weeby running the network? Watch out, world!

But I'm going to Burma, the Mogok Valley, the home of the most incredible, perfect rubies on earth. Oh yeah. Life is good—sometimes.

If the first weeks of working for Miss Mona made me feel like the proverbial gerbil on the exercise wheel, then I can't even begin to describe the next twelve days. We work our way through mountains of forms to apply for visas; we become pincushions for the multiple vaccine shots; we pack, unpack, then pack again, uncertain what we'll really need; and then I'm forced to spend hours upon hours with Danni, because Danni of the super-duper panties becomes a happy camper when she learns she'll be doing the gem and jewelry shows during my Myanmar odyssey. So I have to prepare her. All of that leaves me feeling like a wrung-out washrag.

You see, Miss Mona and I aren't the only ones heading out for an unbelievable adventure.

Oh no. We have to travel with a complete entourage. Of course Miss Mona and I are going, but so is a behind-the-scenes delegation from S.T.U.D. A camerawoman, Allison from makeup, and a couple of others I don't really know too well, all head out for Burma with us.

Yeah, yeah, yeah. Our Ken doll comes too. But you'd figured that out already. Hadn't you? You knew I wasn't going to get to ditch him.

I just pray he doesn't cause an international incident and get us all locked up in some gross Burmese jail.

9<u>00</u>

After a three-hour delay, Thai Airlines finally calls our flight for boarding. I wrestle my carry-on roller suitcase into the overhead bin, slip my laptop under the seat in front of mine, and drop into my window seat. Again, excitement ripples right through me.

I'm going to Burma. I'm going to the Mogok Valley. For real.

There's still that little corner of my mind, though, that true doubting Thomas. So to prove that I'm not dreaming or hallucinating, I pinch myself.

"Ouch!"

"What'd you do that for?" Max asks as he slips his laptop under the seat in front of the one next to mine.

No way! *"You're* sitting here?"

"Looks that way." He flashes me his devastating grin.

Don't look, Andie. He's a gem-dunce, remember?

He adds, "Miss Mona made all the reservations. I'm sure she gave you your boarding pass just as she gave me mine."

Is there any justice? Hours and hours hog-tied by a seat

belt next to Max the Magnificent. *Groan.* I'm really going to have to do something about the Max situation. Hoping against hope, I ask him a very simple question.

"Do you know anything about rubies?"

"I know they're red."

Do I laugh or do I cry? I decide not to go there, so I try another question. "Have you ever seen a real, live ruby?"

"My mother has one. My father gave it to her for an anniversary or something. It's pretty red."

"If you say that one more time, I'm going to scream."

"Are you going to tell me orange is the new red?"

"Are you going to quit with the spessartite stuff?"

"I'm still not so sure you weren't pulling a fast one on me and the viewers."

"I would *never* do that. I'm no fraud, I don't lie, and besides, I'm a Christian. I answer to God for what I say and do. Trust me, I don't want to do something so stupid as to fake people out. God's not likely to let it slide if I do. I've learned the hard way that nothing's worth getting on the wrong side of God's blessing."

He tips his head to the side. "Interesting way of seeing ethics."

"I didn't say anything earthshaking."

"Okay. You're right, I guess." He clicks his seat belt on, then gives me another of his killer smiles. "Tell me about rubies, since you don't think I know enough about them."

"Are you making fun of me?"

"No. It's like I'd love to tell you all about the perfect golf club."

Boooring. "That's okay. I don't have a burning desire to know about golf."

"Too bad."

No way. "You asked me to tell you, and I'm going to tell you. Rubies are corundum, the red variety. All the other colors of corundum are known as sapphire—"

"Are you kidding me? First the goofy garnets, then the dirty diamonds, and now you're telling me that rubies equal sapphires? Are you sure you know what you're talking about?"

I clench my jaw. At the rate I'm going, my dentist is going to retire to his own private South Pacific island off my cracked teeth. "Yes, I'm sure I know what I'm talking about. I have a BS in geology, and a certificate from the Gemological Institute of America that tells all who care to know that I'm a master gemologist."

"You're pretty proud of your pedigree."

"Aren't you?"

He shrugs. "I have a BS in meteorology, and I played football for the Buckeyes."

"For the who?"

He gapes. "You don't know who the Buckeyes are?"

"I wouldn't have asked if I knew."

"Ohio State has one of the best records in college football history."

That's his pedigree? Football?

Okey-dokey. "I . . . see." Better get back to business. "Anyway, I do know gemstones. And rubies and sapphires, both, are corundum, the second-hardest natural mineral known to science. The hardness of corundum comes in part from the strong and short oxygen-aluminum bonds. These bonds pull the oxygen and aluminum atoms close, and that makes the crystal not only hard but also very dense, even though it's a mineral made up of two relatively light elements—"

I quit. He's asleep. So much for wanting to know about rubies.

When the flight attendant comes around with earphones for the movie, I figure I might as well watch whatever they're offering. Hopefully it won't be football. Or golf.

Score! It's a romantic comedy with Reese Witherspoon. I can use a good laugh.

But it seems all the upheaval of the last month and a half has really done me in, and I doze off soon after the movie starts . . .

"Now children," Max says, *"in my right hand is a football, and in my left a golf club. They're both for jocks, but the football's for the sweatier ones."*

"Mr. Magnificent?" a little girl with red hair asks. *"Are you one of the sweatier ones?"*

Max blinks. *"Well, I'm one of the stronger ones."*

Her hand shoots up again. *"And do you hit the football with the golf club?"*

"You mean, you can't tell that football and golf are two different sports?"

She shrugs. *"I like rocks. . . ."*

Something explodes in my ears. *"Aaack!"*

"Are you okay?" Max asks.

"Rocks are fine . . . er . . . I mean, I'm fine. It's the movie. Something happened, and it was loud."

"I'm surprised anything startled you awake. You were out, and you sleep like . . . well, like a rock."

"Takes one to know one. You were out pretty hard too. Did you watch the movie after you woke up?"

"No. I'd missed too much of it, and I brought reading material."

I glance at the book in his hands—*Jewelry & Gems: The Buying Guide*. "No way! You're reading Antoinette Matlins? The world's leading gem author?"

"I figured I'd better learn something about the stuff we're selling. And you're right. Rubies do equal red sapphires equal rubies."

"Has anyone ever told you you have a weird way of saying things?"

"And this is coming from you?"

"Are you implying that I talk strange?" I woke up for this? "I'm tired. See you in Bangkok."

But no matter how hard I try, I can't doze off. My eyes want to open and watch Max the Magnificent read what's known as the "Unofficial Bible" for diamonds, pearls, colored gemstones, gold, and jewelry.

Who'd a thunk the jock would care?

Bangkok is *hot*. Literally.

Since we're in the capital of Thailand only long enough to change flights, I take the chance to head outside while we wait for our flight to be called to board. But the closer I get to the doors, the less I want to go out into that sauna.

I'm a little disappointed. After all, when am I going to get another chance to see Bangkok?

But soon enough, we board, and yes, I'm again stuck with the S.T.U.D.'s token stud as a seat partner. Fortunately for all concerned, this leg of the trip is short.

And then we're in Yangon—better known to everyone as Rangoon. What's with all that name changing? Burma . . . Myanmar. Rangoon . . . Yangon. It's too confusing. At least Mandalay's still Mandalay, and the Mogok Valley goes by its real name.

We reach the Mandalay City Hotel later that evening—the next evening? The evening before? All this time zone changing is hard on the brain. By now I'm so sick of planes, airports, and Max reading Antoinette Matlins that I don't bother to look around, even though I've heard the views from the hotel are incredible. I should have enough time for that in the morning.

But morning comes too fast for my jet lag, and it brings new experiences with it. When we meet downstairs at the restaurant for breakfast, we also meet our . . . what shall I call them? *Escorts* is too tame a term.

"Pssst!" Miss Mona hisses to get my attention. "I'm not sure I trust them."

"I'm sure I *don't* trust them." I nod toward our "guide." "Check him out. That bulge on his belt and under his shirt? That's a gun."

Miss Mona sniffs. "Then that's no guide. I insist they provide us with a real guide, not some thug who'll do who knows what to us. Let's call the embassy."

"Ah . . . the diplomatic relations deal, remember? I doubt the U.S. Embassy can help us." I give our "translator" a good look. "That other one's armed too. And you know the Myanma embassy told us that to get the visas we had to accept a secret service escort for the whole time we're here. That must be the third one, the one who's wearing a suit, and who hasn't said a word."

Miss Mona leans closer. "Let me tell you, I don't like him any better."

"Do you want to go to the Mogok Valley?"

"Of course. That's what we came here for, honey."

"Then we're just going to have to put up with them, deal

with the ickiness of it all, get the footage we want to use, and then hightail it back home."

"Sounds like a plan," Max says from behind me. "I don't like the look of this."

"You mean the Myanmar Welcome Wagon?" Sorry. Sarcasm just pops out sometimes. Okay, okay. Maybe more than sometimes. *I gotta work on that, right, God?*

"I mean the government types that are going to watch everything we say and do until we board the plane for the U.S."

I turn to him. "You know what, Max? They're spies. We know that. We knew the rules from the get-go. But we also wanted these visas, remember? We'll just have to watch our step. None of us has a hidden agenda, and we don't want to check out the inside of a Burmese prison cell."

Miss Mona looks horrified.

Max looks worried.

Me? Beats me what I look like. But I can tell you I'm not loving this. And I'm not feeling the love here, either. They did invite us, but they sure haven't gone out of their way to make us feel welcome. Did we make a mistake by coming? Is filming the legendary Mogok Valley mines worth the chance of getting stuck with a Go-directly-to-a-Mandalay-jail card?

Sigh. I want to see the mines. The other? Not so much.

After breakfast, we head out, and in the parking lot, I get my first glimpse of Mandalay Hill. It dominates the city and the flat plain below.

"Nice, eh?" our translator asks. "You want climb to top? You see city from there, the Royal Palace and Fortress, the Irrawaddy River, and Shan Hills."

I smile. "It's beautiful. But it looks steep."

"You climb the stair, okay?"

"Stairs? Up a hill?"

He nods.

"Okay. I guess that'll work."

Miss Mona comes close. "What'll work?"

"To climb Mandalay Hill. He says there's stairs we can use."

"You and Max can certainly do all the climbing your little hearts desire, Andie. I'm staying by the pool."

Our translator beams. "Pool nice, eh?"

"Sure," I say. "But we have pools in the U.S. Mandalay Hill is here. It's more interesting than the hotel pool."

"So true," Max adds. "But will we have time between working to go for a climb?"

I frown. "We can make the time, right, Miss Mona?"

"Climb away. I have me a stack of good books, and the poolside lounge chairs have big old umbrellas. Add some iced tea, and I'm all set."

Our translator clucks at the unenlightened among us. "When Gautama Buddha visit hill, his hand point to flat land, and he prophesy. He say great city and religion center will be at bottom of hill. Now there's pagodas, *shreeens*, three bones of the Buddha, temple with statue of King Mindon."

Shreeens? He must mean shrines. I shudder. I'm not so cool with Buddhism and all that. It skips God, Scripture, and Jesus. "It's a religious site, then."

"No, no, no. There be many souvenir place, and many astrologers tell you future."

Yikes! I look at Miss Mona, note her raised eyebrows. Laughing right now's not the best idea, so I bite my tongue.

"You want go today?" the man says.

112

"I think not. Let's go to the Mogok Valley. That's what we came to see in Myanmar."

We get into the van provided for us, and our driver greets us with a slight nod. He too is packing . . . something. The bulge at his waist looks much too much like those of his cohorts. Miss Mona and I hold hands to pray.

The drive from Mandalay to Mogok has to be the loneliest in the world. For a while, the one-and-a-half-lane road runs by the Irrawaddy River.

The views are unbelievably beautiful. Pagodas and shrines that look like inverted cones dot the green, green landscape. Every so often along the road, you see a man or a woman loaded down with parcels. The river itself is wide and runs gently between the grassy banks.

At one point, we spot a battered, rusty ferry, loaded to the gills with bag upon bag of freight piled up to the ceiling of the lower level. On the next level up, folks are crammed around tables and benches. Metal barrels wreathed in puffs of smoke have been co-opted for cooking, and a woman behind a counter covered with what looks like Myanmar-style fast food serves the travelers. While we watch, a teenager dumps out one of the cooking barrels overboard—trash removal's no big deal on the Irrawaddy.

"Oh, dear," Miss Mona says a little later. "This doesn't look good."

"This" is what can only be called a military checkpoint. And considering the country is run by a military dictatorship, we shouldn't be surprised. Still, something about AK47s just doesn't conjure up warm fuzzies.

Miss Mona and I cling to each other again, our voices quiet in prayer. When we chime in our amens, I glance at

113

the S.T.U.D.'s stud. Max looks ready to jump out of his skin, so I turn back to the Lord.

"Father God? It's me again, okay? I'm still asking you to keep us all safe, Miss Mona, Max, Allison, Hannah and her camera, and the rest of our crew. We're real strangers in a really strange land, and you're our only protection—those guns our 'escorts' are wearing are just as scary as the ones the uniformed military guys have. Thanks for all the protection you've blessed us with already, and I can't wait to see what you'll do next. I love you, Father."

Miss Mona whispers, "Amen."

I catch a glimpse of Max's expression. Sure enough, he's thinking about my "weird" way of talking faith. It might seem weird to him, but it works for me. I know my Lord hears me. The Bible says he listens, and that's good enough for me.

When I look out the window, I see our "escorts" coming back to the van. Lucky for us, they must have said the right thing or had the right kind of papers or the right color money, because in minutes we're on our way again.

Max relaxes. "Bet our trip would've ended back there if these guys hadn't been with us."

"There's no getting around this place without them," I say. "That's what happens in the communist world."

"Oh, look, Andie!" Miss Mona says. "Isn't this all so sweet?"

If I didn't know better, I would think we'd just boarded a time-travel machine. Very simple, rustic farms dot the flat land every so often. Less frequently, we pass small villages. The locals' favorite form of transportation seems to be foot traffic, but the really wealthy ones ride bicycles and oxcarts. Cars? Maybe two or three.

After a couple of other checkpoint moments, the road begins to twist and turn, taking us into the mountains that had seemed so far away when we saw them from outside the hotel. We pass timber plantations and more quaint hill villages, these springing from the jungle vegetation that seems thicker than when we started. Later still, we see scattered mining operations, and that gets my juices going. It's the first sign that we're coming into gem country.

I can't stop myself. "It's happening!"

Miss Mona leans closer to the window. "Oh, Andie. I do wish your auntie was with us. She'd just love this."

"She would, but can you imagine how much trouble she'd get into? Just think what she might have done if she'd seen those AK47s."

"She'd likely ask the military men to show her how to use the dreadful things. Remember, she wanted to muck out that stall."

"Who can forget? And you know? If she had asked for automatic weapon lessons, we'd all be guests of the Mandalay city jail . . . for-eh-ver!"

Max sleeps.

By now we've passed through five—count 'em, five—checkpoints. I hope there's not a whole lot more of this dusty, rutted road to go. I press up against my window too, and watch, stomach in throat, as we wind through a narrow mountain road with sheer drop-offs on one side, and Gulliver-sized flowers on the other.

Then, all of a sudden, we round a bend on the road, and voilá! We might just as easily have arrived at Dollywood. Just ahead of us, a totally out-of-place, twenty-foot-high sign looms over the road. Our translator turns around in his front passenger-side seat.

"Look. It say 'Welcome to Rubyland.'"

All the comforts of home. Not.

$10\underline{^{00}}$

"*This* is where we're staying?" Miss Mona asks.

I look at the plain-Jane building, our hotel. It's nothing like the beautiful Mandalay Hill Hotel. There's no glam in Mogok. "That's what our keepers say. Come on. I'm sure it's clean. And you did want an adventure."

She sighs. "I did, didn't I? I guess it looks like an adventure. Now you tell me. Why does everybody and their brother always bring up how clean a dump is to try and redeem it in all its dumpiness?"

Oh-kay. "Just think all you'll have to tell Aunt Weeby when we get back."

"I'd better take pictures."

"You better not think of going back empty-handed."

"I miss her."

I never thought I'd say this in Myanmar. "Me too."

"But she really couldn't have handled this, honey, not with that foot busted into bitty pieces the way it is. Oh, and all that hardware they stuck in there. Poor thing . . ."

"Don't feel guilty, Miss Mona. Aunt Weeby's probably

taking your business apart and rebuilding it from scratch. By the time you get home, you might not own a TV network anymore. Who knows what that wacky brain of hers might come up with?"

"I'd best be calling her, don't you think?" Miss Mona runs a hand over her sleek silver hair. "Well, Andie, you're right, of course. Let's get to getting here. We need to bring in our luggage, unpack the essentials, and then . . . then we need to go get us some rubies!"

I glance at my watch. "It's four thirty already. That crazy dirt road trip took six hours. I don't know that there's going to be much happening at the—oh, I'm gonna butcher this name—*Panchan-htar-pwe* outdoor market by now. I think we'll have to wait until tomorrow for rubies."

"Bless you! Now there's a name for you. The who market?"

When I shrug, since I have no idea what the correct pronunciation of that mouthful of letters might be, she chuckles, then continues. "I'm sure we can find us something to eat at that Paunchy-something-or-other market. Don't you want to try some native food?"

Do I look like I want the runs?

"Only," I say, "if it's so fresh it wants to get up and leave, they've fully cooked it, and the cooking utensils are clean so we don't come down with bubonic plague, bird flu, or any of Job's disgusting ailments. You do know we can only drink bottled water, right? If we forget, we'll have to break out the Imodium. Oh, and we can't get on the wrong side of gun-toting locals, if you get my drift. The hotel's dining room looks super-fine to me."

"That's all good with me, honey. Let's finish up here."

We unpack, and in the end, meet the others in the hotel's modest but—you got it—clean dining room. The S.T.U.D. crowd sits at two long tables, where we're served about a dozen Asian mystery-meat-and-veggie delicacies, all with a side of rice. Our armed nannies sit at a smaller table to our right, and while we laugh our way through the meal, they keep their deadpan faces on, say very little, and shovel down their mountains of chow.

It actually tastes pretty good. But between bites, I pray the tons of MSG I'm sure lurks in the mystery mix doesn't sideline us all with permanent migraines.

I don't know about anyone else, but two hours later, I zonk out the minute my head hits the pillow and don't wake up until the sun streams in through our window.

A quick bath followed by a simple breakfast has us on the road to a ruby mine by nine o'clock. When we reach our destination, what I see makes me wince. Yes, I've been to other mine sites in third world countries before, but the crude and primitive conditions never fail to move me.

"This place is rougher than those Hollywood actor types' unshaved chins," Miss Mona says. "Is this typical?"

"Pretty much. But this one's . . . oh, maybe a little worse. You'd think as long as they've been mining here, and with the price of Burmese rubies what it is, their operations would be more upscale."

Beneath canvases stretched between four sturdy sticks, a hole pierces the dun-colored, dusty ground and descends at an angle. In the shade cast by the canvases, I count a crew of about a dozen miners standing around, dressed in shabby, dirt-stained clothes.

I slant a look at Miss Mona, whose expression screams

118

worry. I say, "Hey! Here's the Mogok Welcome Wagon come out to greet us."

Miss Mona smiles. "At least they don't have guns. From what I can see, that is."

"They look poor," Max says. "It's got to be a tough life."

Ding, ding, ding! Give the fellow in the blue shirt a cigar.

"It's one of the poorest countries in the world, Max. These people are caught up in the fist of a communist government—no human rights or civil liberties, you know—and there's not much commerce. It's worse than just poverty you see here."

I stare past the dirt-dusted mine, the tattered miners, and the dingy canvas cover. A short distance beyond, more of that Zambian-emerald rich green landscape reaches all the way out to meet the Ceylon-sapphire blue sky. The sober contrast hits me hard.

Father God . . . how can you stand to see your children in these crummy circumstances? I'll tell you, it's breaking my heart. Remind me how tough it is for them any time I haggle on a price too close to where it could hurt them and their families. I want to be fair, to honor you, and I want to get Miss Mona a good deal. Show me how to do that, 'cause I sure don't see how. Okay? Thanks.

As soon as we park, the men break out in smiles and conversation.

"Oh, listen to them, Andie," Miss Mona says. "Isn't their singsong chitchat charming? I wonder what they're saying."

"I'm not so sure I want to know. I half think they're greeting us and half think they're laughing at the crazy Americans and all their gadgets. Just wait till Hannah sets up her camera and the rest of her stuff."

When the Scandinavian blonde does just that, the miners gawk—bet they haven't seen a girl who looks like her, and worse, who does that kind of work. Their jibber-jabber kicks it up a notch. And while some might think it's a thrill and a half to watch them get a good giggle at our expense, my patience is now as thin as model Kate Moss. I've come to Mogok for one thing.

I rub my hands and open the van door. "Let's go mine some rubies."

"You don't plan to go down that rat hole, do you?" Max asks.

Here we go again. "If they give me half a chance, I'm there."

"Do you have a death wish?"

I step out of the vehicle, and the heat from the hard dirt road burns through the soles of my running shoes, sears my legs under lightweight cotton pants, and roasts my short-sleeved arms. "Just a ton of appreciation for the beauty God created under dirt and weeds."

Max follows me as I approach the mine entrance. "You're really willing to go into an unsafe dirt tunnel."

Enough, already. "Aren't you?"

Horror fills his face. "Any footballs or golf balls down there?"

All righty, then. "Tell me one thing. What kind of qualifications did you feed Miss Mona to make her think you'd make a decent jewelry and gemstone show host?"

He crosses his arms. "My years of experience on TV did the talking for me."

"Reading the weather in Who-Knows-Where, Missouri,

right?" When he smiles that knee-melter grin of his, I steel myself against its impact. Well, I try.

Aren't I too young for hot flashes, Lord?

"Okay, fine." I swipe the damp back of my hand across my sweat-beaded forehead. "Had it been me, I'd've jumped at the chance to peddle stuff too. But didn't you think you might be on shaky turf selling stuff you know nothing about?"

"The network sells more than baubles."

"Baubles!" Now you did it, bud. "I show our customers only museum-quality pieces."

"Hey! You just said if you'd been in my shoes, you would have jumped at the chance to peddle stuff too. So what's the deal with giving me such a hard time for doing just that? Besides, I figure it's only a matter of time before Miss Mona promotes me to hosting the sports shows."

He looks good enough and might know enough to try to edge out our sports guru. But . . .

"Good luck prying Tanya, a former college basketball star *and* international model, off the sports host desk. But let me share a secret. No sane body messes with Tanya. She's six foot three, and moves at the speed of rumors in a girls' college dorm."

"All right, Andie." He rolls his eyes and shakes his head. "Can we get beyond the Max-doesn't-know-anything kick?"

"When you get to the other side of doesn't-know-anything."

"It's already reached the boring and annoying point, so I suggest, for Miss Mona's sake, that you get a life. I'm here, I'm learning, and you're acting like—"

He stops.

121

I glare.

He adds, "Let's just say you're not helping."

The thought that he might be right zips through my brain at the speed of the Roadrunner, but the gemologist in me does a Wylie Coyote and crashes a boulder on top of it.

Maybe Scarlett O'Hara had that thinking about life thing right. I'll think about it tomorrow.

One of the men steps away from the rest and comes up to us. He pulls on a tuft of his dirt-dusted onyx-black hair. "Red." He nods. "You Miss Andie." His accent does some weird things to my name. "I mine manager. I help you here."

Hey, Mom. Thanks for the red-hair genes—not. "Sounds good." I point to the dark hole in the ground. "How soon can you get me inside the mine?"

His eyebrows shoot tuftward. "You no go there. You woman."

At my side, Max the Magnificent chortles.

I jerk to my full height. "I'm a woman, a capable, curious woman, and I've gone into more mines over the last seven years than you want to count. I so want to go into your mine. And I want to bring a camera with me. It's what I came to film, what I was invited to show the world."

He shrugs and goes back to the gathered miners.

"That's going to go over real well with our three armed shadows," Max mutters.

"Until they chase me out with one of their guns, I'm doing what I came to do. Are you with me?"

He shakes his head, shoves his hands in his pockets. "I'll watch."

I head for the mine manager, a million questions zooming in my head. "Can I ask you something?"

He nods. Dust motes drop from his tufts. *Bad hair day, or what?*

I turn to where our crew is waiting. "Hannah! Let's get this on film."

The fascinated manager can't take his eyes off the camera and its pretty operator. But I have work to do. I nod to Hannah, and the film rolls.

I clear my throat to get his attention. "About how much good rough comes out of the mine every day?"

He narrows his eyes and scratches his head. More dancing dust. "Good rough?"

"Yes. Ruby rocks—good for cutting."

"Ah . . ." He holds out a hand, cups it, and draws a circle about the size of a dime.

"That little?"

"Every day? Little, yes, little."

I gesture toward the other miners. "All of them work in this mine?"

He points to the mouth of the mine. "They here."

To the camera, I say, "Ladies and gentlemen, the small amount these men are bringing up out of the mine explains the skyrocketing cost of Burmese rubies, the finest of the red corundum." I face the manager again. "How many hours do the men work?"

Hannah gets amazing footage while we talk about the non-glam stuff. I can see this special's going to kick up a crazy craving for Burma rubies. But where am I going to get enough of the über-rare stones?

Once I tell Hannah to quit rolling and she goes to pack up the van, I ask Tufty—I'll never be able to remember his name—where I should go to find great rubies in decent quantities.

He smiles and looks at the mine. "You go buying office, not market. Market little ruby, no clean." He clams up and his expression becomes kind of sad.

My curiosity flames out of control, but this is one of those times when biting your tongue's the only way to go. The mine manager takes time with his thoughts, and I give it to him.

Finally, he looks at me again. "Yes. I tell you. Sometime small parcel is stole. Sometime so-so parcel is stole. One time, big parcel was stole. Beautiful rubies. Big, good red." He shrugs. "Much ruby stole."

"Oh, that's bad! And no one has found any of them?"

He shakes his head. "No. Last stole two year ago."

"Any idea who might have done it?"

A thin shoulder rises. "Don't know. Anyone can do."

"That's true." What a shame—and such a loss. "There's a lot of evil in a lot of men."

"Evil . . . bad, yes? Much, much bad. Many bad men."

A few more minutes of sad laments go by, and then Max and Miss Mona wave me over. It's time to go. I'm ready for one of those buying offices. I want to be amazed by rubies.

I head to the van. "Hey, Miss Mona! What do you think? Should we go buy us some rubies?"

Max glances toward the van. "Do we ask the driver, the translator, or the armed goon?"

"Well, they're all armed. I don't think any one of them would get queasy about drawing his gun. But I'm sure the secret service one knows we're here to check out all parts of their ruby industry, and to pick up product for the network."

The three of us argue mildly over which one will go ask.

Can you believe they both think *I'm* the most likely to set them off? I smell red-hair discrimination here.

But I know at least two worse at it than me. "Aren't you guys confusing me with Aunt Weeby? She's the one who says weird things, but she's back home in Louisville. And if you ask me, I'd have to say Max loves the taste of shoe leather more than I do. He's always got those big feet tickling his throat, even on screen."

"It takes two," he says, his voice a low growl.

Miss Mona points to the van. "Go! The both of you. I gotta tell you. If you'd only stop picking at each other, you might just figure out you're perfectly matched, and like each other too much instead of too little."

I gape.

He stares.

We both shut up.

When we get into the van—still speechless—she gives the driver a signal, and we take off at his hang-onto-your-life speed. We go down narrow streets clotted on either side with old cars. Kinda freaky, you know? I have to wonder if we'll get to that buying office alive.

We do arrive in one piece. How? Beats me, but not thanks to Speedy Gonzalez in the driver's seat.

The buying office is located midway down a block of old stucco buildings. Some are divided into apartments; others have storefronts, topped by more apartments. Our destination is a plain vanilla two-story structure, no apartments on the second floor. The sidewalk here is made up of chunks of stone; elsewhere in the town I've seen boardwalks. Inside the building, we enter another dimension. Soft cream walls, a nice wooden desk, a sapphire and garnet Persian rug, a vintage copper light fixture, and two bulging bookshelves make the reception area a treat after the ruggedness of the mine.

And the rutted roads.

The slender Myanma gentleman in a dark blue suit shows us into an inner room. Wood paneling covers all these walls from floor to ceiling. A long, library-style table runs down the middle of the room. Eight dark wood chairs, possibly mahogany, are pulled up to it. The three of us take seats, while Hannah does her thing.

Just as she's testing the light, the door yawns into our wood-paneled cocoon, and two men walk in.

"Good afternoon," the one in a tan shirt and khaki pants says. "My name is Mr. Ne Aung, and I have some nice rubies for you."

The very Myanma-looking vendor speaks excellent English with a British accent. His partner, Mr. Win, opens a square, black leather case lined in white satin. It's a nice case, but nothing much can compare with the rich, glowing, pigeon's-blood red rubies that nestle in the satin.

I suck in my breath. "I've seen Burma rubies before, but this . . . Wow! Which mine did they come from?"

Mr. Ne Aung points at two round stones. "These came from the one you visited today."

And how did he know which one we visited? I don't think asking is a good thing. Not right now.

Instead, I say, "Can I loop them?"

Mr. Win holds out a 10x jeweler's loop and a pair of tweezers. I pick up the stone. Mr. Ne Aung turns on a pure-light lamp, and the ruby comes alive. You see, Burma rubies do this neat little trick. They fluoresce, and not just under the "black" fluorescent type of light. Rubies from other locales don't do it, even though they might show off a body color close to that of the Burmese.

"Nice," I say. "Very, very nice. Do you have a carat scale I could use?"

Mr. Ne Aung smiles at Mr. Win. "I told you she would want to verify the weight." He turns back to me. "Mr. Pak spoke very highly of you. Said you knew the business."

Sadness hits me again. "You have heard he died, right?"

Mr. Ne Aung goes kinda green around the gills. "Dead? How can that be? He was here just two, maybe three weeks ago. He was on his way to see you."

"Really? Did he tell you why? What did he say about the trip? And why me? Why was he coming to see me, of all people?"

My rapid-fire questions seem to surprise him. "Don't *you* know why he came to see you?"

"I wouldn't have asked you if I did. What did he say about his trip?"

Mr. Ne Aung glances at Mr. Win. The look they exchange makes me uneasy; the vendor's answer even more. "Only that he would see you after he left here. Didn't he tell you his reasons when he arrived? Or did he not reach his destination?"

"He came to the network studios, but someone killed him before I even knew he was there. We never had the chance to get together. I found him dead. In the vault."

Mr. Ne Aung and Mr. Win swap looks. "Did you receive what he had for you?"

"I did. The police found the invitation from your government to come and film the Mogok mining operations. How

127

else would we have received permission to enter the country? Oh! And I got Rio too—the parrot."

"Parrot? A bird?"

I nod.

He shakes his head. "Then that must be that."

"He was dead by the time I found him. Sure that's that."

"Unless," Max says, "the gentlemen are referring to something other than the parrot or the invitation."

The men trade looks—yet another time. "There's nothing else," Mr. Ne Aung says, his eyes cast downward. "What else could there be?"

Before I have a chance to speak, Max jumps in with another good question, to my surprise. "Aren't you the one who saw him last? Shouldn't you be the one to tell us what else there could be?"

Mr. Ne Aung takes a sharp breath, blinks, then puts on a smile, one that feels just a tad sad. "I'm sorry. I don't suppose there's anything more one can say or do now that he's dead."

"What do you mean, there's nothing more to do?" Miss Mona asks with way too much oomph. I appreciate the effort. "I thought we came all the way 'round the world to buy us some great rubies. We haven't bought a one, and I need Andie to sell rubies for me."

"We can help *you*, madam," Mr. Win says.

He speaks!

While Miss Mona and Mr. Ne Aung haggle back and forth, I can't shake a funky feeling. Something in the cobwebby back corners of my mind screams: that vendor knows more than he's sharing. About Mr. Pak.

And then some.

But what?

I keep my eyes and ears open as I pick out the one-only stones I think we should buy. I nod or shake my head when Mr. Ne Aung talks price; I don't want Miss Mona to pay more than a decent value, where the vendor can make a living and where the network can make a profit.

Then we go on to the parcels we will divide to sell the similar stones in volume at a more reasonable price. They're of lesser quality than the one-onlys, but still better than what one can find anywhere else. The finest Madagascar rubies come close to some of these stones in color and clarity—but no fluorescence.

All this time, Max says nothing more. I suppose he said enough.

And he gave me plenty to think about, Lord. What did all that mean? Aside from those men knowing way more than they were willing to say.

Through the rest of the meeting, my head buzzes with the certainty that Mr. Ne Aung knows more than he's said.

I want to find out what it is before we leave Mogok.

With God's help.

Of course, my curiosity and determination can't hurt.

I hope.

11<u>00</u>

The next day, we return to the mine. Hannah films while I kick up clouds of dry peanut-butter-colored dust with every step I take. It's so bad that by the time I get to the mouth of the mine, my hair looks more nutty than carroty.

Yeah, yeah. Nutty fits me better than carroty.

I continue to interview miners as the mine manager interprets for me, and we film the primitive means by which the world's best rubies are brought out from where God hides them underground.

When the manager shows me the day's production, Miss Mona peers over my shoulder. "That's too bad! There's almost nothing there. And those bitty bits you do have are too small to cut." She looks my way. "Aren't they?"

I hand her a small piece of rough. "This one might make a decent accent stone in the hands of a good cutter. But it's no Hollywood A-lister's rock, that's for sure."

Max holds out a hand. "Could I see it? It doesn't look anything like a ruby."

"Here you go. And that, Max, is why it's called rough. It

hasn't been cut or polished yet. That cut and polish is what brings out the amazing red of Burmese rubies."

He returns the stone to the mine manager, then scratches his chin. "If there's so little stuff coming out of these mines, why are we here? Wouldn't it make more sense to go check out other sources of rubies? Or maybe we just look for some other gems period. Sapphires are good."

Sapphires are good. Sure thing, buddy. And Cartier just sells watches.

Before I say anything I shouldn't—I can bite my tongue every now and then, you know—I offer a quick prayer. I glance down, but when I catch sight of my filthy Nikes, a groan explodes all on its own. I look just like Charlie Brown's pal Pigpen. Ah . . . the perils of gemology.

But I digress.

Back to Max. "True. Sapphires are great, but carat for carat, the best rubies can run many more thousands than even diamonds, alexandrites, or Paraíba tourmalines, never mind sapphires."

"I know diamonds and alexandrites, but what's a para . . . pear-ah—"

I should be used to him by now, but it still rubs me the wrong way. Time to enlighten the gem-dunce. Again.

"Paraíba is a state in Brazil where the rarest form of tourmaline, an electric, neon blue gem, was originally found around 1988 or '89." He leans closer, and I notice his attentive gaze and encouraging smile. Great! Progress is good. I figure I'd better strike while the striking's good. "That mine played out just a couple of years after it was found, and now Brazilian Paraíba gems can bring in tens of thousands of dollars per carat."

131

His baby blues goggle. "*Tens* of thousands? Are you gem geeks crazy?"

"And proud of it. Actually, there was a find in Nigeria in 2001, and another new find of the copper-bearing cuprian elbaite in Africa sometime in 2005. It looks as though the GIA has determined these stones can be called Paraíba even though they don't come from Brazil. Their prices are a little more reasonable."

He holds out a hand, palm out. "Stop. Please. If I didn't know better, I'd say you'd just cussed me out. All those strange words make my head spin."

My smile is just a teensy weensy bit smug. "I said you were in over your head, didn't I? Gemology's not for the faint of heart."

He narrows his eyes. "Neither is the perfect swing or breaking through tackles and blocks on the way to the end zone."

Miss Mona lays a hand on his forearm. "You're a sports fan? I didn't realize that. Or did you tell me and my sieve of a brain let it go down the drain?"

I snort. "He sure is, Miss Mona. He played for the Buckies . . . the Buck-ohs . . . er . . . the Buckaroos?"

He glares. "The Buckeyes, Andie." He turns to Miss Mona. "My BS in meteorology is from Ohio State. I went on a football scholarship and played all four years."

Miss Mona smiles. "I remember listening to my two brothers argue for hours over the merits of the Buckeyes versus the Wolverines."

That's enough to send Max the Magnificent into a mega-psyched defense of his . . . what'd he call them? Oh yeah. Buckeyes.

Just what we need. *Not.*

Sports talk won't get us where we want to go, so by the time they've enumerated a slew of pros and cons for each team, I say, "How about we wrap it up here, guys, and head for the Panchan-htar-pwe market? I'm not so sure they *don't* have any stones of value there. Who knows what we might find if we check out enough vendors?"

"Oooh, Andie!" Miss Mona says, "I've always loved treasure hunts. And I did want to visit the market from the start, remember?"

We wave good-bye to our newly minted miner friends and pile into the van. I have no clue what to expect at the market, but excitement fizzes up inside me. I have to agree with Miss Mona. There's something about treasure hunts that really grabs you. It's the what-if factor.

We reach the market, and I fall head over heels with the whole thing. Pink and blue umbrellas mushroom over the blocks-long open-air bazaar. Burmese folks bustle in and out of the aisles, hustle their way between the tables, and finally vanish in the field of colorful umbrellas. An electric energy radiates from all that activity and draws me in. *And*, as if the exotic aura weren't enough, there's gemstones a-waitin' on them thar tables!

"Let's go," I urge once the driver finds a parking spot on the packed-earth area just in front of the umbrellas. "I can't wait to see what we'll find today."

I scramble out, fighting my natural urge to run ahead. I don't think the demure Burmese can handle a crazed American rushing their prized market. And I have a sneaking suspicion I'm actually allergic to Burmese jails. I itch at the thought.

Our translator follows me into the maze of vendors, and I'm off to the races. The first table I stop at has little to look at. The ruby rough is tiny, cloudy, and nothing I want to mess with.

The next table I visit, though, is a whole other story. While this vendor has no rubies, he does have other goodies. Our translator gestures for me to sit, and moments later, Miss Mona does the same. The gem-dunce follows. Lucky me.

The vendor pulls out a silver bowl and a folded-paper rectangle. My heart starts to pump. As he draws out the moment, unfurling each flap with painful deliberation, I grow giddy.

Tha-thump, tha-thump, tha-thump.

I can't stand the overdone suspense. Finally, the slip of paper blossoms out flat. In the very center multiple stones twinkle and wink at me. I bend closer. They glow stormy-ocean blue. "Ah . . ."

"Nice?" the vendor says.

I rein in my stampeding glee. "I'd like to loop them."

When he nods, I reach into my pocket, pop open my 10x magnifier, and look at the stunning, clean stones. The man's carat scale reveals decent weight. These babies should set up great. "Do you have more?"

"More?" The vendor leans over, digs around in a beat-up old suitcase, and after a few minutes bounces back, a larger folded packet in hand. "More."

You know I buy all those sapphires.

Miss Mona slips the two parcels into her handbag. "Oh, Andie. I'm so excited! Our viewers are gonna eat these beautiful pieces up with a spoon."

"That's what I thought when I laid eyes on the first lot."

"I knew the color was good," Max said.

"You're learning." I hope.

"Everyone knows sapphires. It's all that stuff about other unknown stones that can trip a guy up."

"A guy who doesn't know his gemstones . . ."

"When you know all about football and golf . . ."

"Don't hold your breath."

"D'you see me turning blue?"

To keep from saying anything more, I find another table—not a hardship, since I figure there's about a couple million of them under the umbrellas. Just a tiny exaggeration, but that's how crowded the pink and blue mushroom world feels. I wave at our translator. "Could you please ask this gentleman to show us what he has?"

He nods, singsongs something at the vendor, and after a slew of smiles and more nods, this guy rummages through a white canvas bag slung over the back of his chair. I sit down across from him. Miss Mona takes the chair next to mine. Max the Magnificent stands.

"Spinel," the man says.

I nod. Most people think of spinel as the fake, man-made stuff they put in most class rings, but real-deal spinel is a thing of beauty. Especially the Burmese material. I lean forward and hold my breath.

This man is more progressive with his packaging. He keeps his stones in mini-ziplock baggies. Another silver bowl comes out of the canvas sack, and the gems are poured into its center.

I sigh. "Beautiful . . ."

He has purple, blue, pink, and the big mama of spinel: red.

Max leans forward. "That's not ruby?"

"Isn't it amazing?" I say. "But it's spinel, not ruby. And you're far from the only guy to mistake fine spinel for ruby. It actually tends to be cleaner, more transparent, and the color? There's a whole world of rubies that dream of being spinels when they grow up."

"No kidding."

But enough with the chitchat. Out comes my loop. I wave it at my armed nanny. "Does he mind?"

The men sing out Burmese. When both nod, I take up my trusty tweezers and loop away.

It doesn't get much better than this. To make sure I'm not dreaming, I set down the loop, slip my empty hand under the table, and pinch my thigh. "Ow!"

"Did you just pinch yourself again?" Max asks.

"Yeah. I don't want this to be some dream. Doesn't it freak you out even a little that you're here, all the way around the world, in a country few people have visited in forty or more years, and looking at some of the most spectacular gemstone material *ever*?"

"The travel's cool."

"But not the stones?"

The devastating smile shows up again. Aaack! Even when he makes me crazy, his smile melts my bones.

He crosses his arms. "What can I say? They're okay."

Rather than try to answer, I shake my head and turn back to my gems, soon to be Miss Mona's and the S.T.U.D.'s gems.

We make our way around, up, and then finally down all the vendors' tables. I collect perfectly green peridot; all colors of tourmaline—except Paraíba; amethyst so purple it makes me want to cry; green—you hear that? *Green!*— zircon; squeaky clean aquamarine; velvety navy-blue kyanite;

136

super-rare green kornerupine; and not just the more common colorless danburite but also sunny yellow and fancy pink.

As we head back to the van, exhaustion almost brings me to my knees. Miss Mona, however, is sassy as ever, the usual spring still in her step. How does she do it?

I struggle to keep up with her and Max, but my eyelids get scratchy and my arms and legs weigh about a ton each. In the van, I collapse into my seat. Miss Mona settles in, and Max fills the back bench with his long, lean figure.

Miss Mona hugs her handbag close. A tiny smile curves up the corners of her mouth.

"How does it feel to carry around a king's ransom?" I ask.

"I've never done anything like this," she answers. "But I love it. I'm so glad you agreed to work for the network. I wouldn't have had this chance any other way. And I wouldn't trade this trip for anything in the world."

Even though I'm pooped, I realize how right she is. "I wouldn't trade it either."

I'd consider trading Max the Magnificent for an air conditioner . . .

It's hot in Burma. And it doesn't help that every time the guy looks at me, my temperature rushes right up to stratospheric heights. I'll just have to work harder to control my response. I can't fall for a jock who doesn't know rocks.

You're going to help me, Lord, right? I can't do this alone.

All I know is that Max Matthews is more dangerous than any of the poachers the vendors have told us about.

Maybe I can get on his nerves so much that I'll chase him away—*Whoa!* I can't be that awful. True, I feel as though I'm teetering on the edge of a cliff, and Max is either about to push me over or catch me on the way down. Beats me which, but I'm scared. Still, aside from knowing nothing about my field of expertise, what has Max done? Nothing so bad. Right?

Oh, phooey! The truth is, I'm afraid if I have to spend a whole lot more time around him I might . . . let's just say I don't even want to know what might happen.

He's way too attractive. And I might start to believe there's lots more behind that amazing smile, those twinkling sky-blue eyes, the dumb-jock routine.

Miss Mona's nobody's fool. She hired him. Maybe . . .

Even if he doesn't know his chalcedony from his chryso-beryl.

Heaven help me. *Please!*

Dinner tonight is more of the same mystery mix—fishy-flavored this time—veggies, and rice. The best part of the meal is the fresh tropical fruit we're served for dessert.

Afterward, I sleep like a dog—totally oblivious to everything but my off-the-wall dreams. Okay, so maybe I don't chase my tail in my sleep, but I do spend a ton of time trying to catch Max before he makes another one of those bloopers of his.

In the morning, we follow yesterday's routine of shower and dress, then breakfast in the hotel's dining room. We head out to the mine as soon as we push away from the table.

"Miss Andie," the mine manager says when I do like a dust devil, and my cloud of grime and I approach. "We dig tunnel more today."

"Great! I can't wait to film that. How do you want us to

go about it? Do you need Hannah to go in by herself, or can both of us go down together?"

"I no want you there. Danger in tunnel is big."

"But we came to tape the operation here. If you're going deeper into the ground, I want to get that on film."

I can just hear the rusty wheels in his head cranking around the idea of two loony American women going into his mine while his workers jackhammer their way farther into the earth's crust. Poor guy. Life as he's known it is history. Wait till we leave and he gets a chance to really think about what hit him.

From her practically bottomless tote bag, Miss Mona pulls out two dust masks. "Hold it right there, Andie-girl."

I give her a sheepish look. "Thanks. I forgot we'd taken them out of my suitcase at the hotel. Then I was so ready to get back to the mine, I never gave them another thought."

She grins. "A girl has to be prepared, I always say—so does Livvy, but she's not here, so she doesn't count right now. And don't you go telling her I said that. But I had me a good idea this mining business was going to be a filthy affair, so I wasn't about to leave them back in the room to do you no earthly good."

I slip a mask over my head and hurry after Hannah. She takes the extra one and gives me a mischievous wink. "I see Miss Mona's version of the Boy Scouts' 'Be prepared' motto strikes again."

"I'm glad she was more on the ball than I was." I give her a wry grin. "We're going to walk out of that pit over there with lungs that work. I know a good thing when I see it, and Miss Mona's the real deal. Wacky, but smart too."

"You don't get to make a success of your own cable shopping network at the time of life when others are crocheting doilies if you don't have a good set of brains and smarts. I love the lady."

"We all do," Max says from right behind us. "Even though I'm new to the network, I already think the world of her. She's a class act." He points. "Do I get one of those things? Every time Andie moves, she kicks up a windstorm and chokes us with her dust."

"And you don't kick up dirt when you walk around this place?"

"I don't impersonate tornadoes. I walk."

The nerve of the man. "I walk too. But I'm a woman on a mission. You know—places to go, people to see. What you call shuffling, others more on the ball would call a busy hustle."

With that, I turn to follow Hannah and the mine manager—I can't even begin to torture my tongue into the foreign noises that make up his name. I'm not Burmese. I've never had to utter that kind of sound. I'm now convinced you have to be born Burmese for your tongue to twist like that.

One by one, the miners make their way down the mouth of the mine. I follow, then Hannah comes in, her camera whirring away, capturing every last detail.

"It's hard to believe I'm really in a ruby mine in Burma," I say loud enough for Hannah to get on tape. "But lucky for you, ladies and gentlemen, you get to come along with me."

The mine tunnel is about eight feet high, seven feet wide, and goes into the rock for about twenty-five feet. While I'm thrilled to be here, the candles the miners use to light the way don't do a thing for me. They eat up a whole lot of oxygen, and I kinda like to breathe. The alternative? Not so much.

Now I wish I'd brought one of those Tim-the-Toolman-Taylor kind of three-foot-long halogen lanterns with me. But, back home, I knew getting just about anything past customs into this country would be a hassle. I didn't want to square off against Myanma authorities the moment I landed. And to think Max the Magnificent made fun of my plenteous luggage; I could have brought more.

Where was I? Oh yeah. That's right. I reach out and touch the rough stone walls, etched with the tracks of the jackhammers that carved it out of solid rock.

Then, from somewhere out beyond the other side of the mine tunnel, an explosion steals my voice.

The world tilts off its center.

The earth shakes.

When I lean against the wall of the tunnel to keep myself from going down, it continues to shimmy up a storm. To my horror, a creaking reverberates down from somewhere near the mouth of the pit.

Deathly silence follows.

Then, in hushed tones, the miners start to jabber. Bet they've seen more than their fair share of killer mine explosions in their lifetimes.

Besides all that, clouds of dust eddy around us. Even through my mask, I breathe in the dirt mixed with the scent of humidity, a rare stink of mold, mildew, some sort of organic rot. I don't know what it might be. I just know I don't like it. I grab Hannah, who looks shocked and beyond the grasp of reality.

"Come on! Let's get out of here. This place is about to crash. And I don't want us to be here when it does."

Her face goes gray. Her teeth chatter. But in spite of her obvious fear, she starts to move forward, her camera still on.

141

What a pro. But one in danger. "Run!" I urge her.

The men either hear my cry or figure they'd better do likewise, because moments later, they ooze out of the tunnel and cluster on the dust-clouded mounds outside.

"Hurry, hurry, hurry!" I urge Hannah and wave at the men. No one should stop until they're far, far away from this place.

Finally, I spot the mine manager. "What happened? I didn't think you used dynamite here."

"We no dynamite, Miss Andie." The tight line of his clenched jaw leaves me no alternative but to believe him. Not that I've ever not heard him speak the truth. "I *will* find who do this."

As we reach the entryway, another blast shocks us. I spot Miss Mona at Max's side, all frothed up into a lather. Who can blame her?

I stick my fingers in the corners of my mouth and give a good blow.

They turn.

I point to the van. *"Now!"*

What a change! Max doesn't give me grief. The only thing that does give me grief is the thought that one of us could've been hurt—or worse.

He rounds up the rest of our crew, gets them into the van.

That's when I make my decision. Miss Mona or no Miss Mona. I ask, "Do you have your king's ransom with you?"

She pats her tote bag. "I'd never leave it at the hotel."

"Good." I lean forward to speak to the driver.

The translator turns sideways in the front seat and gives me a leery look.

I don't let him see me sweat. "Get us out of here," I tell the man at the wheel. "Now. And take us straight to the airport. We're leaving."

Just to give you an idea how bad this scene is, neither Miss Mona nor Max say a word about luggage, the hotel, or the hassle of changing flight reservations.

And I'm thankful. I meant it when I said we had to go. Something really bad's going down here. I don't want us caught up in whatever it might be.

Oh yeah. We're out of there so fast that natives can track us by the trail of dust we leave behind.

Lord? Why does this really weird stuff follow me around like one of those evil cartoon shadows? Can you do me one favor? If it wouldn't be too much to ask. Can you take that shadow and retire it? I am so outta Myanmar as soon as we can get standby seats to fly back home. Help us, okay?

"Hurry!" I urge the driver. I'm sure he understands. Fear and urgency don't really come in different language flavors. At least, I don't think they do.

He gives me a nod. The translator speaks Burmese. The secret service guy grunts.

"Please," I say. "We need to get to Yangon. I don't like what's going on here."

And I don't. But I really, really hate what happens next.

That's because bullets begin to fly.

12<u>00</u>

Six tense hours later, we hurry into the airport, check with the airlines, beg for help, and then stake out S.T.U.D.-world. At any other time we would've been guilty of a human-body version of urban sprawl, but today we glom together, needing all the togetherness we can get.

You know what? I'm scared. But if you tell anyone, I'll deny it all the way. I've never been so scared in my life, not even of Max and how he makes me feel. Here I am in Myanmar, at the Mandalay airport, running from crazed locals with guns. Wouldn't you be scared too?

It's so not a good thing.

The next flight out of this rathole isn't until tomorrow morning. And who knows if there'll be room for all of us. We decide, though, that we're all about a Three Musketeers deal—all for one, and one for all. None of this three on this flight, three on the other, and the last poor schmuck's left behind to bite her nails and freak out while she waits. Since I'm responsible for this whole fiasco, and since I can't see the

S.T.U.D.'s stud hanging around here in a burst of chivalry, guess who'd be that poor schmuck?

Now that we're at the airport, one would think we're off the hook, right? Think again.

As we huddle, a braided and medaled, official-looking guy comes up to us, a stamped and sealed paper in hand. Not exactly Big Bird lovable.

Goody.

"Miss Mona Latimer?" he asks. "Miss Andrea Adams?"

We look at each other, squeeze hands—oh, didn't I mention I need that much reassurance? Really? I didn't? Oh, well. Trust me. I do.

"How can we help you?" Miss Mona asks.

In a British-accented voice, he says, "We must do body checks. You've come from Mogok, we know you've been at a mine site, and in the past we've lost too much national treasure to greedy foreigners. There will be a woman to examine the ladies, and the gentlemen will come with me."

Hey! Remember me? The one with the personal thundercloud overhead? It just got darker.

I put on my very best puppy-dog look. "Is this really necessary, sir?"

His eyes narrow and his jaw morphs into granite. "Yes, it is, Miss Adams. Allow me to mention a theft we suffered two and a half years ago. Tourists and gem tradespeople went into the Mogok Valley for two weeks. By the end of that time, Myanmar had lost a parcel of top-gem quality rubies valued at many millions of your dollars. I'm sure you will agree we have every reason to check visitors to Mogok before they leave our country."

Sounds familiar. What are the chances of two identical heists in Mogok?

Miss Mona picks up her tote bag. "I have bought myself a large inventory of gemstones here in Myanmar, sir. But I'll have you know I do have my bills of sale for each and every last one of them. Besides, you can check with that perfectly nice officer over there"—she points to the customs counter—"who'll tell you that when we first got here about an hour ago, I filled out a declaration form for all the gems I bought."

"You do realize you must pay a 20 percent royalty to the government on any gemstones you buy in Myanmar, right?"

What a bargain.

"I'm afraid no one told me a thing about that special fee of yours, but I can pay," Miss Mona answers. "Who do I make the check out to?"

"You must pay the government of the Union of Myanmar, madam, but we cannot accept a bank check, not from another country. We can accept cash or credit card."

"Well, then, why don't you and I take care of that little matter right away. Cash will be difficult, but I think we can make use of my credit card."

For the first time since he came up to us, his expression goes from icicle to mud puddle. "We appreciate your understanding our nation's needs, and we also hope you can extend that understanding to the need for the body searches. We make no exceptions."

Miss Mona looks less happy about stripping in front of a stranger than shelling out the 20 percent. I feel awful for her. "Do you want me to come with you?"

The glance she gives me is full of pure love and gratitude.

146

"If this kind gentleman will allow it," she says, the southern in her accent belle thick, "I would surely be much obliged if you would." She turns to him. "I do so hope you understand."

The mud puddle icicles up again. "That is not how we operate, madam. We prefer to provide privacy."

Miss Mona stands tall, towers over him. "But no personal dignity, sir?" The accent's back to its usual light touch.

Faced with such an indomitable spirit in its statuesque physical form, the government flack backs down. "I suppose we could make a rare exception. But only this once."

One by one, except Miss Mona and me, since we do a Noah's Ark twosies deal, we're searched. Not so pleasant an experience, but not so impossible either. They don't frisk us.

Then we hunker down in our bunker in the terminal to count the seconds until the airline finds seats—we hope— for us. Somewhere in the deepest, darkest bowels of the night, I remember I stink at waiting. I fidget, I pace, I sit again, and then jump back up to start the whole process yet another time.

"Hey!" Max says in a soft voice. "Can't you sleep?"

"Not a wink."

Unexpected gentleness softens his features. "Want to go for a walk? I'll keep you company."

"You can't sleep either?"

He shrugs. "I don't have too much trouble dozing off just about anywhere, but you seem wound up so tight that I feel bad for you. Maybe walking will help. And talking, if you want."

Those blue eyes . . . they're going to be my downfall. Oh, I know I need to have my head examined. It's either that, or run the guy back to the weather job in Podunk, Missouri. Because, against my better judgment—

"Okay."

To my surprise, he doesn't say another word. He matches his steps to mine and seems content to just stay at my side, to let me work the nervous energy out of my system.

Ten minutes later, my gratitude for his sensitivity—

Wait a minute! The gem-dunce sensitive? That, and the moon's made of the green fur on last week's leftovers.

But honestly? I can't fault him for a thing, no matter how hard I try. The whole time we've walked he's been the perfect companion. Not one word has crossed his lips, not even one about football or golf or his . . . Buckeyes. Not that I've said anything either, but thoughtfulness is not something I expect from Max.

Maybe that's my own fault . . . Uh-oh.

And then I yawn. "Hey, Max. I think I am getting sleepy. How about we head back?"

"I was wondering if you'd ever get around to noticing we've gone around this sales kiosk in the middle of the place fourteen times."

I glance toward the stand. "Really? I didn't realize we were doing ring-around-the-rosy. I didn't even notice it there."

"That deep in thought, huh?"

"You could say."

"May I ask why?"

"Sure, but I'm not sure I can put it into words. It's more a feeling . . . maybe a pre-thought." I shake my head. "That doesn't make sense, does it?"

"You're asking me if *you're* making sense?"

I chuckle. "It's okay. You don't have to answer."

"Phew! I'd hate to stomp right into that minefield."

"More like a field mined with piles of dog doo."

"Care to explain?"

I sigh. "Doesn't it strike you as odd that we got shot at only after we bought material down at the market? And after the mine shaft was dynamited."

"I haven't given it much thought. Other than to be glad we got away without any unintended piercings."

"What? You mean you didn't want a freebie? You didn't want to get yourself some of those oh-so-manly earrings or eyebrow thingies . . . Oh no. No, no, no! I know just what would look good on you. You're the nose ring kind, like an ox."

"And here I thought we were making progress."

"Camping out in a third world airport is progress?"

"No, Andie. The airport isn't progress. Talking without sniping is progress."

I blush. Okay. I'm more than a little guilty here, but come on. This is Max, trouble for me. "You have to admit it's kind of outrageous to take a job where you know nothing about the subject matter."

"And you've got to admit I've got plenty of on-screen time under my belt."

"True, but what good are you if you can't contribute a thing to the show?"

"Who says I can't?"

"You haven't yet."

"Doesn't mean I won't."

"Maybe when barbecued sparerib dinners replace those jetliners in the skies."

"And the pigs haven't even left the runway yet."

"I didn't say it. You did."

"Sometimes it's better to take the jab at yourself before someone else throws you the knockout punch."

I step back, look him from head to toe. "You don't strike me like a guy who's had much experience with that kind of punch."

"You'd be surprised what I have and haven't experienced."

"Can't argue that. But I do know you haven't experienced a course in gemology."

"True. But it won't be true for much longer now."

"Huh?"

"I'm thinking of taking a continuing education class on rocks."

"Really?" *Uh-oh!* There he goes again, doing something to make him more appealing. C'mon, c'mon, c'mon, Andie. Think fast! Think of a new brick for that wall you've been building between the two of you.

"Aren't you going to give me any credit?"

I bite my tongue—hard. He's got a point. My conscience stings and I wince in shame. *Oh, Lord, in my cowardly efforts to protect myself, I've been unfair and mean.*

When I don't answer, he throws his arms upward, frustration on every feature. "What kind of super-Christian are you? You don't give a guy half a chance."

Another stab of guilt. "It's not that I won't give you half a chance. It's more that I'm waiting for you to go even half that mile, never mind the extra one. And now you want me to believe you're ready to do the homework you should have done before you started the job."

Arms crossed, he now takes a step back and studies me.

I don't like it.

He doesn't seem to care.

The silence starts to get to me. My back itches right smack in the middle of my spine. Where I can't reach it.

"You're stubborn enough for ten ornery mules," he says after a long while of pitched eye-to-eye combat.

My hackles rise. "I am not." Did I just say that? Oh, am I ever in trouble. But right now, in front of Max, isn't the time to deal with this little personal issue. It's time to take a stab at an answer—a better one, this time. "I'm a perfectly agreeable woman."

Great! I just dug me a bigger hole. I don't know anyone else whose mouth flaps before their brain engages as much as mine does.

"And I'm one of those flying pigs you're waiting for."

"If you want to call yourself a pig, who am I to stop you?"

"Miss Mona was right, but I don't think she knew even the half of it."

I narrow my eyes. "What do you mean? What was Miss Mona right about?"

"You."

"What about me?"

"She said you'd be a handful, but that you're smart and know your business. I'll give you the brains and the book smarts, never mind the handful bit. But what you really are is more trouble than you're worth."

Ouch! "What do you mean?"

"That a guy can crack his head on a brick wall only so many times before he decides it's just not worth it. I really want to make this job work, but I can only do so much. The other half is up to you."

My jaw nearly clips the dingy floor. He thinks he's been trying to work with me?

You'd never know from where I stand.

Right?

Or have I been so busy shielding myself that I've missed his attempts? Could it be *my* fault?

I shake my head. "It's way too late in the night to do this. I'm going to try and sleep. I suggest you do too. Maybe you'll find enlightenment while you grab your z's. You might figure out why this cohosting gig isn't working."

I'm sure I can wait for further enlightenment—know what I mean?

Max looks like he's about to argue some more, but then he shrugs and walks back to S.T.U.D.-world. I follow. And then I groan.

While we were ring-around-the-kiosking, Hannah and Allison must have gone to the bathroom or something, because they're no longer on the couch they'd been sharing. Now each has taken up residence in one of the two armchairs that—you got it—Max and I had used.

The only piece of furniture left vacant in S.T.U.D.-world is that lousy couch. And unless one of us is ready to lie down on the hard concrete floor or wants to wander down to the other cluster of furniture at the far end of the terminal, we're going to have to share.

Yep. You got it. The grounded pig and the dug-in mule and the teensy-weensy little ol' couch. Oh my!

Not a pretty picture.

But I'm too tired. So I drop onto one corner and Max takes the other.

To my surprise, I actually sleep.

I hear clapping.

Then, "People!"

With less than no oomph, I pry open a totally reluctant eye. "Huh—"

Then I yelp. And bolt upright.

If you're as smart as I think you are, you've already figured it out. You see, there I was curled up on Max's broad, warm, supportive shoulder, right in the middle of the airport, for the whole world to see. Of course, I had to bolt.

How am I ever gonna live this one down?

But then it gets worse. When I force my sleep-fogged eyes to focus, I see Miss Mona, who clearly has been staring at us for some time, the most indulgent smile on her face. Betchya Aunt Weeby knows all about that cozy dozing on the Burmese couch by now.

Like I said, I'm never gonna live this one down.

"*People!*" The man's voice is more strident this time. "You want leave, no?"

"Huh?"

Max stands. "I think he's trying to tell us they've found seats for us." He turns to the khaki-uniformed man. "The flight's ready?"

"Flight! Yes." He nods like a bobblehead dog on the back of a land-yacht Cadillac. "You fly to America. Now."

In less than no time, we board and buckle. This time, I make sure I'm next to Miss Mona, even though that poses a peril all its own. We listen to the Burmese version of the airline scare tactics—the life-jacket stuff, the exit slides, mass destruction and mayhem, etc., etc., etc.

Finally, after heavy-duty praying, and by the grace of our merciful God, the plane takes off without any more hitches.

I pray even harder than before, this time all praise and worship for his protection. Plus gratitude, since we're all in one piece.

I sleep.

By the time we land at JFK, I know what I have to do next. I see the rest of our group on to their flight home to Kentucky, book a later one for me, and then hail a cab outside the terminal. A short time later, the NASCAR escapee in a turban screeches to a halt just outside my former place of employment. I pay him the king's ransom he demands. Thank goodness I always kept my purse with me in Mogok. Can you imagine what I would have had to deal with if I'd left all my ID and credit cards in that hotel?

Ugh. And we have to trust that hotel to send us the stuff we left behind? Not holding my breath here.

I step inside the jewelry store where I worked so hard on my ulcers, and before I can say a word, Roger rushes me.

"I knew it! You've come to your senses! I just knew you would. Come on. Let me show you my latest buy—"

"Hang on!" I return his hug, and then extricate myself limb by limb. "I'm not here to work. Well, I'm here *on* work, but I'm not back *to* work for you."

His smile wilts only at the edges. "You don't mean that, Andrea. You know you don't. I knew life in a backwater wasn't for you. Not after all the years you enjoyed the real thing here in the city."

"In your dreams. Do you realize I haven't taken a single antacid since I left?" I marvel at that truth. "And I haven't had even the slightest twinge of pain. It turns out I'm really not cut out for the kind of stress you thrive on."

"I'll triple your salary."

154

"Roger! You have to stop that. I told you I won't change my mind. It has nothing to do with money. It has to do with getting a life—mine! And it's really not here in New York."

All the starch seems to wash right out of him. "If you insist, but I'm telling you now. I'm not giving up."

I let that slide. "I didn't just come for a visit, you know. I came because I have a ton of questions for you."

"Questions? What about?"

"Mr. Pak. He's dead, you know."

Surprise makes him step back, his mouth doing a reasonable facsimile of a goldfish.

"And the minor matter of a parrot."

He shakes his head. "A what?"

"You heard me. A bird."

"That's . . . different."

"Oh, and maybe some rubies too."

That's when he plops his butt on his desktop.

I join him inches away, prepared to wait.

I want info, and Roger's been known to be a fount thereof.

At times. And on his terms.

His office clock *tick-tick-ticks* away.

13_00_

Finally he pulls himself together. "You've lost your mind," he says in a stunned voice.

"I don't think so."

"Well, if you want me to . . ." He waves. "Oh, I don't know. Help you? Beats me what you think I can do, but at any rate, I need to know what you're up to before I can begin to think up some answers."

"What? You can't read my mind?" I give him a sheepish smile. "I guess I do have to bring you up to speed. Maybe then you can tell me if you still think I've lost my mind."

In very broad strokes, I paint a word picture of my last couple of weeks. Aside from a bunch of head shakes, some groans, and a few "I don't believe thises," he keeps his mouth shut and lets me spew. It feels good to go over all the insanity that's struck me since I left New York. Even though the telling makes nothing any clearer than it was before.

At the end, he shakes his head. "Why would you think I'd have answers for you? I've been here, where you should have been all this time, I might add, while you've been . . . oh, practically everywhere."

"I just thought since you've known Mr. Pak for such a long time that you might know something, maybe have names of people he knows—knew—or maybe he said something sometime during those years . . . *anything*." The frustration gets to me and I slap my hands flat on the desktop, then push myself upright. "Oh, I guess I don't know. This is totally insane."

"I agree."

"That's it? That's all you have to say?"

He gives me an exasperated look. "What exactly is it you want me to say, Andie? That Mr. Pak stopped here on his way there, told me he was the victim of a massive international plot, that he was carrying stolen goods—no, crown jewels! That's better. That he has some never-heard-of country's crown jewels or its soon-to-be crown jewels, and that a swarm of killers is after him. Is that what you want?"

I give him a crooked grin. "That's exactly what I want, but it does sound pretty far-fetched when you glue it all together like that."

"Of course it sounds far-fetched. I don't know why he went down to see you. Unless he had some stones he wanted to sell you for the network. Maybe some thief found out what he does for a living, followed him, and then stole the gems."

"That's as good a theory as any. But who would have done it?"

"That's the best I can do. I have no idea who would want to kill him. And I don't know any more than what you've told me."

My shoulders slump. "You can't blame me for trying."

"I don't blame you for anything—other than quitting and leaving me in the lurch."

"Oh, give me a break, Rog. Just think of my departure as my donation toward Tiffany's little splurges. And don't talk about exorbitant raises you can't afford. Look at it this way. Now that I'm gone, you don't have to pay me, so the store's profits go farther."

He runs a hand through his steel-colored hair. "Don't even mention Tiff. I've been working so many hours, I'm in the doghouse."

"Uh-oh. I bet I'm in trouble with her too."

His smile was smug. "She knows who left me to work all those extra hours."

"You know what, Rog?" I cross my arms and arch my right brow. "Your pathetic efforts to guilt-trip me back to work for you aren't going to work. And . . . Tiff's *your* wife—your pro-blem-oh!"

He mirrors my pose. "And the dead ruby vendor's yours."

My spirits deflate. I start to pace. "I don't know why I thought you'd have answers for me. My gut tells me Mr. Pak was murdered for the—"

I catch myself. I haven't mentioned the parcel stolen from the mine. There's no point bringing it up.

A shrug, and I go on. "I'm sure he was killed for his rubies. But if that's the case, the killer has to be someone who knew he'd have stones with him."

"How would anyone know that? Unless he'd called ahead to make an appointment, like he used to do with us. And how are we supposed to know if he made any appointments?

There are millions of jewelers in the U.S. You don't expect me to know them all, do you?"

"Did he ever come to the U.S. just for fun?"

His turn for one of those helpless shrugs.

"Exactly. I'm not ready to start pointing fingers, but we both agree the killer has to be someone who buys stones from him. And I don't buy the random jeweler theory."

That gets to him. He sits way up, his back ramrod straight, his shoulders square. "I hope you're not hinting what I'm afraid you are. Because if you are, then you're dead wrong. I didn't do a thing to that man."

"You think I'm accusing you of killing Mr. Pak?"

"I know how your mind works—if it stinks of rotten fish in Denmark, then there just might be rotten fish in Denmark. Or in this case, in Manhattan."

"Give me a break, Roger Hammond. What you smell is New York fumes. Remember? Trash sits out on the sidewalk for days before the sanitation guys come get it."

"That's not what I meant—"

"Bingo! And what you think I meant isn't what I meant. I didn't come here to accuse you. I came to talk because you know more people in the gem world than Leno knows in Hollywood. Who else would I go to for help figuring out this mess?"

"All right, all right." He rubs his forehead, holds his splayed-out hands in a gesture of pure helpless ignorance, then squeezes his eyes shut, wrinkles his nose, and gives his head a couple of small shakes. "You've got to admit, a guy's going to feel the bull's-eye on his forehead if someone comes in out of the blue and starts talking murder conspiracies."

"I'm sorry. And you're right. I must have come off as some

bad TV gumshoe. But you know? When some creep turns you into target practice while you're crashing and bumping down rutted dirt roads, you tend to look at your world through suspicion-colored glasses."

"Can't say I blame you." He's quiet for a minute . . . two. I prop my behind against his desk again.

Roger tents his hands, then, "His rubies, huh?"

"Why else? I don't think anyone's that sick of his mouthy parrot. At least, not to the point of rubbing out the guy— instead of the bird, that is."

His laugh sputters out. "Rubbing out the guy?" Another laugh. "Andie! What have you been doing down in your back-water? Watching prehistoric B movies? That's awful."

"So's walking into your employer's vault and finding a dead guy—a dead guy you've known for a couple of years and liked very much."

His humor vanishes. "I can't imagine how that must have felt. But look at it from my point of view. I'd heard nothing about Pak's death until you walked in and stunned me with the news."

"I'm surprised. I told the cops I'd met Mr. Pak through you."

"Well, they didn't come here to ask questions. You did."

I wink. "And how did I do?"

"Weird. But that's normal—for you."

I throw a play punch at his shoulder. "That's support for ya." A glance at my watch tells me my flight home might just leave without me. "So you can't think of anything that could help."

"Nothing, Andie. Nothing comes to me. Sorry. Wish I could help. This can't be a good time for you."

"You're right about that." I jump off the desk. "And you can imagine what it's done to Aunt Weeby."

"Her?" He laughs. "She must be in her element, playing sleuth."

"Bite your tongue! Miss Mona left Aunt Weeby in charge of her brand-new, very successful TV shopping channel."

"Are you kidding! For all that Miss Mona of yours knows, your aunt's already turned it into . . . oh, I don't know. Maybe a brokerage for . . . I've got it! Pygmy angora goats with blue fur. Is that insane enough for her?"

Aunt Weeby and a herd of fluffy blue goats. "That's scarier than a Stephen King book."

"Your aunt's scarier than Stephen King."

"But so lovable."

"And way older than you. You're at the age where you need to come back to New York and get a life."

"Look who's talking, Mr. I'm-Working-Too-Many-Hours-For-My-Wife. You want me back here so I really don't have a life, like you!"

"I have a life."

"Sure you do. And an angry wife—"

The bell on the front door chimes into my words. "Roger?" a woman asks.

"And that angry wife's here," I say. I grab my handbag, drop a quick kiss on Roger's suddenly greenish cheek, and head for the back door. "Gotta go. She's all yours, pal."

"Traitor," he mutters, then steps toward the front. "I'm here, honey! What brings you to the store?"

As I let myself out, I hear Tiffany's little-girl voice, but I don't catch her words. I'm glad. I'm not crazy about Roger's trophy wife and her extravagances. Yes, I do like designer

161

duds, but I shop discount—something Tiff would never dream of doing. She's all about that price tag and the "because she can" factor.

I hurry down the back alley to the sidewalk, make my way down to the corner, and check my cell phone. As a proud procrastinator, I haven't deleted New York numbers yet, and right there, on my contact list, is the one for my favorite cab company—the one with English-speaking drivers, since I'm not multilingual—that doesn't have speed issues.

When the company promises a cab in six minutes, I shut my phone and get ready for my short wait. And that's when I get a hinky feeling.

I turn around but see no one. Well, no one but the messenger guy on his bike, the suited exec fixated on his blackberry, the young woman in a tailored tan suit—you get the New York picture. Still, the short, downy hairs at the back of my neck are all lined up like good little soldiers. I know that I know that someone's watching me.

That's all I need.

Lord? More trouble? It's been coming at me for ages now, and I think a dead ruby vendor, gun-happy Burmese goons, a nutty aunt, and a shrieking parrot are enough. Oh yeah. And about the cohost? You know I really don't need him, on any of many levels, so you can send him back to Podunk, Missouri, or wherever he came from. Don't you think I've earned a vacation?

When I realize what a self-serving excuse for a prayer that is, I try again. *I'm sorry. That reeks of pride, doesn't it? Let me put it a different way. I know you know everything, especially what really matters. You also know what's coming down in the future, and while I'd rather think about new designer shoes, I don't think it's looking like that's going to be my top concern anytime soon. So . . . if you could, please keep an eye on me. I wind up in more trouble than anyone else I know. Help me listen to you better—I know, I know. You don't bellow, but sometimes I'm kinda thickheaded and don't catch your warning. I can use some help there too. Especially with that pride thing. It's not pretty. I'm sorry. And thanks.*

The cab squeals to a stop, bringing the traffic to a standstill in the already nasty snarl on the street. The guy in the car behind the cab honks his horn, rolls down his window, and yells an obscenity. The one in the red Chevy behind him is another story. He stares at me, then at the loudmouth, at the cab, and at me again.

Goose bumps pop out all over. It's splitsville for me, especially since I've begun to see a bad guy behind every cab, hot dog stand, and trash can or two.

I collapse on the backseat. The guy behind the wheel isn't sporting a turban, but he doesn't look like the all-American guy next door either.

"JFK, please, and I have to be there yesterday."

"Excuse, please? Yesterday? I no understand."

"Are you new with RideSafe?"

"Yes. I come from Greece three months back."

"Who owns the company now?"

"Own? Company?"

"Sure. Your boss."

"Oh. Cousin Spiros new boss. He good man. Give me work."

I fight to squelch the urge and touch of hysteria that zip right through me. *It's all Greek to me* won't exactly win the driver's cooperation.

Instead I say, "I'm flying US Airways."

"Okay."

While it isn't a white-knuckle ride, it isn't a Sunday drive in the country either. I pay, jump out, and then I see it again. The same red Chevy whose driver stared at me back at the street corner near Roger's store. When I'm about to call 9-1-1, a tall brunette in a designer black suit walks up to the car, opens the rear door, puts in her overnight case, and then sits in the front passenger seat. They pull out, slowly, too slowly for my comfort.

Still, they're gone.

Who says there's no such thing as coincidence?

While my flight home is uneventful, I know that I know that I know something out there made me feel weird. Paranoia isn't usually a problem for me. I didn't imagine what I felt. I also know what I saw the driver of that red Chevy do. On the one hand, he stared. On the other, he drove away when his companion hopped into the car.

So I must have imagined that someone's-looking-at-me feeling before he drove up.

Right?

Wrong?

If someone was staring at me, who could it have been? And why?

Well, I'm pretty sure I know the why. Mr. Pak. And his rubies. But that doesn't get me any closer to the who. More to the point, was it tied to the Burmese shooting spree on the dirt road to Mandalay?

Probably. Mr. Pak dealt with Mogok Valley rubies. And he's the only connection I have to Myanmar.

Why? Why? Why?

Why would he come to see me? Why did he bring me an invitation to Myanmar? Why did someone kill him? Why did they stick him in our vault—or kill him there? Why did someone shoot at us? And to top it all off, why did Mr. Pak bless me with a loudmouth bird?

Back home in Louisville, I'm faced with the reality of parrot ownership. The first thing I hear when I walk into Aunt Weeby's house is that mind-altering *"Squawk! Shriek, shriek!"*

I will my heart to return to its normal sluggish pace, then, "Shut up, Rio!"

A couple more shrieks and a squawk follow, and finally the *clump-clump* of Aunt Weeby's cast makes its way across the upstairs. "Is that you, sugarplum?"

"Sure is!" I grin as she clumps downstairs. When I get my welcome-home hug, I wink. "And how many other late-night visitors do you get?"

"Pshaw! Mona wanders in whenever the fancy strikes her, the girls from the church's benevolence group all have keys—"

"They all have keys? When did you start locking doors?"

She tightens her pale pink chenille robe wrapped around her petite frame. "Since Mona's become a pain about it in the last few months. C'mon, Andie. Tell me. Do you honest-to-goodness think a lock's gonna stop one a' them agents a' Satan if they want to break in and rob me blind?"

"You do have a point. Where there's an evil will, there's always way more than one single way."

"Amen. And that's why them locks are a waste of time—to

good folks, that is. I have to remember to carry a key, re-member what key chain I put it on, remember where I put the key chain . . . it's too much bother. And for what? All of this"—she waves toward the beautiful parlor and foyer—"means nothing before our Father. It's only what we've gone and done for him that counts."

"I know that." The locked/unlocked door argument was making me dizzy. "So do you lock or do you not?"

"When I remember."

"I'd feel a whole lot better if you'd lock. There's no reason to invite the wackos in."

"Maybe and maybe not. Remember that girl the rapist from Atlanta kidnapped after he killed a bunch of folks at his trial? She read to him from *The Purpose-Driven Life*. He didn't kill her."

"But he didn't repent either. He's back in trouble for . . ." What was it he did? I know I heard it on the news one day. "Oh, I don't remember. It's late, we had the weirdest trip, I'm tired, and I'm going to sleep."

"Weird? You had a weird trip? How weird is weird?"

I groan. "I should've known better than to say a thing. There's plenty of time tomorrow—"

"Now you just hold them wild horses there, sugarplum. I get me a call from Mona telling me you and that boy Max are sleeping together in front of everyone and their great-grand-nanny in some airport, then you come home and tell me the trip was weird. Don't you think that calls for a little explaining here?"

I'm gonna kill Miss Mona. Boss or no boss.

"Fine. If you're going to grill me, at least let me make myself a cup of cocoa. I'm going to need it."

I wait for her at the bottom of the stairs, then hook my arm through hers and head to the kitchen. She sits at her favorite end of the ancient farm table that has been in the family for more than a century and a half. I take a pan from a cupboard, splash a generous amount of milk in it, take out the Ghirardelli cocoa—oh yeah!—add sugar, and mix it all together.

The gas stove gives me the willies to light, but I brave fumes and potential obliteration and plunk the pan on the burner. A quick swipe of the counter where the cocoa dust landed, and—

"What are you waiting for?" Aunt Weeby demands. "You've been putzing around this kitchen, plumb giving me heartburn from the anxiety, and you *still* don't say a word. You're like to give a body a conniption fit, you're so contrary."

About that pot calling the kettle black . . . ?

"I seem to remember telling you I needed a cup of cocoa."

Worry creases her forehead. "That tells me, sugarplum, that something's gone very, very bad."

The stool Aunt Weeby likes to use while chopping veggies by the sink offers me a good look into the saucepan, so I perch there and face my aunt. "I don't even want to talk about it. I know it's going to worry you, and that's not so cool. You do crazy stuff when you're worried."

"If you didn't go doing stuff that worries me in the first place, I wouldn't have to be doing crazy stuff to take care of you."

"Sure. Blame it on the victim."

"Victim? I don't see you as any downtrod doormat."

"I shouldn't have used that word." True, but I also know

she's going to find out everything that went on in Myanmar. It'll go easier on me if I'm the one who does the telling. "But it does sorta fit this case."

I go ahead and fill her in on the details of our trip. Then I notice the silence. "What's with Rio? In the short time I've known him he's never been quiet this long. He nearly cost me my hearing when I walked in."

"That's on account of you woke the poor baby up." She preens. "You see, Andie, I've decided to become an expert on sit . . . p-sit. . . . Oh, phooey! It's a long formal name for them Sun Conures like that Rio of yours . . . psittacines! That's it. Anyway, they're right fascinating, let me tell you."

My aunt, the parrot expert. *Oh-kay.* See the consequences of world travel?

"Very well, Madam Expert. Tell me why that loudbox is suddenly so silent."

"I got him a cage cover."

"A cage cover."

"That's right. Parrots like to sleep in cozy, dark places, you see. So I had Mona's Edwina drive me to a pet supermarket. Did you know such places exist? You'd never believe all the things they sell there. Anyway, Edwina drove Rio and me to the pet place, and I got him his very own little cozy cover."

The idea of a bird under a tea cozy doesn't quite cut it. What's worse, the idea of Aunt Weeby turned loose on the greater Louisville population, accompanied by that hearing aid's best friend, is not a thing of beauty.

"How did you get Rio to the pet place? You didn't lug that cage around, did you?"

"'Course not, Andie. That cage's almost as big as I am. I

got myself on that there World Wide Web, and I ordered us a little ol' travel case. It's the sweetest thing! You're just plumb gonna love it. Rio looks adorable inside."

My head throbs like a hammered thumb. "What you're trying to tell me is that they sell cage cozies at that place you went to."

"That's it! And the cage cover almost matches our travel case. It's got all the same colors and the same black piping on the seams. Only problem's that the cage cover has cute little parrots all over, but the travel case—can you believe this?—is covered with cats! I'm telling you, it's an outrage."

My mind conjures the image of Rio entering the drooly mouth of a big ol' meowser. Aunt Weeby's all outraged on the bird's behalf while all I see is a tasty feline snack. And I'm the bird's lucky owner. What's wrong with this picture?

"Why are we talking about the dumb bird?" I ask.

"Why, Andie! Rio's not dumb. He's already talking to me."

Imagine that conversation. What did I get myself into when I moved back to Louisville?

"Fine, he's not dumb, and he beats Oprah at repartee. Can I finish my cocoa and go to bed?"

She crosses her arms. "Only after you've gone and told me every last little detail about that sleeping together you and Max did."

I'd hoped she'd forget. Then again, Aunt Weeby has a mind like a fox trap.

"It's no big deal." I take my now-empty cocoa cup to the sink. "Every armchair at the airport was taken, so we both sat on a sofa. While I slept, I must've slipped sideways, and neither one of us noticed that I landed on his shoulder."

"You landed on his shoulder?"

"Must be. 'Fraid I can't tell you more than that. I was sleeping."

"That's it?"

"Sorry to disappoint. And now I get to go to bed."

"Mm-hmm. You'll need all the rest you can get, sugarplum."

"I . . . will?"

"Uh-huh! Why, you're going to be mighty busy, girl. What with your show and all that sleeping on Max's shoulder and all that investigating you're gonna be doing, that is."

I ignore the sinkholes in Aunt Weeby's words. "Investigating?"

"Sure, Andie. No one's figured out yet why that dead guy wound up dead in our vault. Someone's gotta do it. I figure you're snoopy enough. That's all it should take, some good ol' fashioned snooping on your part. I'd do it, but I got me a cast and a bird to hold me back some."

Okay. Help me here. Do I accept the compliment to my abilities or do I yelp at the insult? After a nanosecond's thought, I decide to do neither.

"I bet you're gonna tell me what I should do." Why am I wasting breath? This is Aunt Weeby. She tells everyone what they should do.

"There's only one thing to do. You're gonna have to sniff out every last little thing there is to know about everyone who works out at that TV shopping network Mona's got herself."

Now there's an appealing prospect. Stick my nose where it doesn't belong to alienate my co-workers. "And how do you want me to do that without landing behind bars?"

"Easy, sugarplum! You just chat them up at work, ask all

170

kindsa them subtle questions they do on TV, and maybe get a look inside their handbags. You know what they say about women's handbags, right?"

They have something to say about handbags? "No, Aunt Weeby. I don't know what they say about women's handbags. But I'm sure you do. And I'm sure you're just dying to tell me."

"I don't rightly know about any dying, but I can most certainly tell you about pocketbooks. They always say you can know all about a woman by the stuff she stashes in her purse."

What's in mine? Gum wrappers, a brush, my favorite Copper Rose lip gloss, my checkbook, wallet, sunglasses, a hair scrunchy, keys. That's it. Pretty boring. And then I remember the no-man's-land at the bottom, the flotsam that litters the lining. Receipts, the four-inch spiral-bound notebook I fondly think of as my brain . . .

Okay. Maybe "they" are onto something. There's just one minor detail. "How do you expect me to get into these handbags?"

She stands and smacks her fists on her hips. "What? Do I have to do everything for you?" After an indignant sniff, she sails out the kitchen doorway. "You figure it out."

Did I tell you I'm squeamish about sneaking around? No? Well, I'm telling you now. I mean, I do have the urge to snoop, but not the guts. That's why there's no way I'm diving into other women's handbags. Dead ruby vendor or not.

No way.

No how.

Not in this lifetime.

14$\underline{00}$

"Are you just the clumsiest cow or what?" Danni demands.

Or what. Time to punt. "I'm so sorry, Danni." I kneel. "Here. Let me help you pick it all up. I owe you that much."

Okay. I'm busted. I accidentally on purpose bumped her purse off the makeup counter while we wait for Allison to show up. And, of course, I'm on those spilled contents like stink on skunk. Against all logic, I'm pulling an Aunt Weeby.

"What are you doing now?" she shrills.

Innocence when you feel like the worst rat doesn't come easy. "Me?" *What to say?* I grab a fistful of rubble, none of which checks out as remotely interesting. "Ah . . . what does it look like I'm doing? I'm . . . uhm . . . trying to help. I made the mess, and the least I can do is give you a hand picking it all up."

"You are the most obnoxious creature I've met in all my born days." Her big brown eyes spit hate my way. "First you come and steal my job away from me, then you score the cutest guy in town as your partner—and don't think I didn't

172

hear all about that cozy little sleep deal during the exotic vacation you took on the network's nickel—you bring down on us some crazed criminal who kills some guy you know, and now you're going through my stuff like an alley cat in a dumpster."

I snag a lipstick from under a cart of fuchsia, lime, and cobalt hair rollers, and stick it in Danni's bag. Is this how people at the S.T.U.D. see me? If that's the case, then I'm in worse shape than I thought.

Oh, Lord Jesus, help me! I know, I know. I got myself into this, but I don't know how to get myself out. I know you can show me, though.

Danni's response is so extreme that it does make me wonder. "You're acting as though you're hiding Queen Lizzie's favorite tiara in there."

I watch her like the proverbial hawk. Will my pointed question get a reaction from her?

Danni yanks her bag out of my reach. "Well, as you can now see—and everyone else too—there's nothing special in my purse."

But as she blindly shoves run-of-the-mill items into the black leather rectangle, I spot something. Okay, yeah, it's interesting. That is, if a mini-ziplock baggie with one large, beautiful ruby in it snags your fancy.

Again, I choose to play dumb. "Oooh, Danni! Did you just treat yourself? You scored a stunner there. And you know I have to ask. Is it Burmese?"

"You are despicable." If her eyes were knives, I'd be hamburger. "You're butting in where you're not wanted. But if you really have to know, not that it's any of your business, yes, the ruby is for me. I've always wanted a nice one, and

Miss Mona said this morning I could go ahead and choose whichever I liked from the vault. And before you ask, I'm paying for it with deductions from my paycheck, Miss Big Ol' Nosy Nose."

What an image! I touch my offending feature before I catch myself. Time for a new topic.

Since there's no way I can pick up the comb and handful of pennies still on the floor without risking bodily harm, I stand. "Miss Mona is a dear, isn't she? Most other bosses would insist on keeping that stone to sell on air. She'd get a whole lot more that way than selling it to you. Employee discounts cut into profits."

Comb and pennies disappear into the bag. Then she stands. "And you working here cuts into my profits. You ready to do the right thing and sacrifice so I don't come up short at the end of the month?" She drops her purse on a chair, crosses her arms, and taps a toe. "I'm on-screen fewer hours than before, and when she started the network, Miss Mona set up the pay scale, as you well know, by hours."

"No way! That's plain wrong. I don't buy your sad story, Danni. You're doing all those underwear shows now that I'm here. That's a bunch more hours a week than I work, so go get a calculator. It doesn't add up to fewer hours for you."

She blushes, glares, and then sticks her cute little button nose way up in the air. "I sell more than lingerie. You should see the cute new spandex Capris we got in this morning. And remember, it's lingerie, Andrea, not underwear."

Spandex Capris? Oh my! "I call 'em as I see 'em. The first things you put on your butt before you put anything else on: what's that if not underwear?"

"No wonder you're not married," she says with a toss of her

blond mane. "No guy's ever going to want to take on someone who knows less than nothing of romance. Poor Max."

She's not married either! But that's not the worst . . . "Poor Max! Are you nuts? I don't even like him as a cohost. Haven't you noticed how dumb he comes across on-screen? He doesn't know a thing."

"He's got a college degree. He must know something." Hers is a feline smile. "And he sure does look good on those camera shots."

"Take him—please! Have him help you sell underwear. I'm sure he'll look a different kind of cute holding up a frilly camisole."

Go with me here. A jock selling women's underwear? Just desserts for the gem-dunce, if you ask me. "Who knows? He might send your sales right through the roof. I bet there's enough women out there who think like you and will order just because he's cute."

She wrinkles her nose. "Cute? That's a stupid word. He's gorgeous, and you're blind."

No, I'm not. I see gorgeous too, but I'll take an order of brains with my serving of gorgeous, thank you very much. Maybe a little less of that potent oozing charm would help. I don't have the experience—or the guts—to handle a guy like Max.

I open the door and step out into the hall. "You know what? I apologized for dumping out your stuff. I offered to help, and all I got for my efforts was abuse. I'd rather clean toilets with a toothbrush than listen to you rant."

I learned all I was going to learn from that fun episode. Danni lusts for rubies. Now all I have to figure out is how much she lusts. And the provenance of that stone she bought.

Did it come from Myanmar?

The only good thing about my encounter with Danni is that no one else was there. Especially not Aunt Weeby.

Or Max.

Mortified, I skulk well away from Danni's radar screen until her makeup's done and she's in the wings waiting for her cue. I hide out in my dressing room, cheeks ablaze, guilt heavy. And then my cell phone rings. "Hello."

"Hey, Andie!" Great. The unmistakable voice of Trophy Tiff. "Who is the S.T.U.D.'s stud? He's hot!"

Did I tell you I hate that term? Well, I do. And I'm not fond of Tiffany Hammond either. Never could see what Roger saw in her . . . except the silicone and the bleach-blond mane and the ten-feet-long legs. "Hi, Tiff. How are you? I'm surprised to hear from you. Is Roger okay?"

She sniffs. "He's fine, but sooo boring, I'm about dying here. Wish I had a stud like yours."

Her spoiled two-year-old whine gets on my nerves, as it always had. And I have nothing to say. This isn't my kind of conversation. So I keep my peace—for once.

Tiffany blathers on. "What kind of guy gets married then dumps his wife inside four walls? He absolutely ignores me. I'm bored. Bored, bored, bored!"

Get a job! I think it, and have to bite it back, but I don't say it. I've earned myself a medal, right? "Um . . . and you figure I need to know this because . . . ?"

"Well, no. I don't. It's just—oh, forget it. I called you because Roger promised me a big, big ruby, and when that Pak guy didn't show up, we didn't get any rubies. I hear you got yourself some when you went off to do your Andi-ana Jones thing—isn't that too cute? I came up with it all by myself. Roger thinks I'm brilliant."

Between the toddler whine and the new twist on my name, she's brought up the subject of rubies. Right? "You called me because you don't have rubies?"

"We do, they're just teeny, tiny little stones. Well, too small for me. I want a *big* ruby. And I figure I got connections— you! Can I come down and get one from you?"

"Our rubies are available to everyone." That's the beauty of TV shopping. "Did something happen to your wide-screen? All our rubies will be featured on Thursday's show."

"Oh no! That won't work. I might not get the one I want, with all those other people calling in to buy. I want to come meet you so I can have my pick of the best."

Swell. I can just see it. Gem trays, Roger's trophy, and me. Since when do I call the shots around here? "I can't make that decision, Tiff. I don't own the network. I'll have to ask Miss Mona and see if she'll agree."

"Ooooooh! Thank you. I'm so there. I've seen you in action. I'm sure you'll work wonders on that old lady. See ya!"

I sit back into my chair. Trophy Tiff strikes again.

Lucky me.

After that fun phone call, it's my turn to surrender to Allison's tender makeup ministrations.

And while I sit in her chair, I talk her into letting me peek into her gear bag. Anyone who really knows me knows I'm a mascara, powder blush, and lip-gloss kind of girl. A satchel the size of Asia Minor filled to the gills with all colors of beauty potions doesn't do much for me.

But there's a plethora of stuff one can hide in a bag that size. Not that Allison does. She's legit; it's all glitter and goop in there.

"When did you become a fan of eye shadow?" Miss Mona asks from the door.

I drop the suddenly scalding turquoise powder pot. "I just find Allison's paints fascinating."

She frowns. "You do? How?"

How does one explain sudden irrational behavior? "Uh . . . I figure I'm not getting any younger, and I'd better learn how to help Mother Nature when the time comes. A little color goes a long way."

Both women give me a "Huh?" kind of look. And here I've always thought of Miss Mona as the queen of the "Huh?" factor. Seems it might just be contagious after all. Either that, or I've deposed her and taken the throne.

Now that I know there's nothing subversive in Allison's bag, I want nothing more to do with it. Especially not since it makes everyone look at me as though I've sprouted an extra nose in the middle of my face.

That reminds me of my encounter with Danni. She might be onto something with that nosy nose line.

"Here." I shove the bag at Allison. "I've looked enough. Am I done yet?"

She looks at me weird. "Only if you want customers calling to ask what's wrong with our camera."

She steps out from in front of the mirror, and I catch a glimpse of my face. My half made-up face. Blush, eye shadow, and mascara adorn my right side. My left? Let's just say the total look is just a hair on the schizophrenic side.

Miss Mona comes up close to stare at me. "Are you sure

you're feeling well? Maybe I should let Danni go ahead and take the show today. You had yourself a mighty stressful time in Myanmar, after all." She taps her lips with her index finger. "I'm thinking she and Max can carry off the show."

Whoa! "No way! Neither one of them has a clue about prehnite, andesine, or amazonite. And that's the bulk of what we're selling on today's show."

Miss Mona backs up a step, her eyes still glued to my face. "I'm going to have to have me a little talk with Livvy. I think you're about due for a good dosing with her Great-Grandmother Willetta's wonderful fish oil."

Oh, joy.

An hour later, I've alienated two other women. I doubt Marcie, the cooking-show maven, will ever speak to me again. She caught me holding one of her deadly knives. Even after I showed her the earring back I'd "dropped" among her arsenal, she isn't buying it. After all, every last one of her desk drawers didn't have to be wide open for me to scrounge around in one for a butterfly back.

Did I mention I hate this sneaky stuff? True, I'm curious, and I don't have a thing against a modest amount of . . . probing, but this? This is gross. These women don't deserve it.

But no one's figured out what happened to Mr. Pak.

And he's been dead for almost a month now.

I head for the ladies' room. And when Julie gets paged out to the lobby, I snag her tote bag and dive right in. Aside from a brag book filled with pictures of her girls and a handful of hair ribbons and diaper pins, I don't find a thing I wouldn't carry myself.

What did I think I'd find?

I give Julie's stuff one last look, and even after this additional perusal, find nothing. But that's not the end of my escapade. You see, she catches me with my hand in the cookie jar.

"What are you doing?" she asks, her hand on her gun.

Yikes!

That steely voice throws a frost all over me. "Looking for a safety pin. I ripped my hem"—true enough—"and since you have kids, I figured you might have one stashed in here. It's big enough for you to haul a bathtub wherever you go."

Her eyes, narrowed and dark with suspicion, don't leave my face for a second. "I don't have safety pins in my bag."

"I figured that out." I wave a plastic ducky-embellished pin. "But one of your diaper pins should do the trick. If you don't mind, that is."

Too late for my own good, the killer stare reminds me of the training Uncle Sam gave this woman. She was trained to obliterate the enemy. Right now, the enemy is me.

I flip over the hem of my black jacquard skirt, show her the small rip, and stick the sharp steel end right through that outrageously expensive fabric. Ouch!

The smile I plaster all over my mug is way too bright—as I can see in the mirror not five feet away. "Thanks, Julie. I don't want the whole hem to come out before I have a chance to fix it. I love this suit, it's new, and . . . well, you know how that goes."

Although she smiles back, the smile doesn't even begin to tickle her eyes. "I guess I do know."

But knowing doesn't do a thing for her suspicion, as those eyes blare back.

And that's when Aunt Weeby prances in. Yes, she does have a foot in a cast. Yes, she's a senior citizen. And yes, she does prance. Don't ask me how. It's a gift.

"There you are, sugarplum! I've been looking for you all over the place."

"You found me, but now I have to head to the set. It's almost time for my show. I'm really jazzed about it. Miss Mona just told me the parcel of tanzanites we ordered before we left for Myanmar arrived this morning. We agreed I should add them to today's list."

"Tanzanites?" Her sniff exudes disdain. "Those them lilac-colored stones I've seen at the mall?"

I slip my arm through hers and put as much space between Terminator Julie and me as fast as I can. "You know better'n that. The lavender stones at the mall are okay for those who like their gemstones washed out and with hardly any color. A real, top-gem quality tanzanite is navy blue with a secondary purple color and tertiary flashes of red . . ."

When we've put some distance between the gun-toting soldier and us, Aunt Weeby stops. "Well? What did you find out?"

"That nobody likes a snoop."

"Pshaw! I'll bet by tomorrow they've forgotten whatever it was you did to tweak their noses outta whack."

"Don't hold your breath. I thought Julie was going to line me up before her friendly neighborhood firing squad."

She tsk-tsks. "You let Julie catch you going through a purse? Andrea! I told you to be subtle, sugarplum. What'd you go and do wrong?"

Why me? "She caught me scrabbling through her bag."

Aunt Weeby's eyes grow saucer-sized. "You went through

Julie's purse? No wonder she has her panties all a-twisted. She wasn't exactly who I would have suspected. Is there a reason you thought a decorated reservist woulda killed your ruby-selling friend?"

That's not the first mistake in my long list of doozies.

"You could say I got carried away, all right? And, it'll teach me to listen to your crazy ideas. There's no one here who would kill Mr. Pak for his rubies . . ."

I let my voice trail off when I remember Danni's red rock. Did she really get Miss Mona's okay to take that stone? Did she really set up an employee paycheck payment plan? Is the stone Burmese?

Is she who Mr. Pak really came to see?

Before I dig myself a bigger hole than the one already swallowing me, I divert Aunt Weeby's attention to the repulsive slime-green, lace-trimmed mini-boxers Danni's trying to peddle on-screen.

"Whoo-ee!" Aunt Weeby says. "Who in her right mind would buy a pair a' them things? Just looking makes me squirm."

"Too much information, Aunt Weeby."

She shrugs. "What are you doing next?"

"Not listen to you, that's what I'm going to do."

"I beg your pardon."

"Yeah. I listened to your nutty idea last night, and all I got is a bunch of enemies. I want no more of that."

"Then you're giving up on finding who killed Mr. Pak."

"No. I'm going to do what every other sane woman would do. I'm going to leave it in the capable hands of the police. And the FBI, who must be involved since the corpse is a foreign national—"

"Don't go forgetting Interpol, Miss Andie," Chief Clark says from behind me.

I fight to keep from making a sound—that groan in my throat might incriminate innocent me in his eyes. I pray, then take a deep breath. Finally, I face him and the silent detective who seems to follow him everywhere he goes. "What brings you here, sir? Do you have any new information on Mr. Pak's death?"

He drags his hat off his head. "I was hoping you would tell me something I could really sink my teeth into."

The way his eyes glom on me, I know I'm in trouble. Again.

How can this man think I had anything to do with the murder? My alibi's tighter than Tupperware. "I'm sorry, Chief Clark. I know nothing more about the death than what I already told you."

"You seem to know a whole lot about the agencies investigating this case."

"I doubt there's an American who doesn't know about the FBI."

The chief's shadow stares at me through narrowed eyes.

Chief Clark scratches his head. "You have yourself a point there. And I do have me a scrap of information for you. Them X-rays were negative."

"X-rays? Who did you X-ray? And why? What did the films not show?"

His gaze flew to Aunt Weeby. "You didn't tell her like I asked you to, Miz Weeby? I told you to check with her before I went ahead with it."

Aunt Weeby dismisses his question with a wave. "I couldn't get ahold a' her. Where she was out there in that Mo-go Valley place she didn't have cell phone service. Plus I didn't want to throw a monkey wrench at your investigation and slow you down, so I figured it'd be okay for me to say yes to you. You don't mind one bit, now do you, Andie?"

"What—"

"So I had no permission."

Aunt Weeby tilts her chin. "She left me in charge."

Are they actually speaking about Miss Mona, then?

Chief Clark shakes his head. "I'm not rightly sure that works as real consent."

"Now don't you go giving me no never mind, Donald Clark. I knew what I was doing, and probably better than Andie here does. Didn't I tell you I've become an expert in the field? If I say it's okay to X-ray, then it's okay to X-ray."

An idea sneaks into my head. A ridiculous idea. Still, it involves Aunt Weeby, so maybe it's not all that ridiculous. "Did you have Chief Clark X-ray Rio?"

Her smile nearly wraps around her head. "Why, sure, sugarplum! We needed to know if your Mr. Pak fed the poor little guy some a' them illegal rubies."

Rubies in Rio's gut is not an appetizing thought. Especially in view of where they would've ended up. But I'm not ready to go down a path that might lead to some answers. Not yet. And not in front of Chief Clark and his shadow.

"Illegal?" I tell Aunt Weeby. "I've never known Mr. Pak to break the law. He's always had documents of authentication for the stones he sells. Did you find anything in the bird?"

"Not at that time," Chief Clark says, a dot of red on each cheekbone. "But there's no way of knowing what's gone all the way through before I got to him."

"Now, Donald," Aunt Weeby says. "You've had me check

184

what's come out on the newspaper in his cage from the start."

That's where I don't want to go. "Gross."

The chief frowns. "Police work isn't pretty, Miss Andie. Not like they make it look like on TV."

"Cleaning Rio's cage isn't pretty either," Aunt Weeby counters, "but I'm not making a big ol' federal case."

The chief's eyes narrow, focus on me. "I don't have a choice. I have to go where the case takes me. I have me a dead body, and Interpol's breathing hot and nasty down my neck."

His shadow shoots him a stern look.

I give the chief the evil eye. "Then how come no one's gone to talk to my former boss in New York? He's known Mr. Pak for way longer than I have."

"Maybe on account of it happened here, not New York."

"True, and I'm not saying he had anything to do with the murder, but with good interrogating techniques, who knows what he might remember from a conversation, something Mr. Pak might have said."

Chief Clark's shadow clears his throat.

The chief shrugs. "I'll be doing the investigating, Miss Andie. There's plenty suspicious to check out around here. Like how you took yourself off on that there trip to Myanmar. Sure can give an investigator something to chew on, you know?"

I square my shoulders. "No, I don't know. I went on a buying trip with Miss Mona, my cohost Max, Allison from makeup, Hannah the camerawoman, and two other staff members. They can all tell you what I did blow by blow. Or minute by minute, whichever you prefer. I was never alone."

The chief's shadow shifts his stance but never takes his gaze off me. I'm getting really sick of him . . . whoever he might be.

Chief Clark takes a step toward me.

I back away.

He comes closer again. "Then, Miss Andie, if you don't think you've done anything suspicious, how do you explain spending your morning going through your co-workers' pocketbooks?"

I hear jail bars slamming on me.

I know better than to listen to Aunt Weeby.

So I have to admit I wanted to snoop.

And it is time to pay the piper.

Hopefully, not with my freedom.

15.00

I'm stunned when Chief Clark lets me go without handcuffs on my wrists. True, it's thanks to Aunt Weeby's ride to my rescue.

"Donald Clark!" she says. "Tell me right now why you're all bent on playing the idiot here."

The look in the chief's eyes gives me the willies. Only Aunt Weeby . . .

He takes a deep breath. "Because—"

"And you may as well know," she adds, unaware or maybe just unafraid of potential consequences to her comments, "it was my idea for Andie to check 'em all out. And a mighty fine idea it was too. What if one of them had had the . . . whatcha call it? Oh yes! The smoking gun?"

Chief Clark looks ready to swallow his tongue. "Maybe you're the one I need to lock up."

Aunt Weeby tips up her nose. "Don't you go sassing your elders, Donald."

"Only by thirteen and a half years, Weeb. Not enough to make you an elder . . ."

To my relief, they go off to carry on their argument.

But then I still have to face the camera. With Max.

Shortly after our show starts, Max leans forward, studies the gem in my tweezers, and then scoffs. "Do you know what you're talking about?"

"Who's the gemologist here?"

"You, but even I know what bad jade looks like."

"Shows how little *you* know, if you're saying this is bad jade."

"That's exactly what I'm saying. It's cheap jade."

"It's top-quality prehnite, you dunce."

"Dunce?" He faces the camera square on. "Who ever heard of this pre . . . pre-hen stuff?"

I look my customers in the—camera—eye. "Ladies and gentlemen, for those who don't know, prehnite is an orthorhombic mineral, which is sometimes found as distinct crystals. More frequently, though, it's found with volcanic rocks, and forms in aggregates with botryoidal habit. Prehnite is rarely clean enough for faceting but can be cut as cabochon. Sometimes it even displays a cat's-eye effect."

When I hear nothing from my cohost, I slant a glance his way. His smirk makes my blood boil.

"Care to share the joke with the viewers and me?"

His smirk widens. "Are you sure you want to hear my thoughts?"

Something tells me I should have ignored him in the first place, but it's too late to back down now. "I'm sure I don't want to, but I'm also sure you're going to share."

With a wink to the camera, he says, "Isn't she cute when she's being smart?"

Guffaws erupt around the studio. My face burns from ear

to ear. And then the memory of my encounter with Danni raises its impish head.

"Ladies?" I say. "If he thinks I'm cute when I bring you information, don't you think he'd look cuter still if he'd help Danni sell frilly pink panties or the spandex Capris we just got in?"

Now his jaw sags. His cheeks turn ruddy. The laughter in the studio reaches the outer heights of hysteria. I settle back into my chair and wait for the hilarity to subside.

But then, from somewhere out in the back of beyond, I hear a shriek, and it's not Rio. Uh-oh. Danni must not have left the premises. I'm gonna have to pay for that zinger. One I probably took too far. *Lord? Am I ever going to learn to keep this mouth of mine from leaping before my common sense?*

"Take note, folks," Max says, an edge to his voice. "She thinks she's a comic." He pauses a moment, forces a grimace that probably is meant as a smile, and then goes on. "While I may not know as much as she does about gemstones, I'm willing to take the challenge. I'm ready to learn. I'm an athlete, and athletes are built for endurance. I can hang in there until the cows come home."

Is that a dare or is that a dare? I know what it is, but I'm not ready to bite. I shove a loose lock of hair behind my ear. In the background, I hear Miss Mona and Danni arguing. I can also imagine what households across America are thinking, saying.

Time to take the reins of my show again and lead it back to where it should've been all along. "So, ladies and gentlemen, what do you think of this gorgeous, soft-green, glowing gem? It *is* prehnite, a lovely stone in its own right, and not related to jade in any way."

At my side, Max fidgets in his chair but keeps his mouth shut. The show goes on smoothly for a while. Then . . .

I pick up a stone from the next tray of product. "I have another gorgeous green gem for you today. And while its soft green hue is similar to that of the prehnite, amazonite is a separate gem in its own right."

"I'll bet it comes from the Amazon," the jock pipes in.

"You'd lose that bet. It comes from Colorado, the Minas Gerais state in Brazil, Canada, Italy, and the Ural Mountains in Russia."

He points at me. "Ladies and gentlemen, I give you our resident encyclopedia."

I choose to ignore the comment. "Some think the name comes from a reference to the Amazons, warrior women of Greek mythology. But no amazonite has been found any-where near the river."

Max leans back in his chair and stares at me. "Wonder if those Amazons had red hair."

Not a word, not a word. I owe him the freebie jab, to say the least. "Amazonite is usually cut in cabochon. And sometimes it shows a schiller effect. That's when you see shimmery, flakelike plates within the stone."

"Really?" No one can miss the interest in Max's voice, his eyes—not even me. Then he leans forward, and that excellent aftershave does its thing again. I feel the warmth of his bulk at my side, hear the soft in-and-out of his breath. How can he be so attractive and infuriate me at the same time?

The show, Andie, the show! "Um . . . really. Look at the stone." I tweeze the amazonite in front of my white velvet drape. "You can see the layers of subtle sparkle inside."

He draws closer, places a hand on my arm. "That's pretty

neat," he says, his attention on the stone and not his now-discombobulated cohost.

And with that uncertain truce, in spite of my bizarre response to his nearness, his touch, we go on with the show. Lots of phone calls help me get through the nerve-wracking experience.

It helps to show the spectacular tanzanites we received that morning. We end with a call from my friend Peggy who congratulates me on the show and buys a top-notch tanzie for herself.

When the theme song wafts over our heads, I wait for Hannah's cue that the camera's off, and then remove my mike. I stride from the desk without a backward glance.

Focus on how little he knows, not how good he smells. Aftershave's cheap, so to speak. A good gemologist, not so much.

Max's stare burns a hole between my shoulder blades.

But I'm a woman on a mission so I just keep going. I have to corner Miss Mona before my oomph goes away, not to mention before Max the Magnificent gets to her. She thinks he's great.

"Andie, Andie, Andie!" Miss Mona wraps me in a huge hug. "You are incredible. That show was the best, honey, the absolute best."

"Huh?" She's still the queen of the "Huh?" factor.

"The phones are ringing off the hook again! The viewers went and bought up every last little thing you showed, *and* they were all raving over you and Max. They really missed you while we were on our trip!"

"But—"

"You're a hit, an honest-to-goodness star!"

191

Oh-kay. Help me out here, will you? I thought I was leaving the gerbil-on-an-exercise-wheel life in the Big Wormy Apple, but here I am living my worst nightmare in Louisville. How did I land in the middle of a mess complete with a dead vendor, bullets, a suspicious cop, a co-worker who hates me because she thinks I stole her job, and a cohost who rattles my world and makes me look like a fool with his lack of knowledge?

And let's not forget my nutty aunt and the "Huh?" queen. Who, as we speak, is staring at me with questions in her gaze. It's enough to give a girl a migraine.

"Let's go somewhere to talk." I slip my arm through hers. "Just us girls, okay?"

"Sure, honey. We can brainstorm some great new ideas for the show. I know! Maybe we can coordinate your wardrobe with Max's clothes. Wouldn't that be sweet—"

"Aaack!" My response brings about the hoped-for result. Miss Mona stops rhapsodizing over Max and me.

I close her office door, then turn to face her. "*That*, Miss Mona, is just what I wanted to talk about. You've got to get rid of Max. Now. He's just awful. He doesn't know a thing about gems, and he makes me look stupid."

"Andie!" Forget saucers; horror makes her eyes big as trays. "How can you even think such a thing? The viewers are in love with you two. We can't break up a perfect match."

That makes my head pound. "We'd better break up a poisonous pairing before it blows up in our faces."

"It's blown up in our faces in a big, good way. We can hardly handle all those calls. Our wonderful shoppers are just buying up anything you and Max argue about, and all of them can't tell us enough how much they enjoy you."

"But *I* don't enjoy us!"

Miss Mona doesn't answer right away. She stares. I get itchy and squirmy, as if I'd done something wrong. But I haven't. Max has. Right?

Still, it's probably best if I keep my mouth shut, let Miss Mona think about what I said. Try and catch my breath.

She goes behind her desk but doesn't sit. Her posture whisks me back to grade school and that one visit to the principal's office.

What for, you ask? Nuh-uh. I'm not telling.

Fists on the desk, Miss Mona leans forward. "I never thought I'd have to do this, honey, but I'm going to have to be your boss more than your friend right now. Listen up, and listen good."

I bite my bottom lip. This doesn't sound so good. My stomach lurches.

She goes on. "Max is the perfect cohost for you. You spar *and* sparkle together like the best of old-time movie couples. And I've told you this before. More important, it's the viewers who tell us that. I'm telling you, honey, he's your perfect foil. The customers recognize this. It's time you do too."

"But I left New York to get away from the stress. I can't work under this much tension." The kind that's making me feel sick right about now.

She waves away my concern. "You're just going to have to find a way to make peace with him. He's staying right on that chair next to yours."

"But he knows nothing about gems!"

Miss Mona raps her knuckles against the desk. "That's why he's so perfect for you. You're brainy and beautiful, but the customers aren't. Brainy, that is. And not all will be beautiful either. But they see Max as one of them—they identify with him. He asks the bumbling questions they would ask but can't, and he looks great while he's doing it. It's the perfect mix."

"That can't be. They can't possibly want to see a dunce try to sell them gems."

"He's not trying to sell them anything. *You* are. It works. You can't fight with success."

"But—"

"There you are!" Aunt Weeby cries as she barges in. "Whoo-ee, Andie! You could probably sell them folks rotten tomatoes and make them like 'em with that routine you and Max got going on. How long does it take the two a' you to work it out ahead a' time?"

"Hey! You're so wrong about that. There's no 'working it out' going on." I shoot for calm and reasonable. "Explain this to me, please. How can people who want to buy something unusual and very special think it's great if one of the two salespeople is a total dud?"

"Max is no dud!" Aunt Weeby waggles her index finger at me. "He's a handsome, smart boy, and he sure knows how to play to a crowd. He's just playing to it at your side, and you might could learn from him, Andrea Autumn Adams. Don't you be letting that pride a' yours get ahead a' your smarts."

When the queasy feeling hits my gut, my defenses leap to attention. "Are you saying I don't know how to play to the audience?"

"You don't," the source of my irritation says, as he too walks in. "You're too serious, and you just rattle off facts and prices at the viewers."

I wish I could just wiggle my nose and make him disappear. "Last I heard, that was exactly what I was hired to do."

Miss Mona comes to my side and places an arm around my shoulders. "Yes, honey, I hired you to tell our customers all about the treasures we offer for sale, but you also have to entertain them while you're doing it."

"So now I'm dull."

Max whistles a few random notes. "You know, Andie, if the glass slipper's yours, then you'd better put it on."

Aunt Weeby juts out her chin. "Now, Max. Andie's not dull, it's just that them facts and chemicals all fascinate her more'n they interest you and me and the man on the moon. You might could help here by learning a little about 'em, and helping her make them more interesting."

"It's called," Miss Mona says with a grin, "cooperation, kiddies. And it works real well."

I slant Max a glance. Satisfaction is smeared all over that gorgeous face. I groan. "Do you know what you two are doing? You're making him even more conceited."

"Conceited?" Aunt Weeby asks.

"Huh?" Miss Mona offers—for a change.

"Sure. He thinks he's the best thing that's ever happened to American television broadcasting." But me? I'm thinking I might just be allergic to the guy, I feel so bad.

Max's eyes give off sparks. "I do not. I just know how to present myself to an audience. Better than you. You might want to learn."

When I don't dignify him with a response, Miss Mona says, "Andie?"

I don't like her thoughtful expression, but I can't refuse to respond. I'm not that rude. "Yes?"

"You might have a point," she says, "but not the one you tried to make. Max may or may not think he's the best thing that ever happened to American TV, but he *is* the best thing that's happened to you, your show, and our network. When he baits you, he brings on the entertainment. Then you can bring the information. It's brilliant. And it works."

Max blushes—a true rarity.

Aunt Weeby nods. "You might just want to give this some thought, sugarplum."

A sense of betrayal simmers up in my gut—my roiling gut, mind you—but before I can say anything, Miss Mona jumps in.

"Just don't go overboard with all the peace and love. I need you two to keep on arguing on the show. It's the formula that works."

Feeling cornered, I back up toward the office door, my head throbbing. I rub my temples. "I'm confused. You want me to cooperate with Max, but you also want me to argue with him."

Miss Mona claps and beams at me. "That's exactly it!"

My head's spinning, and I can't think past the pounding in my temples. I look at Max, and the thoughtfulness on his face makes me even more jumpy. When I look at Aunt Weeby, I know for sure I'm in real trouble. There's a whole lot of matchmaking going on.

I square my shoulders and press a hand to my woozy middle. "Maybe I ought to make Danni happy and just quit."

"No!" Aunt Weeby yelps.

Max steps toward me, stops inches away. "Please, don't."

"The network needs you!" Miss Mona wails.

I've just learned a new medical truth: being ganged up on makes a woman lightheaded. "This is too bogus." I rub my forehead. "You guys don't play fair. It's three against one, three nuts against the only sane one."

"It's not a battle, Andie," Max says. "We all want what's best for the show. You just happen to take yourself too seriously."

Eeuw! Who wants that? "Okay. Fine. Ya'll think I'm the problem here. And maybe I do need to think about what you've said, but it's so not fair. I can't think while you're all ganging up on me."

"Go home," Miss Mona says, her voice gentle. "Think about the shows you've done. Think about what we've said. Think about what you really want—for the show and yourself, and pray. Then come back and we can talk it all through."

Do they think I can think about anything else? "You got it. It probably is for the best if I go. My head's spinning and it's all made me queasy—"

"Out!" a man calls from the hall. "Gas company here. There's a leak in the building. I need everybody out. And don't go crazy on me and panic now."

I, of course, freeze.

Aunt Weeby *clump-clumps* past me. "C'mon, sugarplum. Let's get to getting."

Miss Mona hugs her small office safe to her chest, and hurries out.

Max says, "Move, Andie."

But I can't move. A gas leak. How can that be? Gas leaks don't happen out of the blue.

Then big hands clasp my shoulders. "Andie?" Max says. "Are you okay? Did you hear we have to leave?"

I nod in slow motion, but still can't make my feet work. So Max takes action.

He scoops me up in his arms and heads out the door.

I let out a weak excuse for a shriek. Worse, I can't bring myself to fight him. Instead, I give up to the dizziness, lean my head against his shoulder, and let his strength work for both of us.

You know I'm scared. More scared than even when bullets came flying at us in Myanmar. And let me tell you, that was scary.

Even when we get out into the fresh air, I can't shake the certainty that this is no accident. This gas leak is part of something bigger, part of everything that's gone really wrong.

It's part of the murder.

And the rubies sit front and center of it all.

Not just any rubies either. It's all about that missing parcel of multimillion-dollar Burmese rubies.

No one's had to tell me.

It all adds up.

16$\underline{00}$

When I open my eyes, all I see is putrid green walls. Something sharp and detergenty irritates my nostrils. And I feel so bad, I figure I must've lost a close encounter of the steamroller kind.

Last thing I remember is fleeing from Miss Mona's office in Max's arms. Just the thought of it tears me in two. I mean, most girls dream of a knight in a shining business suit who swoops them into his arms and whisks them off into the sunset.

On the other hand, it *was* Max who did the swooping.

Not exactly the stuff of my dreams. No, really. He's gorgeous, but . . . oh, I don't know. Something about him makes me throw up an incoming missile defense shield. Know what I mean?

I open my eyes again, wider this time. When they focus, I see I'm in a hospital. And then the memory of the gas leak *thwaps* me between the brows.

That would explain why I'd felt lightheaded and queasy in Miss Mona's office. I'd blamed it on the snarling fight on screen with Max followed by the gang-up-on-Andie moment, but now I know that wasn't the cause. I've always been sensitive to smells and fumes. Nothing's worse than gas fumes. They don't just stink; they can kill.

"Oh no!" Is everyone else okay? Did anyone succumb to the fumes?

My heart begins to pound. I fight the sheet over my body. I realize I'm tethered to an IV fluids pump, which makes my efforts nearly futile. I wriggle. I twist. I find the nurses' call button and give it a healthy push.

I have to make sure everyone else at the studio got out okay.

A middle-aged woman with dark hair in a ponytail walks in. "Well, hello there! I'm Wilma, your day nurse. It's good to see you awake."

"Is—" My dry throat catches my question on its way out, but I push through the discomfort and make myself try again. "Are the others okay?"

"Everyone's fine." She pushes a button on the side rail of the bed.

My head goes up. The world takes a whirl. "Wow!"

"You still woozy?"

No joke. "How long will it last?"

"Not much longer. The doctor gave you a mild sedative so you would rest. You had a little trouble breathing, but after you got some oxygen that was fine. You, on the other hand, weren't taking this all too well."

Uh-oh. "What does that mean?"

She chuckles. "Let's just say you're not the easiest of patients."

I blush. Half of me wants to know the ugly truth, while

200

the other half wants to hide under the covers. The braver half wins. "What did I do?"

"Oh, you just fought like a wildcat when we tried to start your IV, you didn't want to have your pulse taken, you didn't much care for the nasal cannulas the doctor put in your nostrils for that oxygen you needed, and you kept calling everyone a dunce."

Groan. "You were right. I really didn't want to hear all that."

"Oh, I don't know," Max says from the door.

I groan again.

He laughs. "It was all in character. You behaved just like you always do. You were stubborn, snippy, cranky, and you called everyone names."

I slink down in the bed but keep my eyes just above the edge of the crisp white sheet. "You're never going to let me live this down, are you?"

Smirking—again—he crosses his arms. "Would you if you were in my place?"

The sheet I now pull over my head does nothing to block out his question. "I'd like to think I'd be . . . oh, magnanimous—"

His whooping laughs cut me off. "Yeah, right," he says. "The woman who tried to get me fired because I'm not a gem geek like her now wants me to believe she'd be generous when catching me at my worst."

My cheeks burn hotter than jalapeños on nachos. *Lord? Do I have to eat crow? Can't I just let this blow by?*

God doesn't answer, but I feel worse by the second. I guess I know the answer.

"Okay, Max. You win. I've been a brat. I sorta knew it when

201

I was giving you grief, but I didn't want to see beyond my idea of what a gem show host should be."

He doesn't respond. I peek out from under my sheet. And groan. Again.

In my best, überpolite voice, I ask, "Do you think you could wipe off that smirk? I did give you what you wanted. My apology should work, plus I admitted I've been a pain . . . for too long."

He grins. "At the risk of raising your hackles again, you're cute when your own behavior backs you into a corner."

"You really know how to kick a woman when she's down."

A knock at the door keeps him from answering. In walks Chief Clark. Where's that sedative when a girl can really use it? My day can't get much worse. I hope.

"Miss Andie." That drawl is getting to me. "I'm right sorry you were hurt by the gas leak at the studio. How're you feeling?"

I blink. I don't expect kindness from the chief. "I figure I'll live so you can suspect me some more."

Max does the groaning this time. "I think we can safely assume she's going to be fine. That mouth of hers is working overtime again."

The chief arches a brow. "And why should I be so suspicious of you, Miss Andie?"

Remember my red hair? Well, my temper's flaring just that bright. "Give me a break. I'm not dumb. You've had me in your crosshairs since Mr. Pak turned up dead in the vault."

He leans against the sickly green wall, sticks his hands in his pockets, and crosses one ankle over the other. "Can you look at it from my end? I have me a dead foreigner in my

202

jurisdiction. He brought a fancy invite for a woman to visit a country our country doesn't do business with, and then he dies when he gets to where she works. Don't you think I'm going to have a passel of questions for that woman?"

"Questions are reasonable," I say. "But suspicion? That's a whole 'nother thing, sir."

"Not if you haven't given me any good answers. You haven't. And I've asked for 'em."

"Ahem!"

The chief and I turn to Max.

"I hate to have to agree with Andie, but on this one, sir, I think she has a point. She didn't know this man was coming to see her. I believe her. Especially after we were shot at when we were in Myanmar."

"I heard all about that." He eases upright, takes a few steps to the room's window, then faces me again. "But that's no evidence of innocence. There's always trouble between crooks, you know. When one tries to rip off another . . . well, things go bad more often than not."

With my unshackled fist, I shove myself up on the bed. I stare at the chief until he meets my gaze. Then, between gritted teeth, I say, "I didn't steal anything. I don't have any-thing of Mr. Pak's—except that loudmouth bird. And even you say there's no contraband in its innards. So what would I know about anything?"

"Y'see, Miss Andie. It's like this. I have no idea what you did with the bird's . . . er . . . poop when you first got him. How am I supposed to know you didn't find something . . . um . . . coming out that other end?"

"Probably because I didn't clean Rio's cage. Aunt Weeby told you she's fallen head over heels over that dumb fowl, and she's taken care of him from day one. Are you going to suspect Aunt Weeby of international intrigue?"

Even Chief Clark sees the idiocy in that idea. He smiles. "'Fraid you do have another point there. Miz Weeby's the last woman I'd suspect of committing a crime. She'd be more'n likely to nab a crook and drag him by the ear to confess at church."

"And what makes you think I'd be any different?"

"I can't see you yanking anyone anywhere by the ear."

"Donald Clark!" the ear nabber herself chides as she walks in. "What are you thinking, badgering this poor child? Wait'll I tell her daddy how you're treating his little girl."

"She's not a little girl, and this has nothing to do with your brother."

"Sure, it does. Your best buddy growing up's not going to take it too well when I tell him what you've been up to."

I goggle. "No way. You mean *my* father likes *him*?"

Max's laugh snorts out.

Aunt Weeby chuckles.

Chief Clark frowns. "We swap letters at least once a month, Miss Andie, so I'd have to say he does like me. At least a little."

I plop back on my pillows. "How come I don't remember ever meeting you before?"

Another "ahem" draws everyone's attention to Max. "Can we get back to what really matters here?"

"And what would that be?" the chief asks.

"I'd think the topic of the moment has to be the gas leak at the studio."

The chief juts his jaw. "What do you want to know about it?"

"Everything," I say.

"How did it start?" Max asks.

"Did anyone croak?" Aunt Weeby, of course.

"Well . . ." The chief's reluctance stinks like last week's leftovers. "I think you can all figure out for yourselves that it's no accident, since I'm here."

The breath whooshes out of me. I'd known it, but just like that gut feeling I've had for a while about the missing Burmese rubies, I hadn't wanted to accept it. "Go on."

"Sally Thomas called the gas company. They called me and said she told 'em that something smelled funny, and that she didn't know where Miss Mona was right then. They told me she was all apologetic about bothering them and all, but they thought it best to go check things out. And they did. So did I. Lucky for all you all."

"What *did* you learn?" Max asks.

"There's evidence of tampering with the gas line into the studio. And then someone messed with the valves that control the flow of the gas inside."

I shudder. "I guess we do need to ask Aunt Weeby's gory question. Was anyone . . . killed because of the leak?"

"No, but two other employees are here under observation. Just like you."

My curiosity raises its head. "Any reason why some are just fine and others of us aren't?"

"I've been listening to the three of you all this while," Wilma, the nurse, says. "Y'all are fascinating. But I didn't have anything to add to what you've said up to now. Now, I do. Have something to say, that is. Some folks are just more sensitive to any particular toxic substance than others. It

205

seems you're more sensitive to natural gas than these two here."

"Figures," I mutter.

"Is that all you learned?" Aunt Weeby asks. "In all this time? What were you and your boys doing, Donald? Playing Barbie's gone to Malibu with those stupid Capri things Mona ordered for Danni's show?"

The chief, Barbie dolls, and Danni's spandex Capris in one sentence is too much for me. I howl. And then my sore throat makes me hack.

Chief Clark does not approve. "No, Miz Weeby, I weren't playing dress-up and neither were my men. We went over that there building of Mona Latimer's inch by inch. And, if you really want to know, we found plenty."

I lean forward. "What kind of plenty did you find?"

"It wasn't just the tampered gas line we found. We found a rummaged mess everywhere else. Whoever trashed the place knew what he or she was doing, and worked mighty fast, since he only had the time while we got everyone out and settled with the EMTs and ambulances."

Rummaged. "Come again?"

"It's not so hard, Miss Andie," the lawman says. "Someone ransacked the studio. And they didn't miss a room."

Great. He might not know what the intruder wanted, but I do.

It's all about the rubies. The missing Burmese rubies.

After the chief dropped his bombshell, I didn't say much more. What could I say? And even now, hours later, I still don't have much to say; I don't have a clue how to go about this business of figuring out who, what (well, I know what), when, where (know that too . . . sorta), and why. And that last one, the why of it all, is the real doozy.

Why did anyone do any of this? Well, stealing a fortune in legendary rubies is a no-brainer for the shadier element among humankind. But nothing else is.

At least, nothing else is easy for me or the chief or Aunt Weeby. Not for Miss Mona either, and forget about Max.

I do know who knows what it's all about, but he's not talking, not loud enough for any of us to hear, at any rate. As I always do when I'm in a mess, I reach for my faith, and give him a ring on my prayer line. But as usual, God's keeping his peace.

When too much thinking makes my head hurt, I doze off. Later, beats me how much later, the phone rings. Even in the hospital, and half dopey from sleep, a call-deprived woman like me can't let a call go by. "Hello?"

"It's Peggy. How are you? Is everyone okay? The gas leak's all over the papers and the evening news."

"I never aspired to fifteen minutes of this kind of fame." I crank up the bed, and this time only wince at the slight dizziness. "Everyone's okay. There are three of us still in the hospital, but mostly for observation."

"I hope they keep a good eye on you, woman. You're a magnet."

"Don't you start with that. I do a good enough job of beating myself up."

"What do you mean? Why would you beat yourself up?"

"Look at all the trouble that follows me."

Peggy doesn't answer right away, and I realize I haven't talked to her since I got back from Myanmar. "You know what? You're at a disadvantage here. You don't know what happened on our trip."

She chuckles. "Well? Are you going to tell me?"

I do. Once I'm done, she says, "Who do you think stole the rubies?"

"So you agree that's the key to everything."

"Hello! Two plus two still equals four."

I sigh. "I don't know what all's going on. And I don't know who stole the rubies. I can't see Mr. Pak taking them. He always struck me as the most honest man. But . . . who knows? Maybe he did. And if he did, why? Why would he do something so unlike him?"

"Could he have stumbled on them? You say he travels all over the world. It's not impossible that he . . . I don't know. Saw them, identified them, and snagged them."

"I suppose he could've found them somewhere where they shouldn't have been. Maybe he was trying to return them to the rightful owner—I suppose that would be the government of Myanmar. But then, why did he come here? Why didn't he just take them back to Myanmar?"

"How about this? What if Mr. Pak was killed by mistake? Could someone have fought him for the stones, bashed his head in to get the stones from him but killed him instead, and then taken off to avoid getting caught?"

"Are you saying someone followed him? Or do you think some garden-variety thief found out he carried gemstones with him and pulled off a plain old robbery?"

"Either one could work."

"Aaarrrgh!" I don't do frustration well, as I'm sure you know by now. "Okay, okay. How about this? If Mr. Pak did have the rubies, and if he was bringing them to . . . I don't know, maybe sell them, who was he supposed to meet? You know it wasn't me. No matter what that dopey cop thinks."

Peggy giggles. "Chief Clark's okay. He catches his crooks, and he does a great Santa for the kids down at the police station."

"I can't see him being all that jolly. And Aunt Weeby says he was my dad's best friend growing up. The guy even says he gets a letter from Dad every month. I can't see how he could ever be my father's friend. Dad's a serious man, totally sold out to God and the ministry he feels called to. Plus he loves our family, and he's not the kind to jump on an impulse. Dad wouldn't have much patience for this good ol' boy who jumps to conclusions like frogs hop across lily pads."

Now Peggy hoots. "Can't see Chief Clark on lily pads. Let's just say he's a little . . . um . . . hefty for that."

I chuckle at the image, silly as it is.

Then, "There's one thing, Andie. And I don't want to upset you, but I can't shake it, no matter how hard I try."

"What is it? You won't upset me."

"Hasn't it occurred to you that . . . Max showed up at a very . . . interesting time?"

I suck in a breath. "He did, didn't he?"

"The same day your vendor turned up dead."

"But he was on-screen with me. He has the same alibi I do. If I couldn't have done it because millions were watching me, they were watching him too."

"Who's to say he worked alone?"

It had occurred to me the minute she mentioned his name. "You're right. He could have had a partner."

"Has he done anything strange?"

My laugh has more than a little hysteria. "You don't know the guy. There's not much he does that isn't strange."

"But could it be suspicious?"

My brain channel surfs through the events of the past few weeks. "You know? Now that you mention it, it's more than a little strange that he wants to stay on this show with me so much. Especially since he's a big-time jock."

"Maybe he's keeping an eye on you. Mr. Pak did come to see you."

"Swell. Another thing to worry about around him."

Peggy doesn't say anything right away. Then, "Have you prayed, Andie?"

"Practically nonstop."

"Have you stopped to listen?"

I pause. "I *think* so."

"You don't sound all that sure."

"Well, there's been so much going on, and every time I pray lately, I wonder if God's still out there listening to me. I've always thought he was, but I'm kinda getting my prayers bounced back by the ceiling here. At least, that's how I feel. Can he hear me? In the middle of all the craziness going on? All this has happened, I've prayed and prayed, and I have no answers for any of it!"

"Don't give up. Sometimes God's answer is just to hang on. That the solution's just around the next corner."

"I'm hanging, but my nails are ripping off, if you know what I mean."

"Duct tape! Do whatever it takes, but don't let doubts steal your faith. Remember. Faith's our spiritual duct tape. Tell you what. Let's pray. Right now."

We do, and then hang up. Pain creeps up my neck from my

210

tense shoulders. My head hurts from thinking too hard, and the gas episode has left me with some crummy symptoms of its own. But there's still one question I have to ask.

"Why, Lord?"

The heavenly silence is deafening.

But deep in my heart, I know that question is the one that needs answering. And I don't know where to go dig up the answer. Or the answer to any of my other million questions.

Again, it comes down to God. And trust. Which leads to patience. Something I missed back when God was giving it out. Trust is the key.

Trust . . . a little word with a huge meaning. And prayer.

It's not as if Peggy's the only one who's prayed with me. Before she left, Aunt Weeby prayed with me. After our amens, she took my face between her hands, stared me in the eye, then dropped a kiss on my forehead, just as she has done since I was a little girl.

"Don't wrassle your brains into a big ol' tangle, sugarplum. You don't have to do it all. You don't even have to do any of it. God's with you, and all he wants is for you to trust him to work it all out."

"But—"

"No, Andie. No buts work here. Only trust in God. Faith, the real deal, girl. That's what we're talking about. And the next time you start wrassling thoughts again, pray. Toss it all over to God. He's the man with the answers, and you know it. Oh! And forget all about that snooping thing. I . . . uh . . . was all wrong about that."

I do know she's right—in my head. It's ironic how in this hospital room, after hours of prayer, self-examination, and too many thoughts, I come to such a huge epiphany. For years now I've been a Christian, since my teens, when I gave my life to my heavenly Father. But it's only now, today, just weeks before my thirtieth birthday, that I realize I haven't really sold myself all out to God.

Aunt Weeby is right. I do try to "wrassle" answers all by myself. And to my shame, I finally know that's not self-reliance or independence or even talent, ability, or a gift of some sort. That kind of "wrassling" I do is nothing more than a lack of trust in God. Instead of moving out of his way to let him do his thing, I barge in where his angels fear to tread.

What I really need to do is surrender, to say, "Thy will be done," and mean it with all that is within me, every single time, and about every single thing that affects me.

Heaven help me, what I really need is to be more like my aunt. Nutty, wacky, and all the rest, she has, though, figured out this whole life and living thing. She does life in a constant state of trust in God.

And it's only my helplessness while laying flat in a hospital bed, while under suspicion of horrible crimes, in a fog about all the awful things that have happened to me and others I care for, that brings me to a deeper knowledge of what it means to know Christ.

"Thy will be done . . ."

17<u>00</u>

A stay at Hotel Hospital is no fun. I cut mine short as soon as I trumped Aunt Weeby's and Miss Mona's arguments. The two other S.T.U.D. employees who'd been under observation were heading home, so why shouldn't I do the same?

The daunting duo's strong suit isn't logic.

And now, three long days of Aunt Weeby's not strictly necessary pampering later (picture tall me on the not-so-tall parlor sofa, since she can't clump up and down the stairs to do her ministering), I'm heading to the studio. My beady little eyes want to see what Chief Clark has assured me. He insists the vault wasn't breached. How does he know if someone didn't figure out the combination, open the door, and once inside, help himself to a fortune in gemstones? He doesn't know what we have in inventory.

Well, Sally and Miss Mona do, but still. Seeing is believing.

After a quick shower, I take my time to put together an outfit that has neither Tweety Bird nor Taz on it, like my pajamas do. Sure, I'm designer most of the time, but I've also got a thing for handsome cartoon males, with the likes of whom I've spent a great deal of time during my convalescence. I score a bagel for breakfast, then head for the front door. When I get to the parlor, I hit the brakes and come to a screeching halt. Aunt Weeby and Miss Mona are there, on their way out, stacks of shopping bags and cardboard boxes at the ready.

"What are you two doing?"

They swap looks, grin, and Aunt Weeby waves the newspaper in her hand. "Check it out. We're going on a flea market safari. This one's only about twenty-eight miles away. Want to come with us? See what kinda trophy you can bag? It'll be such fun."

Hmm . . . let's think about this. Two giddy senior citizens, a place boiling over with more of the same, tables and booths bursting at the seams with people's dusty junk . . .

"I think I'll pass."

"Aw, sugarplum. You're gonna have to come with us one a' these times. You don't know what a thrill it is when you spot a treasure in the middle of a bunch a' garbage. And then the *real* fun starts. That's when you haggle the price down to bargain-basement pennies."

I'd rather volunteer for a root canal. Without Novocain.

If ever there was a time for diplomacy, this is it. "I just don't get the thrill of it all. Dirt and trash aren't my thing. And as far as arguing goes? You guys know I get more than my fair share working with Max."

Miss Mona gives me one of her laser-beam looks. "And here I thought you were going to play nice."

Was he playing nice when he first showed up? Murder's not nice.

214

But I can't bring that up. "Sure, I agreed to work with him, but that doesn't mean he suddenly knows enough that he won't make me crazy the next time he comes up with some dumb comment while we're on-screen. And besides, you did tell us you wanted the, um . . . er . . . *disagreements* to go on."

Aunt Weeby chuckles. "See, Mona? I told you there's not a thing to worry about. They're not gonna be billing and cooing anytime soon. The viewers are still gonna get lots a' sparks coming their way. They're the perfect couple."

I fight the urge to blab, to warn them, and face Miss Mona. "Any reason why you'd be heading out on a junking junket instead of coming in to the studio on the Friday morning after it was sabotaged?"

"Andie, honey, Max was right on at least one thing he said. You do take yourself much too seriously. That's the why-for behind your ulcers. You need to be more like Livvy and me. We know how to have us some fun."

Max, Max, Max.

"I'll give you that I've become too focused on work over the last few years, but I don't find anything about junk particularly exciting. I'm more the Queen of Clean kinda girl, not the kind who goes around collecting endless piles of more stuff."

Aunt Weeby purses her lips and looks toward the ceiling. "You Philistine, you. We don't buy us any junk stuff. We find us real good antiques, sugarplum. You have to give it a chance—"

The ringing doorbell cuts her off. I rush to see who came to my rescue, but wrinkle my nose when I spot the—suspicious—male on the front porch. "What brings you here?"

He seems clueless about the . . . um . . . lack of enthusiasm in my voice. "I knew the ladies were headed out for some R&R, and I thought you might like a ride to the studio."

Uh-oh. "I usually drive myself in to work. Aunt Weeby's been letting me use her old VW Jetta."

Max snaps his fingers. "That's right. I've seen you. But wouldn't you like to travel in style? And the company's not so bad either."

A date with Jack the Ripper. "Ah . . . well . . . I never thought about it."

"Tell you what. How about you do something wild and crazy today and give it a try? Come with me. I promise not to sabotage you and your gem geekydom. You'll be safe with me."

Really? "Okay."

"Lighten up, Andie. I can't find even a hint of humor in you."

I don't see the humor in a corpse in a vault. But he can stand some surveilling. I grab my purse from the table in the foyer. "Okay, pal. I'm taking you up on your offer. And just so you know, my sense of humor's just ducky, thank you very much."

"Oh my!" Aunt Weeby says. "I don't know what'd be more fun today. I love flea marketing, but refereeing these two could also be a barrel of fun."

And I traded ulcers for this? "I'm outta here." And outta my mind.

Max holds the door, and as I head for his SUV, he calls out, "Have a great time, ladies. I'll take good care of her."

My suspicion-o-meter starts beeping like a trash truck in reverse.

We get into his car and buckle up. "I'll have you know I'm a perfectly capable adult, Max Matthews. There's not gonna be any of that 'taking care of Andie' going on."

"Let me worry about that."

Fear waves hello, but then my conscience pipes in: Try more prayer.

I give it another whirl. *Lord? Can you make sure murder's not on his agenda? And while you're at it, please send me an extra dose of calm coolness in the face of . . . well, Maxness.*

We drive away in silence—a sticky, icky silence. What's the deal with this guy?

After a few minutes, he says, "I've been playing around with an idea. Are you willing to listen?"

"I'm your captive audience, but that doesn't mean I'll take the bait."

"Fair enough. Why don't you check out the bag in the backseat?"

I give it a glance. The brown paper sack looks innocent enough. Will it blow up when I open it?

A peek at Max gains me nothing. Nothing but the reminder of how close we are. And that answers my question. I doubt he'd have a bomb in the bag. He doesn't strike me as suicidal.

When I open the sack, I'm stumped. It contains nothing suspicious, just strange. I spread out on my lap a pair of plastic Groucho Marx glasses, a hot-pink ruler, an eight-inch-square blackboard, and an apple.

"What's all this?"

"Where's that sense of humor you told me about?"

"Right where it's always been, but that doesn't mean I get your shopping habits."

"Let me spell it out for you. The reason you hate me is because I'm not gem savvy—"

"Wait! Wait, wait, wait. I don't hate you. I just don't think you're the right man for the job."

"All I want is for you to give me a chance—even though I'd much rather be selling sports equipment. That's what this is all about, *Teach*."

"Are you serious?"

"Yep."

"Whatever happened to your old folks' course in rocks?"

"You're never going to think I know anything unless you're the one who does the teaching. So how about it? If you know as much about gems as you say you do, then go ahead and share. Teach me what you think I need to know."

Talk about being between a rock and a hard place—pun totally intended. I don't want to spend any more time with Max than I have to. He's too attractive, even with all his flaws. Then there's that coincidence that might not be so much coincidence.

I mean, really. What could be worse than—

No. I'm not going there. Not while we're in his car.

You have your own flaws, remember? Figures my working-overtime conscience would kick in right about now. But flaws don't compare with guilt. We're talking murder here.

And maybe not.

On the other hand, Max does have a point. If he's innocent, and if I'm going to be stuck with him, I would want to make sure he gets his facts straight. So maybe it's not such a bad idea after all. "I guess we can give it a try. But if it doesn't work out, then you're off to sell sports junk."

He lets out a sigh that tells me he hadn't been sure of my answer. And he'd been sweating the wait for my decision. Why would he want to spend so much time with me, if he feels I hate him? Especially, if all he wants to do is sell sports stuff. I don't do sports.

Suspicious, don't you think?

I slant him a glance and notice his smile, no smirk in sight. In spite of everything and with no effort on his part, his easy good looks hit me in a way I don't really want to be hit. At least, not by him, and especially not now that Peggy's got me to thinking.

Focus, Andie, focus. "When do you want to start?"

Max the Magnificent jumps on that. "How about tonight? After work. We can grab something to eat, and then you can knock yourself out throwing gem basics at me."

Beep, beep, beep. My suspicion-o-meter's on double-time. His cozy little gem lesson could be construed—*mis*construed—as a date. Or something more sinister.

Since I don't want to give him any crazy ideas of either kind, I let the thought slide into oblivion, where it belongs. And will stay. I hope.

My nerves do a jitterbug in my gut. "Where do you want to go?"

"D'you like Chinese?"

"Love it!"

"See? We have something in common."

"Oh, and last time I looked, you walk upright. That makes two."

He chuckles. "One can work wonders with a lot less than that."

Before a comeback can roll off my tongue, my cell phone does Beethoven's Fifth. "Hello?"

"Miss Andie?" Chief Clark says.

Those nasty nerves of mine kick up another fuss and my heart beats a triple-time cadence. "Yes. What's wrong? Why would you be calling me?"

"I'm afraid I do have some bad news for you. There's been an accident."

Try talking when your heart's imitating a jackhammer. "Who?"

"I'm sorry, but your aunt and Miss Mona took off going east, east of I-65, that is, down by where there's them hills by the farms?"

Sorry? Then he rambles? "Get to the point, please!"

His sniff comes across the line. "Well, Miss Andie, it looks like the brakes in Miss Mona's fancy car—that Jag thing—gave way. They musta been faulty, 'cause that car's pretty new. Can't have wore out or anything like that so fast."

"So far you've told me there was a crash, but you haven't said a word about what really matters. How are my aunt and Miss Mona?"

Max pulls the SUV to the berm, watches me, but keeps silent.

The chief goes on. "It's like this, Miss Andie. They're on their way to the hospital right as we speak. Once they get them there, and the emergency folks do what they need to, then you and I, we'll both know more. I do know Miss Mona weren't conscious when the EMTs got to her."

I totally free-fall inside. "Uh . . . thanks. I appreciate the call. And I'm on my way . . . to the hospital—Oh! Which one? Where'd they go?"

"Baptist East. It's the biggest and closest to the accident."

"I'll be there."

When I close my phone, my hands are shaking and I feel like I'm about to throw up. I'm chilled. Everything around me feels unreal, hazy, and fragile.

"Andie," Max says, his voice caring and gentle. "Tell me where we're going. We don't want to waste time."

That unexpected gentleness of his again touches me, and I smile. "Thanks, Max. We need to get to Baptist East as soon as we can. Miss Mona's Jag seems to have had some kind of brake failure, and they crashed."

"Hang on. I'll get us there." He turns the key in the ignition, then gives me a wry grin. "But I'm going to need directions. I'm new in town, remember?"

As we hurry to the hospital, I notice how sure he is at the wheel of the SUV, how steady his actions. I take comfort in his strength, and turn, as always, to prayer.

By the time we reach the hospital, even though my stomach's knotted and my shoulders are tight, I'm in a more peaceful place thanks to my faith in God's mercy and the power of prayer. I'm also thankful for Max's surprising sensitivity.

"Hey," I say softly. "I guess you're not a three-headed monster with a glowing green halo, after all. Thanks again."

"I told you I'm human." He turns off the car. "How boring of me."

"Ya think?"

"I think you really get something out of arguing with me, but I don't really know what. Or why." At my sputter, he puts a hand on my arm. "Wait! I'm not done. I just want to put you on notice, Teach. I intend to find out why you're so prickly around me. And you also need to know I'm a pretty determined guy."

I read between his words, and come up with—I think, I hope—the right conclusion. He wants his job, and he's going to fight to keep it, even though what he really wants is a sports spot. He's also going to knock down the wall I've built up between us.

I hope there's not another murder in his plans.

Blinded by tears, I stumble into Aunt Weeby's room. Under the covers, she looks tiny, worn out, and for the first time ever, her age is a sobering reality. I can't stop the sob that slips through my lips, but for her sake, I get a grip right away. "It's so good to see you!"

"Aw, sugarplum. I'm so sorry to worry you like this. It's not what we were wanting, you know."

"Of course I know. Nobody wants to crash their car."

"It was really strange." Her voice can't hide her exhaustion, or maybe it's pain I hear. "We were riding along just fine, but then when Mona tried to slow down to make a turn, nothing happened. She couldn't get that crazy car a' hers to slow or stop. We were going down this small hill, a bitty thing, you know. It shouldn't've done much to speed us up, but the problem was them brakes. They just wouldn't grab, so Mona couldn't get the car to stop."

I reach for her hand. "I can imagine how scared you must have been."

"And Mona." A tear rolls down her pale cheek. "I feel right awful about all this. I'm the one who came up with the idea for that safari today. We should've just stayed put. She wouldn't be so bad off if she'd gone ahead to the studio like she planned to do."

"How is she?"

"They told me she's in critical condition."

"That's what they told me too."

"But, Andie? I didn't need any one a' them to tell me anything. I couldn't wake her after we hit that light post. She . . . she hadn't come to, even when we got here."

"Hey! You're the one who always tells me to hang on to my faith. Where's yours hiding out today?"

She draws a shuddery breath. "You didn't see her yet, did you?"

"What's that got to do with God?"

"She looked . . . she looked dead."

"Don't think about that, Miss Weeby," Max says from the doorway. All of a sudden I realize how quietly he walks. Hmm . . .

Oblivious to my suspicions, he goes on. "I just checked with the nurses, and they say she's in critical but stable condition. She hit her head, so they have her sedated. They want to make sure there's no hemorrhage around the brain."

"Oh, that sounds awful. Poor Miss Mona." I reach a hand out to my aunt. "Let's pray."

We bow our heads, and, as we've done so many times, we turn to our Lord, lift Miss Mona's condition to him, pray for his blessing upon her, for guidance and wisdom for her doctors. As always, Aunt Weeby ends by saying, "Your will, Father, yours and not ours. Amen."

The deep, masculine "amen" catches me by surprise. "You were praying too?"

"What?" He looks uncomfortable and defensive. "Are you the resident expert on that too? Or can mere mortals reach out to God for the sake of a nice lady who's badly hurt?"

That really zings me. "Sorry, Max. I keep forgetting how stupid it is to assume stuff about people."

"I have gone to church since I was a kid."

"That's not the same thing—"

"Miz Weeby!" Chief Clark tumbles through the door and comes to the side of the bed, leans over, and my aunt wraps her arms around his neck. "How're you doing? You did give us one awful big scare."

"I'm fine." Her voice cracks just a bit. "But Mona's not. They still have her out . . . and she's still in critical condition."

I glance at the doorway, and sure enough, his shadow's hanging there. Who *is* that guy?

But before I get a chance to ask, the chief says, "Now, you know these doctor types really know a lot. I'm sure they won't let anything go wrong with her."

"It's in God's hands," she murmurs with more resignation than hope.

Not good.

Then she adds, "What brings you here, Donald? I already told that other officer all he wanted to know about the crash. There's not a whole lot I remember. It all happened too fast."

He drags off his hat. "I saw all that in the witness report, so you don't need to go over it again and again. You're pretty clear on what happened, and there's no need to doubt you."

Wish he'd go that easy on me.

"Then what'd you come over here for? It isn't the most cheery place to spend a day, you know."

"I do know, and that's what makes coming here worse. I . . . I have something to show you."

He reaches into his uniform pocket and pulls out a ziplock baggie with a folded piece of paper inside. "The investigating guys gave me this. I thought you should see it, and maybe you might could give me an idea who's done this."

"I'll give it a try." She lifts her head just a little bit. "Let me tell you, Donald, I can't wait until you get your hands on the little creep what did this to us."

The chief pulls out a pair of latex gloves from his other pocket, slips them on, and then opens the bag. He unfolds the paper so he can hold it out for Aunt Weeby to read.

Shadowman steps into the room, silent as always.

Aunt Weeby reads, and then turns, if possible, even paler. "Oh no! This is dreadful. Sick! Sick, sick, sick. Why would someone do such a thing? And who? Who would do it? What are you going to do about it, Donald?"

"I'm trying, Miz Weeby. I'm trying as fast and hard and everything I can."

I come up to his side. "Could I read it, please?"

"Here. See if you recognize the writing."

The block printing doesn't look like anything I've seen before. But I'm not surprised. It's clear someone tried to disguise their handwriting. And the words? They're just disgusting and disturbing.

Hand them over, or this is only a taste of what's coming your way.

"Well?" the chief says.

Max comes closer. "Could I take a look?"

"Sugarplum?"

"Never seen it before," I say. "How about you?"

Aunt Weeby shakes her head. "So what do you think?"

"It's all about the rubies," Max says.

My aunt gives one of her trademark sniffs. "That's what *I've* been thinking for a while now."

Knock me over with a feather. "You have, have you?"

"Why, sure, ever since you and Mona told me about that mine, the market, the shooting, and them missing stones. I reckon your friend knew about the multimillion-dollar stolen rubies. It just works, don't you think?"

If someone like Aunt Weeby, who has no knowledge of the gem world, never met Mr. Pak, and didn't get shot at in Myanmar feels this way, then I know my gut's been right all along.

"What's this about multimillion dollars?" Chief Clark asks.

The shadow comes within inches of where I stand. I glare and he backs off. I definitely feel stalked right now.

I turn back to the chief. "There's a parcel of multimillion-dollar rubies out there somewhere. That's what killed Mr. Pak—well, not the rubies themselves, but someone involved with the theft, or someone who knew Mr. Pak. Mr. Pak must have known what happened to the stones. And I'm sure there's more than one person out there who wants them. The man most desperate to find them is the one you have to find."

He narrows his eyes. "Or woman, Miss Andie. Women kill too."

Why do I feel he'd like nothing more than to lock me up?

18<u>00</u>

After two days filled with flurries of shows and hospital visits, I bring Aunt Weeby home. Her head's fine. Well, there's no concussion, just normal nuttiness. And although Miss Mona shows no sign of intracranial bleeding, the doctors want her to stay a bit longer, since she was out for so long.

Every time I look at her, see her hooked up to machines that blink and beep, I get angrier by the minute. You know about my temper, right?

Why did Mr. Pak come see me? That's what started it all.

After more thinking than my mush-for-brain wants to handle, I'm so confused that I can't tell what's what. I decide to revisit all that's happened and in the order it happened. After helping Aunt Weeby to bed, I sit at the kitchen table. Armed with notebook and pen, I list events, observations, feelings, anything and everything that comes to mind about the last few weeks.

At eight thirty, the doorbell rings. I'm so involved with my lists that I'm tempted to ignore it, but in the end, I can't let it go. It could be important.

But guess what? It's Mr. Magnificent. "What are you doing here?" I ask.

"Wow! Is that a welcome or what?"

Or what. "I wasn't expecting anyone. I'm kind of busy. Is there anything you need?"

He stares at my Pooh slippers. "I see you weren't ready for a state visit. What's kept you so busy?"

Wouldn't you want to know? "Stuff."

"Hmm . . . conclusive." He shifts his weight and shoves his hands in his pockets. "Can I come in? I couldn't stop thinking about the death, the shooting, the gas leak, and the accident. I wondered if you wouldn't mind doing some brainstorming. Maybe we can make some sense of the situation."

Something fishy going on? "Ah . . . sure. Go ahead. I was in the kitchen, doing just that."

"Really? Did you come up with anything interesting?"

Is he here to brainstorm? To check out what I know? Or worse, am I in his crosshairs?

I gesture for him to go ahead. Right on cue, Rio lets out his "*Squawk! Shriek, shriek!*"

Max stumbles, trips over his feet. "Whoa!"

I fight the urge to laugh. "Just ignore him. He's saying hi. It turns out Aunt Weeby's cage cover really works. He'll be quiet now after that first blast."

"Lucky you!"

"I won't dignify that comment with an answer. Why don't you sit? Want some coffee? Or maybe iced tea? Water? Soda?"

"Tea sounds great—as long as it's sweet."

"Come on, Max. We're in Kentucky. Tea only comes sweet here!"

He grins. "Then tea it is."

My heartbeat speeds up, but I don't know if it's from his smile or from fear. And while I fill the glass with ice and tea, I ask myself how much I really fear Max.

Did he kill Mr. Pak? Would he hurt—kill—me?

What shocks me most is my lack of instant reaction. I glance over my shoulder and watch him study my lists. His expression is serious, intent. But at the same time, his posture is relaxed. He doesn't exactly give off murderous vibes.

Besides, he'd have to be Oscar-worthy to pull off the gem-dunce act. To want those legendary rubies, you have to know your gems. And ignorance of gemological data doesn't necessarily equal murderous tendencies.

I put his glass down on the counter, and to gain some time, I reach for a paper towel to wipe it off. *Lord? What do I do? Can I trust him? Or did he kill Mr. Pak? Please guide me—I can't see my way clear.*

"Here you go." I put the glass within easy reach. "I see you've been looking at my lists. What do you think?"

"You're pretty thorough."

"So you don't think I missed anything."

"Not that I can see. But there's still nothing here to go on."

"That's the problem." *Okay, Lord. I'm going with my gut here. I'm gonna trust him, so keep your eye on me. Aunt Weeby needs me alive and kicking for a while longer. I wouldn't mind hanging around some more, either.* "I've been wanting to call Mrs. Pak, but I have no idea how to go about that. All I know is that they live in Bangkok. But millions of people live in Bangkok."

"And there's no way to know if Pak is the Thai equivalent of Jones or Brown."

"Exactly. I've thought of calling the Thai embassy, but what do I say? 'Hi. Your citizen was killed in our vault, and I want to talk to his wife about him.' I can see them sending out the loony-tunes patrol for me."

"You're right. It won't fly." He picks up one of my lists, takes a sip of tea. "How about tracking down the bird?"

"I thought about that, Max. Mr. Pak couldn't have brought the parrot from Thailand. There are strict export rules, and since that whole bird flu scare popped up, you can bet no Asian bird is getting in this country without every health expert checking it out. Besides, I don't know if they have tropical parrots in Thailand."

"That means he bought it here. Can you check bird . . . what? Farms? Hatcheries?"

I chuckle. "I think hatcheries are for fish, not necessarily eggs. And I tried to Google parrot breeders. Guess what? I got 35,200 sites! I don't think either you or I will live long enough to check them all out."

"True, but where did Mr. Pak go? I mean, how long had he been in the country? And what airport did he go through? Since he must have bought the bird here, I don't think he would have traveled far from the airport where he arrived."

"Good point, but good luck trying to get any info on incoming passengers. There's something called Homeland Security, remember?"

"There is that." He takes another sip of tea, then returns to the lists. "How about your old boss? Wouldn't he be a good one to talk to? You said he's the one who introduced you to Mr. Pak. He must know something."

"That's where I went after we landed from Myanmar." Should I mention the *woo-woo* feeling I got while I waited for the cab? Nah. He already thinks I'm half-baked. Which I may very well be, after all I've done. And said. "Roger hadn't even heard about the murder."

"He hadn't? That's strange. You told Chief Clark about the connection between the two of them. I was there. Why wouldn't the cops question him?"

"Hey, I asked the chief that very same thing. It did nothing for him. He said he had plenty to investigate here."

"That's crazy. And didn't he mention the FBI?"

"No, I did. But he brought up Interpol. Where are all those guys?"

He shrugs. "Interagency jealousy?"

"Beats me."

"Maybe they've been staking him out without anyone knowing."

"Maybe, but that sounds a little too James Bondish to me. All I know is that there's a dead man in the picture. That should trump all the other garbage."

"I know the chief's your father's friend—"

"So he says, but I've never even heard of him."

"Anyway, your aunt seems to like him, and she's okay by me. I have to wonder if he's really that much of a good ol' boy cartoon character. What if he's really doing his job, and lets everyone think he's kind of slow?"

"I don't think he's slow, just nasty. He thinks I'm behind all this, and there's no way! Besides, the FBI hasn't even talked to me. Doesn't that smell fishy to you?"

"Maybe they're staking you out too. And maybe that's the first thing we should look into. Has it been reported to the right authorities? And if not, then why not?"

We? Is there really going to be a we here? And why? "How do you think we should go about doing that?"

He wiggles two fingers in the air. "Let your fingers do the walking. Check the phone book. I'm sure there are government listings. We'll start there."

"No. Better yet. Let me call Roger. If no one's talked to him yet, then we know something weird's really going on." I flip out my cell phone. "I'll try his cell. He never goes anywhere without it."

The phone rings a couple of times, three, then, "Hello?"

Dulcet feminine tones do not equal Roger. "Tiffany? Where's Roger? Or did I dial your number by mistake?"

"Andie?" She sounds as surprised as I am. "Ah . . . I wasn't expecting the phone to ring. Neither was Rog. He's, um . . . unavailable. You do realize it's late, right?"

"It's not that late. Could I please speak with him? I only have a question or two for him. I won't keep him for long."

Tiffany sniffs. "I can tell you've never been a bride, Andrea. We need our privacy."

Eeuw! TMI. "All right, all right. I'll call him in the morning."

Then, to make my discomfort even greater, Max looks at me. "Well?"

I blush hotter than . . . well, than the fire of a Burmese ruby. "Trust me, Max. You don't want to know. It has to do with the two of them and their privacy."

To my mischievous delight, Max turns pigeon's-blood red. "You're right. I don't want to know."

Neither one of us speaks, and the grinding of our mental gears is almost deafening. Then something comes to me. "You know what else I want to know?"

He leans forward, empty glass in hand. "What's that?"

232

"Who Chief Clark's silent shadow is. Aren't you curious?"

Max leaves his glass on the table, sits back in his chair, tents his fingers. He doesn't answer right away. When he finally speaks, he does so in a quiet and thoughtful voice.

"Maybe he's one of the Feds on the case. They have to be involved. The chief even brought up Interpol, like you said. That guy with him looks like a Fed. He's always worn a suit, white shirt, and navy tie. He's almost a cliché."

"Well, the chief wears his dress shirt and tie, but I think the missing suit jacket's his style choice." Or lack thereof. "But wouldn't an FBI agent ask his own questions? Wouldn't he introduce himself? How about homicide detective? Maybe that's what he is, but in some junior, training job."

"No way. The detectives came in right after the chief and the responding officers the first night. I think you were just too out of it to notice them collecting evidence."

"And the chief's the one that keeps coming after me. Interesting he's not let the detectives take over. At least not with me. Sounds like control issues, you know."

Max chuckles, but says nothing.

I go on. "Okay, if he's a Fed, like you say, why didn't he question me?"

"I've heard all these different law enforcement types tend to be territorial. The Fed might be deferring to the locals, as long as he feels everything's being done right."

"Still sounds strange to me."

He pushes away from the table and stands. "Nothing about this is normal. Strange is the least I'd call it."

"Then I know I'm not missing anything."

"Unless I'm missing the same thing." He shakes his head. "I guess I'm just not cut out to be a detective."

I wink. "Or a gemologist."

"Not fair! I asked for lessons, but the accident got in the way. How about we start those up?"

If tonight is anything to go by, I think I'd survive. "Okay. Tomorrow looks good."

"After the show we'll get a phone book, check out some government agencies, eat, and do gems."

"Sounds like a plan."

A sudden awkwardness hits us both, and just as my cheeks start warming, he smiles and heads down the hall. "I'd better get some sleep," he says. "Otherwise Allison's job tomorrow's going to be harder than usual."

"You're not worming any compliments out of me."

He winks. "Can't blame a guy for trying."

"Good night, Max."

"Good night, Andie."

As I close the door behind him, I can't make myself believe he's the killer.

"Lord? Am I right? Because if I'm wrong, I'm *really* wrong. You know what I mean?"

The silence is thick, but I remember Peggy's duct tape. I'm hanging. Still.

Faith. It'll see me through.

The next day, our show goes off with less nastiness than usual. True, Max teases me a couple of times. I give him grief right back on his lack of knowledge. But I go easy on him. After all, most people would think a gem-quality kunzite looks like a washed-out amethyst.

"That wasn't so bad," Max says after we take off our mikes.

"Okay, it wasn't horrible."

"Should I get that in writing?"

I head for the green room. "Don't push your luck, bud."

"How long do you think it will take you to get ready?"

"For lunch and a lesson?"

"What else? Oh, and the phone book. Don't forget that."

Our cease-fire feels good, but I wonder if I'm just falling for a charmer's spiel. People did say Ted Bundy was a nice guy. Until he started killing people.

One thing's for sure. I've got to keep my eyes peeled every moment I'm with Max. My life might depend on it. Not that I'm calling him a mass murderer or anything.

I glance at my watch. "I can meet you in the parking lot in say . . . about fifteen minutes. I'll just take off my makeup and stash the sample trays in the vault."

"Great. Gives me time to get rid of my war paint too."

His grimace makes me laugh. Is this for real? Mr. Magnificent acting this near to normal? Or am I the one that's taken a turn for the extraterrestrial? I have to stop myself before I pinch my thigh. With my luck, he'd catch me and laugh. Again.

I cream my face, wipe off the heavy goop, then suds off the residue. I'm excited about the chance to track down Mr. Pak's steps after he entered the country. I would imagine he came in through JFK, since he'd more than likely go to the diamond district in New York first.

Even though it's called the diamond district, way more than diamonds are sold there. Mr. Pak had loads of contacts among the other jewelers there; we were only one of his usual stops. I know at least a handful of the others, and I'm all about making calls today.

I snag my Coach bag and hurry out, not wanting to give Max

any more reason to tease, and I'd be willing to bet that anything he construes as "primping" would bring on the teasing.

"You're quick," he says when I run out to the parking lot.

"I want answers to our questions."

Over General Tso's chicken and kung pao shrimp, we come up with a plan of attack. I'll call the jewelers, and Max will take on the FBI. The more I've thought about it, the more I think Max is right. Chief Clark's shadow is probably a Fed, just giving the chief his space.

An hour later, I slap my phone shut. "Let's talk about equality here. There was none. You had the easy call—only one. I've been on the phone all this time, and no one I spoke with had an appointment with Mr. Pak."

He turns his hands palm up in fake helplessness. "What else was I going to do? I don't know every jeweler west of the Atlantic's shore. And it's not my fault that when I called Chief Clark, I had my answer. He was surprised I was asking about your 'shadowman.' He didn't realize, or so he says, he hadn't introduced the man. The shadow's John Stewart, the Special Agent assigned to the case—a man of few words, and driving our good chief crazy with his silence."

I give Max an impish grin. "Couldn't happen to a better man. Any word on why Roger didn't get grilled?"

"Let's just say Chief Clark isn't one for sharing information."

"No joke." I rap my fingers on the table. "You know, I'm convinced the answers are with Mrs. Pak."

"You want to try to hit up the FBI guy?"

"Hah! If Chief Clark can't get him to talk, what makes you think we'll get anywhere?"

Now he's the one with the mischievous grin. "You can start

236

lecturing him on rocks. Sooner or later he'll yell *STOP!* I'm sure you'll think of something once you've broken the ice."

Against my better judgment, I laugh. "Get real! That's the dumbest thing I've heard."

"I get an A for effort. And you laughed. But you're right. It's all about the rubies—like you said before. Who's tried to track down the stolen stones?"

"I'm sure the government of Myanmar has. Remember our secret service babysitter? And how about the guy at the airport and his searcher buddies? Don't forget, Chief Clark mentioned Interpol, so I'm sure they're in the hunt."

"Wonder how the original theft happened."

I snort. "Did you forget that mine already? Security's not their thing. Anyone can come and hold up the miners. Or even the buying office where we went. There wasn't much there besides a regular lock on the front door."

"Then that's that, and we've made no progress. How about we head out? I don't think this'll be a good place for a lesson on gemology."

While we ate, the normal hum of the restaurant didn't register, not even while we talked. Now, though, I notice the Asian music that underscores the constant murmur of diners, and the occasional burst of laughter. Not exactly conducive to learning.

"You know, it's not quite one thirty. How about we go back to Aunt Weeby's kitchen? I have my personal collection of stones at the house, and it's better to learn with the real thing in front of you. Books only go so far."

"You keep valuable gemstones in the house? Aren't you afraid someone might break in and steal them?"

Is that his plan? To lull me into trusting him, bringing out my collection, killing me, and then adding my gem trays to the missing rubies—

"Oh no!"

"What's wrong?" he asks.

"You're not going to believe this. I forgot to return the sample trays to the vault. I left them in the green room. Anyone could have taken them."

"Come on. I'll get you back to the studio."

We fly through traffic. Although Miss Mona has carefully screened each and every employee, the Bible's right about temptation. It's a powerful thing. There's no need to leave temptation out there to happen.

At the S.T.U.D., Max agrees to wait for me in the car. I run into the green room, and to my pleasant surprise, the trays are right where I'd left them—untouched. There's a lot to be said for Miss Mona's instincts.

Who says you can't get good help these days!

Trays in hand, I make my way down the hall. The audio system is blaring Tanya's baseball card show, but other than that, everything's quiet on the S.T.U.D. front.

And then things take a turn for the bad. Really bad.

Something small pokes through my Diane von Furstenberg silk just below my ribs. My blood turns to ice. My knees, to linguine. My heart does the tympani thing again.

Then a rough voice whispers in my ear. "Don't stop, and don't say a word. It's a gun, it's loaded, and I know how to use it. Let's go to the vault."

As much as I love rocks, I never really thought I'd give my life for a fortune's worth of them.

Strangely enough, I'm not horror-movie scared. More than anything, I'm mad. And I want a chance to see my killer.

$19\underline{00}$

Where's Football Max when I really need him?

Shoulder pads or not, he could tackle whoever's tickling my ribs with a gun. Maybe if he realizes how long it's taking me to put away the gems, he'll come looking. Otherwise, I'm toast. I'm not dumb enough to think for a minute that this is a run-of-the-mill holdup.

"Could you just tell me why you had to kill Mr. Pak?"

I figure if I'm going to die, I might as well die knowing what went down.

That harsh voice says, "Shut up, Andie. The vault. Let's go."

"I'm going, I'm going." Figures I'd wind up with a cranky killer. One who knows my nickname.

And then I get it. I'm not nearly as shaky, scared, intimidated, as I probably should be. Which says one of two things: either I'm really certain that God's watching out for me—

You know what? I am, and I figure whatever he decides is fine by me. I mean, I'd rather not be this creep's target practice of the day, but when push comes to shove, I'm ready to see my heavenly Father face-to-face.

Wow!

On the other hand, maybe I'm too stupid for words. Because somewhere in the cobwebby corners of my mind, something tells me I'm not about to bite the dust. At least not without a fight.

Focus, Andie, focus.

A familiar sound penetrates my thoughts. *Click, click, click, click, click, click . . .*

There's only one thing that makes that sound: high heels! The creep's a woman—or a guy in drag. But if he's going to kill me anyway, why would he bother with stilettos? No one in their right mind is going to want those on their feet when they might have to make a quick getaway.

So it's a woman.

As I turn the corner toward the ladies' room, I glance down and slightly behind me. Before I can catch myself, I gasp. You're not going to believe this, but the creep and I have the same taste in shoes.

She's wearing a pair of the same green velvet Stella McCartneys that Rio's water ruined the day Mr. Pak died!

Okay. Does that tell me anything about her? For one, she knows me—she called me Andie, and I don't use my nickname professionally. Second of all, she likes great shoes. How many people do I know that share my weakness?

Well, there's Danni of the multi-hued panties. And she hates me. Not only that, but she's got a thing for rubies. Then . . . well, half the female population of New York loves designer shoes, but would they know my nickname? And would they want to kill a ruby vendor?

240

I don't think so. I'm taller and bigger than Danni. I figure I can take her. If I can distract her long enough to steal her gun, that is.

Let me tell you something. I'm not crazy about guns.

At the door to the ladies' room, I realize I'm about to learn the creep's identity. Right across from the door is a massive floor-to-ceiling mirror. As soon as I walk in, I'll see her face.

I reach for the doorknob, and the gun in my ribs gives me a sharp jab. "Don't be stupid. Let's get to that vault."

Something about that husky whisper is familiar, but I can't quite place my finger on it. The best thing to do is what they do in bad B movies—keep the perp talking. "Trust me. I don't like this one bit. I'm not being stupid. You know and I know the vault is in the ladies' room. It's a pretty clever way to throw someone off, don't you think?"

"Remember Mr. Pak? He thought he was clever."

A shudder runs through me at the memory of the poor man's corpse and his spilled blood on the floor of the vault. "I'm not about to forget. It's not every day I find a friend murdered at my place of employment."

That's when pieces of the puzzle start clicking into place. So many images rush through my head that I get dizzy. Mr. Pak . . . the invitation to Myanmar . . . the missing rubies . . . the vault . . .

"He left the stones in the vault, didn't he?"

"Shut up! And move."

I open the door, but can't move forward. Why would he have brought them here? Why come see me?

"Look," I say, hoping to bargain, at least for answers. "You've got a bullet with my name on it, so it's no big deal if

241

you tell me what it's all about. Let's face it. Who am I going to tell once I'm dead?"

"The vault."

"All right, already! You're like a broken record."

"I know what I want."

It's gotta be Danni.

Feeling a bit more confident, I push open the door, step into the ladies' room, praying Julie's at her post, and when I catch a glimpse in the mirror, get the shock of a lifetime.

"TIFFANY!"

At the same time she mutters a curse, my former boss's trophy wife jabs me harder with her stupid gun. Mad? D'you think you've seen mad? You ain't seen nothin' yet!

"What do you think you're doing?" I yell. "Are you crazy?"

She tosses her bottle-blond, extension-boosted mane. "Are you forgetting who's holding the gun?"

Yeah, you guessed it. Julie's not at her post. Why should she be? If she were, I wouldn't be in trouble. And you know how it goes with me and . . . well, trouble.

"Fine. You're holding the gun, and if poor Mr. Pak's anything to go by, you know how to use it. My question's why?"

"Why?" Her blue-contact-enhanced eyes narrow. "Why not? Why shouldn't I have the nice things I want?"

Huh? "For one, because they're not yours!"

She shrugs. "They're only pre-mine. I make sure they become mine when I decide I want them."

"Like Roger?"

"He was a mistake."

"What does that mean?"

Another flurry of faux fur . . . er . . . hair. "I thought he

242

wanted the same things I do. All those years he's been wheeling and dealing, and now he gets cold feet!"

"Cold feet?" Try ice in my veins. And Roger? *Roger?* "What does that mean?"

"He chickened out at the last minute. Pak had told him about the stolen rubies awhile back. Roger made sure Pak knew he wanted the stones—if Pak ever got his hands on them."

I feel sick to my stomach. "Are you saying Mr. Pak stole the stones?"

She waves her gun. "Are you kidding? He didn't have the guts to do something like that. He had nothing to do with it, but since he traveled to . . . ah . . . Magoo? Magone? That place they get the rubies. Anyway, he traveled there a lot, and he was scared the government would think he stole the stones."

That's better—but not all good. Not yet. "Roger wanted to sell stolen goods?"

"How 'bout that safe, Andie? Your rent-a-cop's going to be back soon, and I'm not sticking around long enough for her to see me."

Another stomach lurch. "What did you do to Julie?"

"Nothing. She got a call saying her kiddies were throwing up. She went to her day care to get them."

"And she's going to find out no one from the day care called her, right?"

She shrugs. "A girl's gotta do what a girl's gotta do."

"And that means killing a nice man who . . . what did he do for you to think you needed to kill him?"

"What's it to you? Open up the safe. Mr. Pak knew how to break safe codes, but I don't. And I know you know the combination, so don't try to play that game. I'm not dumb."

But you're not smart either. No one with an ounce of sense kills to get a bunch of rubies. "How do you know the rubies are in the vault?"

"I don't. Not for sure. But he didn't have them on him when I got here, and he did tell Roger he'd found them."

"Really? How'd he find them?"

"You don't give up, do you?"

"Do you?"

"Don't get smart, Andie. I'm holding the gun."

"You'll be holding cell bars sooner or later," I mutter as I head for the wooden panel. "How do you intend to find a parcel of rubies in our vault? Do you have any idea how large it is? How many thousands of parcels we store there?"

"I only got a quick look that other day before you barged in."

"That's right. You checked it out when you rubbed out Mr. Pak."

Tiffany rolls her eyes. "That's nasty, Andie. Mr. Pak was just a problem I had to deal with. Now let's find the rubies."

Certain I have no other alternative, at least not right now, I open the vault door. "Knock yourself out, Tiff. Tell me how one parcel looks different from another—unless you know exactly where he put them, what he put them in . . . you get my drift."

"I know where he was when I found him."

"Show me."

"I plan to. You're going to be the one doing the touching. Not me. I know about fingerprints. I watch CSI."

But you haven't figured out they always, one way or the other, catch the crook.

Inside the vault, I flick on the light, and gaze down the

length of the vast, shelf-lined room. Multiple millions of dollars' worth of jewelry and gemstones fill the trays on the shelves.

I gesture for her to come inside. "What do you plan to do with the rubies?"

She motions with the gun for me to go farther in, then pulls the vault door behind her. "Sell them."

Great. She's not dumb enough to let me get between her and freedom. I'll have to keep her talking until I think of something else. "You have a buyer?"

"Roger does. But he chickened out, Roger did. Suddenly he doesn't want to have anything to do with stolen stuff."

"And Mr. Pak was bringing the stones for Roger to fence them?"

"Not hardly. There was a bunch of other people after him. Everyone wants those rubies. But he had some crazy idea that *you* could take them back to Myanmar. He didn't want the government to say he'd stolen them, and then ban him from the country. His business would shrivel up if they did that."

"Me? Why me?"

Tiffany shrugs. "I guess he figured no one would ever think you're smart enough to pull off something like this."

And you're a rocket scientist, right?

"How did Mr. Pak wind up with the rubies?"

"I'm not sure, but I think they went from the guy who took them, to another guy—a couple more, really—then they went to a cutter in Thailand. Somehow, Mr. Pak got hold of them, and Roger's wanted them since Mr. Pak first told him about the stones."

The longer I keep her babbling about how smart she is, the better my chances of Julie getting back here.

"So I was supposed to return them. Because I'm too dumb to steal them. That makes a whole lot of sense."

Tiffany shrugs. "I never said Mr. Pak was smart. He should have sold the rubies. They're worth a lot of money."

"So's Roger. Why do you want more?"

Her eyes bug out. "Are you serious? There's lots and lots more stuff I want."

"So it's all about what you want."

"Isn't that what life's all about?"

"No. Not really. Life's about meaning and service and God's plan." Where's my copy of *The Purpose-Driven Life* when I need it?

"You can do the God thing. I'll stick to what I can touch and see. And right now, I'm not touching or seeing those rubies. Find them!"

I wave. "See all those racks? They're full of gemstones. Why don't you take a bunch? They'll sell for plenty."

That was the wrong thing to say. She jabs the gun my way. "Get going, Andie. You know what's in the parcels. You know they won't bring as much as the rubies. Find them. I already have that buyer."

I act helpless—not a stretch right now. "Where do you want me to look?"

She points to a spot on a shelf right by where Mr. Pak died. "There. And don't waste any more time."

Things can't get any worse, right?

Wrong.

The bathroom door opens. *Clump-clump, clump-clump.*

"Back," Tiffany says, checking the door. It hasn't clicked, but to an uninformed onlooker, like Aunt Weeby, it would looked closed.

246

The cast clumps closer. "You did say she came to put away the pretties she had on the show, right, Max?" Aunt Weeby yells.

Tiffany's eyes grow wider. Her forehead begins to dew. She looks surprisingly like a caged rat. I fight the hope that springs to life in my heart. That's my injured, elderly great-aunt out there.

"That's what she said," Max answers.

Tiffany presses her gun against my temple. "Not a sound."

"She'll see the open vault door."

Tiffany smiles. It's not a nice one—if shaky. "This"—she jabs the gun against my head, pinning me against the shelves, her back to the door and Aunt Weeby—"is what they'll find. They can choose. I shoot you *and* them. It's a win-win situation for me."

I doubt Max is armed, and I know Aunt Weeby isn't. All I can pray for is the Lord to protect them from this madwoman.

"Sugarplum?" Aunt Weeby calls. "You okay to your stomach? Is it them ulcers acting up?"

When I don't answer, she goes on, her voice closer with every word. "Are you in here? Max says you been gone forever—what's this?"

Sure enough, she yanks open the vault door. And that's enough for Tiffany to move the gun just a fraction away from my temple. I take my chances, and jab out with my elbow. It connects with her middle.

"*Oooof!*" She doubles over. The gun goes off.

"MAX!" Aunt Weeby bellows as she trips over her cast and lands on the floor.

"Max!" I echo.

Tiffany straightens up.

"Leaving?" I ask. Then I lunge. Maybe I should have listened to Max on some of that football stuff. I'm sure my technique is lacking, since I almost land on my face. It's not exactly what I'd call a tackle, but I go with what I have. I grab Tiffany's foot, and being a shoe girl, I give the Stella McCartney a yank. Tiffany crumbles.

The gun skitters from her hand, the momentum carrying it out into the restroom after it bounces off the vault door—thankfully without discharging again.

Aunt Weeby grabs it and squeals with glee. "Put 'em up!"

I groan.

Max runs in, followed by Julie, gun at the ready. In the doorway, I see two more figures, but I'm too overwhelmed to identify anyone right off the bat. A moment later, I make out Sally and Miss Mona's new camerawoman huddled together, their jaws agape, their eyes a-bulging.

The welcome *whee-oh, whee-oh, whee-oh* of police sirens draws near.

Now that the cavalry has arrived, I can't find the oomph to move, much less stand up. I lay flat on the ground; I don't register more than a general buzz of action and sound around me for seconds, minutes. And then strong, gentle hands grasp my shoulders.

"Are you okay?" Max asks.

"I think all the parts are still attached."

"Want to stand?"

I give him a crooked smile. "How about we try sitting first?"

He holds my hand, and I use his strength to haul myself up to a sitting position. "Who called the cops?"

"Julie did as soon as she got to the day care center. She realized someone had lured her away on purpose."

"Is Chief—"

"While you were kissing the floor there, he hauled Tiffany away."

"I wasn't kissing the floor. I was just too wiped out to move. *You* try having a killer hold a gun to your head. You might just lose all your macho football jockiness too."

He backs up, hands in a defensive position. "Hey! I'm on your side."

"All right, all right, all right," I mutter as I stand up. "Where's Aunt Weeby?"

"With Agent Stewart, giving him her side of the story."

My eyes goggle. "Poor guy! He doesn't know what he's in for."

"He can handle it, I'm sure. But you're in for a date with him too."

"Don't remind me." My knees don't remember how to do their thing, and it's all I can do to stay upright. "Do I really have to go through a grilling right now?"

"Maybe we can talk them into letting you get checked out at the hospital first—"

"Hold it right there, Max Matthews! I'm not going back. I want to go home. Let me at Agent Stewart."

I wobble out of the vault, nod hello to a couple of Chief Clark's officers, one of whom has the gun in a ziplock bag, and then I stumble toward the door. There, in Julie's usual seat, is my aunt, retelling the tale in her own unique—wacky—way.

"Miss Adams," the shadow . . . er . . . Agent Stewart says. "I'm done with your aunt. I have a few questions for you—"

249

"Could you give me a couple of hours? I'm shaky and I'd like a shower and a nap. There's nothing like a gun at your head for making you . . . well, sweat."

Aunt Weeby groans. "Andrea! A woman never sweats, sugarplum. We only—"

"Yeah, yeah. I know all about dewing, and all that. But I can tell you, I was sweating. If it's all right, I'd rather go home. I can promise you'll get better answers from me after I quit shaking."

We agree, I head home, thanks to Max and his SUV, and I collapse on my bed. In the safety of my room I recognize a few things. Tiffany is rotten. My gut had told me that from the start. The most I can say for her is that I hope and pray someone can lead her to Christ.

I also realize that all of Roger's wheeling and dealing skates the edge of illegal. Although I hadn't participated in any of it, I'd excused it for a long time as part of "doing business" in New York's cutthroat diamond district.

"Lord?" I whisper. "I'm sorry. I guess when I told you I wanted your will for real, it really means looking at things your way and not the way everyone else does. I have to ask your forgiveness for my . . . oh, I guess it was willing blindness, and even some fudging. It's hard to look at the world your way, but I'd rather be with you than without you."

From down the hall, I catch the *clump-clump* of Aunt Weeby's cast. "Oh, and thanks for watching out for Aunt Weeby and Miss Mona. Me too, but they didn't have anything to do with this mess, and still they got caught up in it. Thanks, okay?"

And then I sleep.

An hour later, Agent Stewart shows up and asks his millions of questions. By the time he's done, I need another nap. But I don't get the chance to take it. A short time after he leaves, I have more visitors.

To my surprise, the secret service guy from Myanmar, the uniformed and medaled one from the airport, an official from the Thai embassy, and tiny, sweet Mrs. Pak stop by. She'd wanted to meet me, so the three officials had brought her to Aunt Weeby's house earlier in the day. Aunt Weeby, dying to get out, had them drive to the studio. And that's how she wound up in the vault.

When they leave, Aunt Weeby takes off to her date with the church's choir director. Poor man. He doesn't know what's about to hit his well-planned program for this next Thanksgiving.

About a half hour later, Max walks in.

"Hi," I say as I pull the tray full of bird-poop-covered newspaper out of the bottom of Rio's cage. Oh! Didn't I mention the glamour in parrot ownership? Sure. It has to do with cracked bird seed and dropping-littered cage bottoms that must be cleaned day after day. Yesterday was Aunt Weeby's turn; today is mine.

"I hear you're an international superstar," Max says, a wicked grin on his face. You can be sure he's not about to offer to help.

"I don't think so."

"Last I heard, you had dignitaries from two Southeast Asian countries here to see you."

I shrug, head for the utility room, and start to scrub the

thick, heavy-textured plastic tray. "They brought Mrs. Pak. She wanted to meet me. At least I was able to tell her how sorry I am about her husband's death."

"Did they say why he brought the stones to you?"

"The cutter in Thailand who wound up with the rubies was killed for the stones, but before he died, he'd told Mr. Pak about them. Mr. Pak wanted them returned to the government of Myanmar, but he was afraid. He thought his connections to the cutter might tie him to the thieves. He did visit the mines at least four or five times a year, and he thought that would instantly make the government doubt his story."

"So then, why you?"

I roll my eyes. "According to Tiffany, because I'm too stupid to plan and get away with a heist like this."

He laughs.

I smack the tray against the side of the sink. "Hey! Some sympathy would be welcome, buddy. I've been traumatized here."

His laughs slow down to chuckles. "What about Mrs. Pak? Did she have anything interesting to say?"

"That Roger had lusted after those rubies ever since Mr. Pak mentioned the theft. He wanted the stones because they're incredible. Tiffany heard about them, and she wanted the millions they'd bring. Roger didn't care about the legalities, but he didn't hurt Mr. Pak either. Tiffany, on the other hand, threatened Mr. Pak. She even threatened his family, but he refused to hand over the stones. He felt they should go back to the government, then be sold on the open market to the highest bidder."

Max doesn't say anything for a while, but instead stares at

me. I get itchy and squirmy under his scrutiny. "What? Do I have spinach on my teeth?"

"No. I'm just thinking what a compliment Mr. Pak paid you. He trusted you, your integrity. He knew you'd do the right thing."

"But I didn't. I never even found the stones." I turn to yank a wide ribbon of paper towels from the wall-hung roll, and the tray teeters on the edge of the sink. "Ooops!"

Max dives after the drippy tray. "Look out!"

The tray hits the floor. A thin sliver of plastic slides out the left side. On the sliver of plastic is a wide swathe of duct tape.

I stare.

Max sucks in a breath.

My knees begin to shake, and I wind up on my butt right by the tray.

Mr. Magnificent joins me, oblivious to the puddle of water in which he sits.

"Do you think—"

"Could that be—"

Our gazes meet. We both reach out, but then he draws back. "Go ahead," he says. "You've earned it."

With shaking fingers, I ease a corner of sticky silver adhesive from the white plastic and tamp down my excitement when I feel the lumps below the tape.

Millimeter by millimeter, I work the glue away, and then . . .

"Wow . . ." Admiration fills Max's voice.

The beauty of the stones steals mine.

We've found the rubies.

And the gems are as stunning as anything God has placed on the face of his earth.

We stare, silent. Then, I don't know how much later, Max reaches out and laces his fingers through mine. I curl mine around his.

Our gazes meet again.

And hold.

After the police, FBI, Interpol, Myanma dignitaries, and Mrs. Pak have again left the house, Max and I collapse on the couch.

"Bird poop, huh?" my most eloquent cohost asks.

"You gotta admit, not many are going to go looking there for a fabulous fortune."

"Aunt Weeby thought of it. She had Rio X-rayed."

"You're right. She did." I wink. "See? Brainy women run in my family."

He laughs.

So do I. Then I sigh. "Still can't figure out why, of all the people Mr. Pak knew in the U.S.—the whole world, actually—he chose me."

Max's admiring gaze makes me warm all over. *Oh my!*

"I started to tell you earlier," he says. "You didn't want those stones for yourself. You never really went looking for them. You cared more about Mr. Pak and who'd killed him than anything else."

I shrug. "Mrs. Pak said he believed I'd return the stones once I figured out where he'd hid them. What else was I going to do? You know? I couldn't keep them. I sure couldn't sell them. They're not mine."

He smiles.

I'm so glad I'm sitting. This guy's more lethal than Tiffany's gun.

"That's it, Andie. That's what I mean. Tiffany saw the stones for what they could do for her. Roger saw the stones as another trophy. You see the stones as someone else's property."

I give his answer some thought. "Actually, Max, the stones, and everything else, are God's. He only puts things here on Earth for us to use and give him the glory. We all come to an accounting before him sooner or later. When that day comes, I want to be on his good side, since he's done so much for me."

My cohost again says nothing, studies me some more. Then, in a quiet, serious voice, he says, "I think there's more I'm going to learn from you than just about gems. You up for it, Teach?"

Oh boy. What do I say?

I came home for a more peaceful life. Who'd a thunk I'd find so much excitement doing TV in plain old Louisville? Who'd a thunk I'd be forced to share the screen with a California gem-dunce surfer boy?

And live to . . . what? Tell about it? Do another show? Get along with him?

What? What's next, Lord?

I look at Max, take a deep breath, and say, "Let me get my gem-jar trays."

Ginny Aiken, a former newspaper reporter, lives in Pennsylvania with her engineer husband and their three younger sons—the oldest is married and has flown the coop. Born in Havana, Cuba, and raised in Valencia and Caracas, Venezuela, Ginny discovered books at an early age. She wrote her first novel at age fifteen while she trained with the Ballets de Caracas, later to be known as the Venezuelan National Ballet. She burned that tome when she turned a "mature" sixteen. An eclectic list of jobs—including stints as reporter, paralegal, choreographer, language teacher, retail salesperson, wife, mother of four boys, and herder of their numerous and assorted friends, including the 135 members of first the Crossmen and then the Bluecoats Drum and Bugle Corps—brought her back to books in search of her sanity. She is now the author of twenty-six published works, but she hasn't caught up with that elusive sanity yet.